Cassius Station:

Heist

BY

GUSTAVO BONDONI

2025 JIM BAEN MEMORIAL AWARD WINNER

Also by Gustavo Bondoni:

From Guardbridge Books:

The Emily Plair Saga
OUTSIDE
SPLINTER
AMALGAM

Off The Beaten Path, short story collection
Back to the Well: An Argentinian Ghost Story

From other publishers:

Siege
Incursion

Ice Station Death
Jungle Lab Terror
Test Site Horror
Lost Island Rampage
Desert Base Strike

The Malakiad
The Swords of Rasna

Pale Reflection: A Collection of Dark Fantasy
Love And Death: A Series of Stories
Tenth Orbit and Other Faraway Places

Cassius Station:

BY

GUSTAVO BONDONI

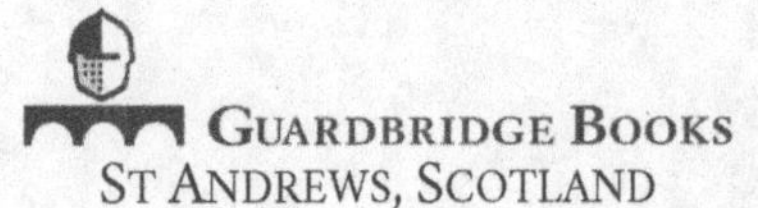

GUARDBRIDGE BOOKS
ST ANDREWS, SCOTLAND

Published by Guardbridge Books,
St Andrews, Fife, United Kingdom.

http://guardbridgebooks.co.uk

Cassius Station: Heist.

Cover art © David Lascelles.

ISBN: 978-1-911486-95-4

*To Connie,
to whom I'll dedicate as many books as I
possibly can.*

Chapter 1

The air smelled of fried pork and cheap cotton candy, food staples of the Old Corridor. That meant the recyclers must be getting clogged again.

I ignored the hawkers and sliced through the throng, almost tripping over a group of children out on a cultural appreciation tour from some more affluent neighborhood.

The Tiantáng Sector, as the structure around the Old Corridor is formally known, is the heart of Cassius Station, the ancient orbiting platform around which the entire sprawling complex congealed.

And it was always packed. First, second or third shift, the crowds made it nearly impossible to move.

I pushed aside a guy blocking the doorway I needed. He looked up at me and decided not to make an issue of it. It was a good choice since I didn't have time to beat him up. I would have had to put him down via electronic means… and that was never fun.

The store was full of junk, but I didn't let the dusty electronics and abandoned furniture fool me. Rime Tristano was rich enough she could indulge her fantasy that she was a pawn shop owner out to give the little guy a break. But she was smart, you had to give her that. Her real business was a spinoff of the front.

When I walked in, she was yelling at a couple of uglies from the docks. By the time I started for the counter, they were heading toward the door. One of them, a bald guy as wide as he was tall—not much on the height, but big around the shoulders, and with mechanical augments—gave me a sour look with a blue scanner-eye. The other guy didn't even bother to look my way as he stormed down the corridor. All I saw was that he was a head taller than his companion. Nearly as tall as I was.

I didn't flinch, but I politely gave way so they could leave. I had a feeling these guys would be a lot harder to budge than the guy at the door. I could probably do it... but the hardware I'd need to use would leave a couple of smoking bodies on the floor of Rime's store.

That would put her in a mood, and right now I needed a favor.

"Deck Leonid," she said when she spotted me. She was a small woman, particularly for Cassius, where the spin gravity in most public areas was only three-quarters of Earth norm. It made me think she might have been born planetside. The Tau Ceti system had a couple of planets, neither of which was a place I'd want to live. She was beautiful, too, with blue-tinted hair that complemented her dark skin beautifully. "Of all days you should show your face around here, of course you'd choose this one."

I nodded back towards the door. "Trouble?"

"Those guys? Nah. I can handle them. I'm more worried about you. What do you need?"

"I'm here to add to your bank account. A lot."

"And you couldn't call?" she said, raising an eyebrow.

"Not the kind of thing you talk about over a network," I replied.

That earned me a sour look. She knew as well as I did that if I was worried about people cracking encryptions, it was a big situation.

I held up my hands. "No danger involved, though."

"You always say that."

"And it's always true. Have I ever gotten you shot at?"

"Not yet. What do you want?"

"Cleanup job. A two-person rooming unit out near the station rim, a new bedroom built from a shipping container. You'll like it. High end computer equipment just there for the taking." I shot her the list of abandoned possessions via IR.

Unless the cops were actually in here, in line of sight, they wouldn't intercept the transmission between my Panorama and hers.

"And the owners? High-end computers usually means hackers."

"They won't trouble you. They were in the unit when it unfortunately suffered a freak and unexpected structural failure that vented all their air into space."

"You bastard. There won't be anything left."

"Fly around. Pick stuff up. Wipe away DNA. The computers were held in by the wires. That's the stuff you can really use," I said.

"What I can use is the fee. Five thousand for a full clean."

"I have a budget of ten," I replied. "Half now, half when I receive the scan of the place."

She whistled. "Someone is on an expense account." But her eyes softened. She knew as well as I did that I could have kept the extra five and no one would have asked a single question. It hurt to give it to her, but it would serve me well the next time I needed a cleaner. "What about the data? Someone had to have a record of the inhabitants' presence there."

"Don't worry about that. It's being taken care of."

She raised an eyebrow at me. It looked good on her, because normally she had the perfect elfin features and full lips popular among the inhabitants of Cassius Station who could afford to look however they wanted, but the expression revealed her unique personality. "You're playing with the big boys again?"

"Just a small job. I have no idea what this is about."

"That's a good recipe for getting killed."

"I try not to think about that. So will you take the job?"

She shrugged. "It's a living, I guess. I'll have it done and send you the proof in an hour."

"It needs to be perfect."

"All right." She shrugged. "Two hours, then. It won't actually take more than one, but if it will make you feel better about it, then we'll pretend my basic service isn't perfect already. Now get out before someone sees you and my reputation goes to hell."

I refrained from commenting on the state of her reputation, but before I left, I called back, "And how about that dinner date?"

She glared at me. "I already told you. Get your nose fixed and we'll talk."

That was unfair. Guys felt threatened by my crooked nose. They thought it meant I was prone to violent altercations. Women loved it: it made me look dangerous.

Besides, Rime really shouldn't complain about it, seeing as she was the one who broke it the first place.

* * *

The air outside smelled no fresher than it had earlier, but with my work done—I was being paid very well by an individual known only as The Earthling—I decided it was time to get something to eat. And in this part of the station, that meant Dongee's.

I looked both ways in the corridor, trying to catch sight of the bright yellow awning that signaled his stand, but it was impossible to spot it through the crowd. Of course an annoyance for me would be a boon for someone trying to sell fried pork, so I aimed at towards where the crowd was thickest.

There. I turned a corner and his electric cart stuck out like a yellow metal tent which had inexplicably sprouted stools from its side. One guy was just finishing as I approached, so I timed my walk to arrive as he pulled away. I got his stool in front of a couple of other potential customers who cursed me—albeit good-naturedly—for my excellent timing and simply stood while they waited for their food.

"Yo, Deck," Dongee, the proprietor, said. His green dreads and pale skin made him look sickly even for a denizen of Tiantáng. "How's the confidential operator racket these days?" He didn't ask me what I wanted. He didn't need to.

"Going well. Taking a little break and decided to see if your food is still poisonous."

"It never was. I make it with real pork."

He pulled away for a minute as he piled strips of meat smothered in thick red sauce onto a rigid white taco and handed it to one of the guys I'd displaced. Then he repeated the operation and gave it to me. In all the years I'd known Dongee, I'd never seen him fail to serve his customers in the exact order they arrived at his cart, regardless of what kind of scrum developed around him at lunch time.

"You haven't seen real pork meat in your life, Dong."

"That's what you think. Once, when I was a kid..." He served a woman with glowing blue hair and returned his attention to me. "I was at a farm where they had twenty thousand pigs. Down on Tau II it was."

"I've heard of that place," I said. "It's called Dongee lying to me."

"Yeah, that was the name," he replied.

The meat was reconstituted vat product, of course, but it was supposed to be identical to real pork meat in texture and nutritional composition. Whatever... it smelled divine and I munched down on it, leaning well forward to let any stray sauce fall onto the coated metal counter of the cart.

Just as I did so, Dongee leaned in and asked, "You're aware of the people tailing you, right?"

"Huh?" I asked through a mouthful of shredded meat-analogue. Every instinct told me to look around and find the people I'd missed, but Dongee would never forgive me if my pursuers realized he tipped me off. Instead, I kept my head down, pretending to eat, and waited for him to return from handing food to another customer.

"Yeah," he said when he returned from serving a couple of kids in school uniforms who really shouldn't have been in the Old Corridor unchaperoned. "One heavy and one beauty. They pretend they're separate, but they're definitely together. Lady in purple by the scramble arcade and the big dude in grey pajamas beside the massage parlor."

Pretending to straighten out after a bite, I sneaked a peek. The woman was dressed in a knee-length coat. She was tall and thin, a sign of someone born on Cassius. The guy looked like he'd been built from spare parts: he was bigger on his left than on his right, and also bald. Probably cyborged to within an inch of his life... or to extend his life. I didn't know. Unlike most people in my professional circles, I was still working on my original body and organs. Hell, the only thing really damaged had been my nose, and that was when I was playing, not working.

"Thanks, Dong. I owe you one," I said.

And then, breaking with my long-standing habit that anyone who wanted to follow me around would have known about, I abandoned my stool and carried away my food. I also grabbed the coffee of the guy sitting next to me, a nice steaming cup with the word 'Caff' written on the side. He was arguing with a pretty little drug dealer on the other side, and he didn't notice.

I strolled casually in the direction opposite the two people watching me while I tried to think of a place where I could lose them.

The maintenance alley between the two retail blocks to my right might work, if there weren't too many people inside. Or it might be a disaster.

I would have to risk it.

Pretending to study a rack of scarves, I went around it, saw that my pursuers were about ten meters behind and pushing through the crowd, and dove into the alley. I went three steps and stopped, pressed against the wall.

Seconds later, the cyborg man came around the corner and got a cupful of scalding coffee in the face. He screamed, but mostly, his face made gear-gnashing sounds as whatever exposed electronics I'd hit went berserk. Just in case, I also zapped him with my taser and turned to face the woman who'd just rounded the corner.

She stopped in time for me to get a good look at her face: light brown skin, big brown eyes and straight black hair made a combo I wouldn't be forgetting in a hurry. She was beautiful. But I only looked at her face for a fraction of a second before I recognized what she was carrying.

"Is that a gun?" I asked.

A trembling hand lifted the weapon.

Chapter 2

I didn't stop to think. I threw myself to a side as an enormous explosion stunned me. A chunk of the metal wall disappeared behind my head.

Ears ringing, I did the only thing I could think of: I threw my taco into her face and followed up with a charge that sent her flying.

Then I headed down the Old Corridor as fast as my feet could carry me, and anyone who was too slow to get out of my way ended up flat on their backs.

I didn't make any friends that day, but I needed to get out of there. I was used to having people come for me. It came with the territory: sometimes I did jobs for people who had enemies who didn't want the job to get done. Sometimes it was a courier mission they wanted to interrupt. Sometimes they wanted to hide someone I wanted to find.

But never, not once in the course of my investigations, had I ever seen—or even heard of—someone discharging a projectile weapon inside Cassius Station.

Which is why I ran. Normally, I'd stick around and work a couple of incompetents like these two until I knew who was coming for me and why. Then I'd go twist that individual's arm until they promised to stop.

The projectile weapon changed the math completely. Cassius station was fine with civilian beam weapons. Those might cook the target to a nice well-done level, but they wouldn't punch holes in the walls and kill everyone. Projectile weapons weren't just forbidden; they were actively confiscated and tossed out the nearest airlock along with the people holding them. It didn't happen very often, but I remembered a couple of instances: no trial, no argument, no due process, just an all-expenses-paid trip into the cold hard vacuum outside the station.

So if this lady was willing to fire a gun out in the open like that—not some homemade lash-up, but an actual, factory-produced slug-thrower—it meant she had some serious clout. Which probably meant this had something to do with The Earthling's enemies.

Anyone who could stand up to The Earthling wasn't someone I could go after alone.

I needed help.

The alley sloped upward against the spin gravity and soon I came to a locked door leading to a connection nexus, the passages used by workers to avoid the crowds in civilian areas. I didn't know this area, but I had a universal door code override, a small black disc that was absolutely illegal but easy to get hold of if you knew who to ask, which I slapped onto the door. As it hissed open, I looked back down the alley. No one appeared to be following me.

Which meant nothing. Cassius Station was too small to hide in. A guy could walk from one end of it to the other in a couple of hours even though you had to cross several transfer areas between spun zones and a few zero-gee intervals. There was no need to follow someone: you just waited until he showed up on a camera you had access to and sent people there.

Of course, there were no publicly-owned surveillance cameras… because, other than the air supply, there was no publicly-owned anything on Cassius. The single flat tax everyone paid covered the cost of air and cops. If the population went down, the station fired cops until the books balanced.

I wondered where to go. My own office and rooms were a non-starter. They'd have people waiting for me there. Rime was close, but I wasn't sure she would stick her neck out for me. There was a time she would have. A time when she would have done anything for me. But that ended the day she broke my nose.

I came to a spot where two maintenance corridors crossed. Of my three options, two were well-lit and clean while the third was equally well-lit but streaked with oil, a clear sign that whatever was at the end of the corridor hadn't paid for a cleaning bot to go through this week. I headed that way.

A minute later, I arrived at a junction.

Junctions were places that allowed one to pass from spinning sections of the station to zero-gee spaces. They consisted of temporary doorways on both sides that would unseal when they were in phase, giving you five seconds to cross between the spaces before a safety door sealed the junction against the vacuum and and pushed you back. Without the safety door, the movement of the spaces would chop you in half as they went out of phase again.

I dove through just as the safety door began its sweep, and floated into a wall.

The corridor ahead was even dirtier than the one I'd left, but at least it smelled of chemicals and not garbage. Probably worse for me in the long run, but I wasn't planning on sticking around.

I pulled myself through the passage as fast as I could go, popped another sealed door and wondered why I'd headed for the industrial zone. If someone wanted to get rid of me without witnesses, this was the perfect place. Most of the area was automated, and big chunks of it were actually off limits to anyone not wearing rad protection.

But there were no surveillance cameras here. The people who owned the industrial pods made do with security bots that were not only much more effective at actually catching trespassers but were also easy to scrub and could never be used as evidence of… whatever they wanted to hide. Unlike cameras which were dumb and recorded everything for later interrogation.

As long as I stayed on the open paths between the unpainted, rust-stained walls, there was no need to worry. Surveillance bots were programmed only to attack people who crossed into restricted areas.

I started down the corridor, which was just a bunch of parallel cables that crossed through the center of an industrial cube a hundred meters to a side, on which factories clung to all six faces. There were no safety rails, of course; it was impossible to fall. However, I made certain to fly straight, since it was very easy to drift off into the void. You'd eventually reach a wall you could push against, of course, but drifting slowly through a zero-gee cube while people with guns used me for target practice was a scenario I preferred to avoid.

I hit a cloud of sticky vapor in the middle of my crossing, but I just closed my eyes and tried to get through as quickly as I could.

The next module over was another big cube, but this one had been converted to small-factory use. It was split into hundreds of ten-meter cubes, and the passageway ran in the spaces between them like a cramped three-dimensional maze. Of course, the factories themselves weren't cubical, which meant that the pathways wended between pipes, around boilers, over cooling towers.

The preferred colors were grease and rust, and only the basic minimum lighting—as mandated by Cassius Station—showed me where I was headed.

Except I didn't know where I was headed. I had decided to come this way to avoid the cameras. But now I wasn't sure it had been a good idea.

One of the factories vibrated and thumped as I passed, some kind of miniature metal press, probably. The next one just hummed and hissed. None of them were unoccupied: Cassius Station might not be the perfectly regulated and controlled society that reigned in the rest of the Tau system, but it was definitely a good place to become extremely rich if you were willing to work at it. All of the places vibrated with the activity of commerce, and I guessed there were probably some people around, even though none were in sight at at that moment.

If your attempt to make it in a commercial environment failed, you could always go back to Tau Ceti II, where the centrally-controlled nanofactories would meet your every need... boringly.

I normally shuddered to even think of the bland existence of the groundsiders, but from where I floated, boring looked really attractive right about then.

Hell, I was so non-bored that I didn't even know where I was going.

That's when I got the sinking feeling in my stomach. It wasn't the microgravity that got me but the fact my subconscious mind chose that moment to stop pulling my strings and actually tell me what was going on.

I knew why I'd chosen this direction. It wasn't just because my pursuers wouldn't be expecting it or that no one wanted cameras recording their activity.

There was someone out here who could help me.

But only if she felt like it. And she was hard to reach.

I finished crossing the cube and reached another crossroads. This one had eight tubes branching off in every direction. I checked the codes and realized I wasn't too far off.

Two cubes later, I entered The Complex.

I hated this place, but there was no choice. I needed Sileon's help.

The Complex was a recent addition to Cassius Station. It had been a starship once—a foldship, not one of the big multi-generation jobs—which the owner, a woman who went by the name Sileon the Unwinder, had paid to graft onto the station. No one knew where she'd come from or what her real name was, and rumor said that the databases of early space exploration showed no record of the ship she'd brought with her.

I suspect that is exactly the way Sileon wanted it. She was pathologically secretive to the point where, if you wanted to visit her office in person, you had to go through her maze.

I'd only been forced down that path once. A client had needed a particularly knotty simulation resolved in order to take down an artificial personality who wanted to block a will... and only Sileon had the skills necessary to get through.

Of course, when it comes to network stuff, it's much safer to keep all conversations offline, so I'd been forced through her maze, a place of shifting corridors, pulsating lights, endless dead ends and the occasional drone programmed to zap you with just enough voltage to be slightly painful without being life threatening.

Microgravity and having to operate in three dimensions hadn't helped things in the least. It had taken me four hours to navigate the thing.

Now I had to do it again, with armed people chasing me. I was pretty sure Sileon wouldn't sell me out... but if she was of a mind to do so, having me stuck in the maze would make things perfectly simple for her.

I walked in. The door shut behind me and the red light I remembered from the first time came on. I sighed and walked forward.

"At least, if Sileon doesn't sell me out, no one is going to find me in here," I said to myself, as I pushed on the first of the doors ahead of me.

It swung open and I walked through. As the door hissed shut behind me, I heard machinery reworking the passage I'd just passed through. The maze was variable, which is how it could keep you occupied for so long in such a small space.

I opened the next door. I figured I'd go straight until I couldn't do that anymore. Another door. This one had blinking lights. It was followed by another.

I stepped into a carpeted reception hall. Sileon stood in front of me, an angry look on her face. "What in the world makes you think I would ever sell you out?" she said.

Sileon was thin and athletic, with short-cropped brown hair and delicate features. She dressed in leather pants and a beige shirt, like someone from a tri-D show about medieval swordswomen. I could imagine her scaling the wall of a castle by night, to steal a magic diamond.

"I see you turned off the maze."

"Yeah," she said. "From what I hear, you didn't need the distraction."

"Why is the gravity on?" I asked, ignoring her hint that she already knew what was going on. She was probably hoping I'd ask so she could show off.

The last time I'd dealt with Sileon, I'd done my damndest to figure out who she was and where she came from. I'd heard any number of theories ranging from the ridiculous—she was an alien being sent here to scope out the Tau system for a future invasion—to the plausible—she was somehow riddled with machine implants undetectable to the kind of scanners we had on station.

Just about the only information I believed, mainly due to its source, was she was definitely human. A particularly insistent criminal organization had gotten hold of a sample of her DNA and tested it thoroughly. Such a prosaic result lent the whole thing an air of legitimacy.

She shrugged. "The maze also serves as a junction. I can spin the ship when I want to."

"You didn't do it last time."

"Last time you were just a customer."

I paused. "And what am I now?"

"A supplicant. There's a different set of rules. Sit down. You want a drink?" She plopped onto a big, upholstered chair and gestured. A sleek autonomous robot—a *humanoid* robot—walked over.

Those are illegal, I didn't say.

"Yes, it's illegal," Sileon replied to my unspoken question. "And it's waiting for your drinks order."

"I'll have wine. White."

She raised an eyebrow. "I would have expected something else from you."

"I need to keep my wits about me. We can get hammered once I'm safe."

"You're safe now," she said.

Sileon was hard to read. She spoke softly and never made eye contact. Yet her words belied any shyness, and her confidence in the sanctity of her home seemed strange coming from a small woman I instinctively wanted to protect from the world. I remembered that from last time: of all the female operators around, she was the only one I felt protective towards. Maybe it was the fact she'd either been born with one of the prettiest faces I'd ever seen or, if not natural, whoever had done the work on her face had built it exactly the way I liked them.

"The people after me are heavy hitters," I said. "Earthling-level heavy, unless I'm wrong."

She shook her head and spoke softly: "Actually, the people after you are rank amateurs. If that woman had simply dropped the gun and blamed you for it, she would have had people doubting what they saw. Hell, half of them told the cops you were the one they wanted." She shook her head. "But then, they did this."

A floating image appeared in the air between us. I hated

those things because they were always fuzzy, but this one didn't need to show too many details. It displayed the alley I'd left earlier in turmoil. I must just have made my exit, because the woman I'd clobbered lay on the floor, gun still grasped in her hand, and the other goon got up. I watched in fast motion as they were surrounded by onlookers. Things seemed to get ugly: the woman pointed her gun at them.

Then, out of nowhere, four more goons in grey swept in and began knocking heads before the six baddies made their escape.

"Yeah," I said when the image flickered and vanished. "That did look kind of stupid. Or maybe they're just too big to care."

"If they were big, you'd be dead," Sileon said, staring at her shoe. "My take is if anyone big is involved, they hired these guys through some intermediary to keep one layer of insulation between themselves and you."

I looked her over, I'd have to let her show off. "How did you know I was coming?"

Instead of crowing, though, she looked away. "I have event alarms set on certain people. You're one of them."

"Why?"

She shrugged. "Makes business sense to keep track of what's going on with the other players. The field we work in isn't huge, after all." Then she looked up. "And besides, I like you."

"Huh?"

"I enjoyed working with you. You are one of the few people who treats me like I'm a normal person you can criticize and stuff, instead of like I'm someone who will crush them and shove their belongings out of an airlock if I get mad at them."

I laughed. "I treat everyone like that. Which is how I got my nose broken."

"It looks good on you."

I raised an eyebrow. "Are you flirting with me?"

"Not yet," she replied, matter-of-factly. "I need to decide whether you'll live long enough to bother, or whether I should kill you before you get me killed. But later, maybe."

"That isn't comforting."

"You didn't come here for comfort. You came here because you need a friend other people are afraid of. Someone who can figure out what is happening and how to get you out of it. Don't answer that."

I sat there for a second wondering what she meant until my Panorama buzzed. I glanced down. "It's just Rime, calling to tell me she finished her cleanup."

"And if someone is piggybacking the call? As soon as your Panorama goes active they'll try to triangulate. And when they find they can't locate you, they'll know you're in a radiation-damped area. Not many of those on Cassius station."

I grunted and ignored the call.

"Besides, are you sure you can trust Rime?"

"We go way back."

"Yeah. Were you expecting her to break your nose?"

Damn. She had me there. Rime had been right that time—her suspicions about the girl from groundside were spot-on—but the right hook had caught me completely by surprise.

"Thought so," Sileon said quietly, still studying her shoes.

I toyed with the idea of asking her how she knew—before I did—that a call was coming into my comm, but I decided I didn't want to know.

CHAPTER 3

A couple of hours later, Sileon's put-upon sigh woke me. One might have expected it to be difficult to drop off to sleep in the lair of one of the most notorious underworld players extant—notorious mostly because no one really knew what her game might be—but after the morning I'd had, I zonked as soon as my lay my head on the armrest of her reception couch.

"What?" I slurred.

"It makes no sense. The rest of it? Fine, I'll buy it. But that makes no sense."

I focused bleary eyes on her. "Goons coming after me? Yeah, I know. I'm not working on anything this big."

Sileon rolled her eyes. "Not that, you doofus. I mean the gun. I've identified the make and model: it's a Beretta 107, produced on Earth before the Tau Ceti colonization. There is no record of one of those ever arriving in-system. Even more interesting is that I can't track any unidentified guns entering Cassius Station in the last two hundred years."

"That's not surprising," I said. "Anyone crazy enough to bring a gun up here would also have to be stupid if they don't cover their tracks."

"Deck," she said. "You came to me for a reason, even if your subconscious apparently forgot to tell the rest of you what that reason is. You came to me because you know that data is where I live and breathe. I know all about your dealings with The Earthling, and I know all about a lot of other stuff that people don't want anyone to know about. I keep them to myself, but I know them"

She let that sink in.

"Which means I can tell you where every illegally smuggled gun on the station is stashed. There are actually seventeen in all. Some of them are stashed so well that they'll never be found again." She chuckled. "Unless I need them. That's because the last people who knew about them are long dead."

"So when you say it didn't get smuggled in…"

"You can believe me," she said.

"So where did it come from?" I asked.

"Another dumb question. It came from Earth…"

"But if someone hacked a nanofactory and pushed this design through the failsafes…"

"I would have been the very first to learn about it, and I would have logged it. This gun simply wasn't here," Sileon declared.

"It obviously was."

"Yeah. And that's what makes no sense. It's a good thing you got to me before you went anywhere else. I have a feeling you're going to need my help."

I shook my head. "I don't think I can afford your help. Not with the way this case is shaping up. I doubt this will be over in a day." Her rates were astronomical even by the standards of Cassius Station.

"So you came here because..?"

"Because I need someone who can hide me from the goons coming after me. If anyone can make me invisible, you can. I want to pay for a cloak job."

She cocked her head. "That's stupid. You can't hide on a station this size. Not if they have anyone competent chasing you."

"So what do I do?"

She thought about it. "Strategic retreat?"

"What?"

"Leave the station, go to one of the asteroid colonies." Then she shook her head. "No. That won't work, they'll track you down. Go further away. An outlaw outpost would probably be safe, they'd have to search hundreds of spots, and that takes enormous manpower."

I snapped my fingers and slapped my head. "Of course," I said. "I'll just jump in my interplanetary tug and fly away. Why didn't I think of that before?" I paused. "Ah, now I remember… because I don't have a ship."

"But I do," Sileon said.

"That's very nice, except I can't pay you for its use."

"I'll let you have it for free. One-way ride to one of the Outlaw rocks."

Every hair on my body stood on end. This kind of offer always made me suspicious. In my world, when something was too good to be true, you did well to count the fingers of your hand after the handshake that sealed the deal. And this was orders of magnitude more too good to be true than the usual stuff that was too good to be true. "I'm not buying it. What's in it for you?"

"Information," she said. "Seeing what happens when you disappear from Cassius completely will tell me a lot about who's working with whom and against which third party. That is the kind of information that will keep my lights on and docking fees paid."

Then she grinned at me. "Actually, though, that's only part of the reason. The real reason is I like you and want you to stay not dead for a little while longer."

Screens flicked to life on the smartwall nearest me. She frowned at it. "Oh, and you'd better decide quickly. Your friends are here."

The image showed a group of men surrounding…

"Is that a tank? Like in the police Tri-ds?"

"Yep," Sileon said. "Except that one is real."

"Where the hell did they get a tank?"

"Factory 11B, sector 7. There's an impact lab that lends out its acceleration tube to paying punters. But it's a front. They've been hiding the tank there for ages. The acceleration tube is actually the barrel of the gun, using low-expansion charges."

The barrel aimed for the camera and I saw the faintest hint of a flash before the image went out, to be replaced by a split-screen view taken from ground level. "Backup cameras," Sileon explained. Then she turned to me. "Anyhow, if you want to leave, you'd better make up your mind fast. The maze is built from thick steel armor... but then again that thing out there is a tank. I give us ten minutes, tops."

"Dammit, dammit, dammit," I muttered. "Get us out of here."

Sileon snapped her fingers and acceleration tossed me back onto the couch.

CHAPTER 4

We drifted a few dozen kilometers from Cassius station.

"One minute," Sileon said. "I'm checking for trackers someone might have tried to hide on the ship and also adjusting the records of our departure from 'Irregular' to 'Authorized'. I want to come back here, after all, and I don't want to have to bribe every official on the station to do it."

"There aren't that many officials on the station," I replied. "We tend to keep government to a minimum."

"Yeah, and they know it, so they have an inflated notion of their value to the universe and the price tag for bribes reflects that notion." She tapped her screen. "Oh, come on, are these guys actually serious?"

"What?" I said.

"They shot a torpedo from one of the airlocks. That has to be the dumbest thing I've ever seen."

"So why aren't we evading?"

"You're a dear, Deck, but sometimes, I wonder how you ever survived this long. Evasion is for people who aren't prepared. Personally, I find all that running around undignified. Here, look."

She waved her hand and another image appeared on the smartwall. This showed a lozenge-shaped grey missile drifting in circles just fifty yards outside something recognizable as Cassius Station.

"What's it doing?" I asked.

"Nothing," Sileon said with a smirk. "When you're a missile and all your navigation algorithms get wiped, apparently you go around in circles. Ah, the tracker check is complete. We're clean."

I was pressed down onto the couch as the ship began to accelerate.

"How did you crack into that torpedo?" I asked.

She tsked at me. "You're a big boy. You should have learned by now that all girls—well, the interesting ones at least—have their little secrets. If I told you all of mine, you'd get bored and look for someone else."

For a second, I considered surrendering to the people who wanted to shoot me. Sileon seemed like she would be more dangerous than anyone else on the station... and at least the people chasing me were likely to be motivated by greed, which was something I could understand.

Sileon? I didn't know. She'd arrived on Cassius Station less than a decade before, looking exactly the way she did now. Of course, that meant nothing: with enough money to your name, you could pretty much buy eternal youth on Cassius. But a starship was a different story. Those weren't a question of money, there simply weren't enough of them to go around, and no one was interested in building them, mainly because fold drives needed to be built to extremely high tolerances if you didn't want to end up a million light years from your destination. You couldn't just ask a civilian nanofactory to build you one.

Moreover, Sileon's ship was a design that didn't match any of the three or four standard vessels the government used to travel between the human colonies on the half-dozen settled systems.

Sileon herself was no less of a mystery. She had been introduced to me as a librarian, which made no sense, even when she explained she was more of a data collector than a librarian per se. From what I'd seen, she was a ninja hacker of the highest order, and no data or system was safe from her.

Not even a torpedo which, I assume, would have been kept in secret somewhere the authorities couldn't get at it.

Now, I was essentially at her mercy. She might be completely true to her word, or she might just be waiting to sell me to the highest bidder. I was twice her size, but on her ship, she would not be helpless. In fact, she probably had automated weaponry tracking my every step. And no matter what she said, of how she pretended to bat her eyelashes at me, there was an angle in this for her.

The problem was, by the time I found out what that angle was, it would be too late for me to do anything about it.

"Let's see about getting you settled," she said.

"What? No need. I'm fine right here. This couch is comfy."

"Don't be ridiculous. We're going to be on this ship for five or six days, and I don't want you underfoot in central areas. Besides, you'll start to smell. I've got spare cabins, and I'm pretty sure there's clothes that will fit you somewhere in this tub. Come on."

I shrugged and followed her. The first four or five rooms we crossed were similar to her reception room. Plush, thickly-carpeted, with imitation wood on every surface. It was decadence that seemed completely out of place on a spacegoing vessel. Then we crossed over into what had to be the crew areas.

They were utilitarian: grey-blue walls and polished metal.

Apparently, however, Sileon had just taken me down a shortcut because we emerged into another sumptuously decorated corridor. This one was bedecked in some kind of green leather.

"Ah. This should be a good room for you," she said. She opened a door by waving her hand in front of it, and we entered the place. It was decorated like one of the fantasy suites you could take a hot date to on Cassius station, except those were cut-rate and tacky, while every surface in this room appeared to be covered with materials of exceptional quality. Though I knew it was impossible—it had to be, didn't it?—I would have sworn the burgundy leather covering much of the room was real animal hide and the dark wood was actually from a tree. But that would have made this ship worth more than a large segment of Cassius Station.

I noticed something else. Other than the slight push of the engine which you had to lean against, we were standing perfectly upright... but we hadn't gone through any slide-locks.

"Holy shit," I said. "This ship has artificial gravity."

Sileon sighed. "I was hoping you wouldn't notice that."

"But... how?"

"A girl has to have her secrets. Can we leave it at that?"

"Do I have a choice?" I asked.

"If by that you mean if I'll tell you who built this ship or how the artificial gravity works, no, you don't have a choice, because I'm not going to tell you. But feel free to ask me over and over again and become a total nuisance. I won't try to stop you if you absolutely must do it."

"All right, I won't ask."

But I was definitely going to wonder. The mystery around this woman got deeper and deeper.

"I think there's some men's clothing in the closet. Why don't you try some of it on to see whether it fits?" she said.

I slid the door open and pulled away. "Ouch," I said. "That is hard on the eyes."

Bright oranges seemed to be the palette the former occupant of the cabin favored; a long way away from the steel grey I preferred for my own look. But the closet was packed, and there were a few serviceable items. I pulled out a pair of trousers in a muted brown, and put them over my legs. "Looks about right," I said.

"You should try them on," Sileon said with a half-smile.

I held her gaze. "I'm not wearing any underpants."

"Try them on anyway."

I decided to call her bluff and unlatched my trousers. Sileon didn't flinch. In fact, her gaze never left mine until, after a moment, she deliberately looked down.

Then she frowned and looked back up at me. "You lied. You are wearing underpants," she whined.

"I just wanted to see what you would do. I thought you'd run."

"Well, I didn't. What are you going to do about it?"

"I'm going to try on these trousers." I pulled them up. "A little loose around the waist, but I see some belts that might help."

She took that without complaint, without even the slightest disappointment. Which hurt a little, to be honest. But could you blame me for not playing her game? She was a major power broker in a place where you could throw a burrito and the odds were it would land on a criminal. That she looked like a little elfin dream girl made no difference. People with money or power like hers could look any way they wanted.

To cover my thoughts, I reached into the closet and pulled out a white shirt. It was a little frillier than I preferred, but not anything that would call attention to itself.

Sileon wrinkled her nose at it. Then she stood and walked to the closet. She pulled out one of the orange trousers and a green shirt. "I'd love to see you in these for dinner," she said. Then she pointed at the display, which told us it was 4:26 PM ship time. "I expect you in the dining lounge at 9 PM sharp for dinner. In the meantime, feel free to wander around the ship. Most of it will be unlocked, but if you find anything that isn't, don't try to get in. Also I think you should take a shower. I believe you'll find the bathroom facilities quite adequate."

She turned and walked away, closing the door behind her.

I let her get a bit of a head start and tested the door. I was surprised when it actually opened. I shut it again.

Now what? I asked myself. If she was using this time to sell me to the highest bidder, I was screwed. There was nothing I could do but let it happen. Oh, I could go on a rampage and damage the expensive décor of her ship, but what would I gain from that? Probably nothing except, instead of waiting for a good offer, she'd sell me at a discount.

Somehow, however, I trusted her. The fact that I was still alive was certainly a point in Sileon's favor, although, if she was trying to sell me—or use me to gain information about what was going on—she would want to keep me that way for as long as it suited her.

My drinking buddies—I didn't have many real friends—had enormous fun at my expense. All they had to do for a good laugh was to enumerate my problems. And the first thing they invariably mentioned was I would do anything for a pretty face and a smile. Which, they said, was fine, as long as I didn't make the mistake of trusting the woman.

When I replied I knew how to take care of myself, they'd point at my crooked nose and say unflattering things about my ability to learn from past mistakes.

I sighed and headed for the bathroom. I stood in shock for a few moments.

"Adequate, she said. Who is this woman?"

A roughly circular tub nine feet in diameter—but not quite circular, because it had organic-looking protuberances and indentations along the edges—dominated the bathroom. It was made of translucent glass and stone, illuminated from within with blue light. The effect was stunning.

A shower pod and toilet each had their separate glass partitions, and as I relieved myself, I studied the second toilet beside the main one. This one didn't have water in it, but a shower faucet that shot water upward, and I concluded it must be some kind of sex toy.

I left it alone and headed for the bath. I had had a tense

day, and I smelled like it. Not finding the controls for the water, I gave up and headed toward the shower.

But the bath was so inviting, I couldn't resist one last look at it, and a plaintive cry of: "Why can't you be simple to use? All I want is some warm water."

Water began to pour from the sides of the tub, resplendent in the blue light.

"Voice activated. Of course."

I dropped my clothes and put a foot into the tub. "Warmer," I said.

The water got warmer.

I climbed in and sat down. "Aah. A guy could get used to a place like this."

* * *

I soaked for an hour, but even after I took another half hour to dress in the garish outfit Sileon had picked for me, and studied myself in the mirror trying to figure out just how ridiculous I looked, I still had a couple of hours to kill before dinner.

I wandered around the ship, looking into the nooks and crannies and learning how the other half lived. My main question was more where this other half existed.

I had been born on Tau Ceti II, in the city of Copernicus, which was the largest city on the planet. Like everything on Tau Ceti II, the city existed not for economic reasons but for social ones: people liked to congregate and enjoy the company of their fellow colonists. It also made sense to keep the administrators in one place.

The city was small by the standards of the past, with a reasonable population spread out over wide areas of low housing units and manicured parks. Life in Copernicus was one of tranquility. Everyone had a housing unit comfortable for the size of their family, and food and furnishings were centrally produced by farms or vats or nanofactories—to everyone's specifications. There was no such thing as poverty or need, but there was also no such thing as accumulation or excess.

I'd gotten to know what poverty meant when, utterly overwhelmed by the everyday sameness of existence in Copernicus, I'd taken a train to the space station and then a rocket to different settlements within the Tau Ceti Administrative Sphere. Still unhappy, I'd managed to sell my services as a general space monkey to a freighter bound for Cassius Station.

I'd been seventeen at the time and arrived with nothing but the contents of my backpack, none of which had any monetary value. I spent my first year scratching around the alleys of the station doing odd jobs for stall owners before I realized that my intelligence made me good at finding things and my size made me hard to push around. My first client as a private investigator arrived just ten minutes after I told Dongee that I was going to give the racket a shot.

I knew he'd talked the guy into hiring me and ever since, I'd never, not once, bought a burrito from another vendor. I had been happy enough in my days of poverty, but I was in no hurry to go back.

This ship represented something completely new to me: opulence on the scale you only saw in the old tri-D adventure films, before the current fad for minimalism came in.

I thought Sileon had chosen my room to mess with me, to make me feel like she thought I belonged in a cathouse, but every room on the ship was equally decadent. Some of the beds were filled with water, others vibrated. One bed actually floated on a bubbling pool of some kind of viscous orange fluid. I tried to imagine who would want such a thing, especially when the ship was under acceleration.

The entertainment rooms didn't exude the same overtly sensual air, but they were also well above what private individuals would have on Tau Ceti. Tri-D immersion theaters for twenty people. Adaptable multi-sport ball courts. Meditation rooms with image, sound, scent, and temperature controls.

I'd seen all of those things before, but always in a community nexus area.

On a ship? Not so much.

This ship had never been from Tau Ceti. It came from a different colony with other values, which ruled out Wolf and Gliese, too. I was stumped as to what it might be. Surely if some colony dedicated itself to utter decadence, the legends would have reached us at Tau Ceti. But I'd heard nothing.

At the very least, I could confirm the theory that she was human. This ship might not reflect Tau Ceti values, but everything about it spoke straight to my darker sensual side. It made me think that, while it was certainly tasteless, I wouldn't mind bringing a hot date here after all. At least the furnishings were real.

The library nearly stopped me cold. There was a fad in Cassius Station for disguising portable libraries—electronic devices holding books—in simulated leather with simulated embossing to resemble an ancient paper-volume. A number of my friends had them.

In front of me stood three walls covered in shelves with one of these after the other. The leather came in all colors, from the deepest maroon to the brightest white. Some were even weathered to look old and dusty. I'd heard that each one had a memchip big enough to store a million books on it… I tried to do the math, but there were too many of them to count. But even considering duplication in the files, there might have been a billion books stored on those devices.

I wondered what was kept there, and whose it had been

before Sileon somehow got her hands on it.

I'd need to ask the second question of Sileon, but at least I could check out the contents for myself. I pulled one of the volumes from a shelf in front of me.

It fell open to show cream-colored paper with dark close-packed lettering filling two columns on the page. A musty, organic smell wafted from it.

"What the…"

I nearly dropped the book in my surprise and tried to remember my history lessons. When had the last paper books been made?

I couldn't remember. But it was back on Earth well before humanity launched the *Umberto Eco*, the first starship. I reverently placed the book back on the shelf and was about to step away when curiosity got the better of me: were they all paper books, or had I happened to stumble on a priceless treasure, hidden in plain sight among thousands of commonplace items?

Two meters to the left, I pulled a blue-bound example out of its space. It was a paper book, too. This one had illustrations in it, and modern typeface, but it still felt incredibly brittle and ancient in my hand. I replaced it.

I looked up to the roof, and from wall to wall, trying to take it all in.

"There's a thousand of them," a voice said.

I turned to see Sileon leaning on the doorjamb. "How…. I mean… how…" I said, eloquent as always.

She smiled. "You mean the books."

"Yes. But all the rest of it, too. This ship isn't standard issue."

She strode into the room and I watched her. She'd worn a grey smokesuit, a garment of gauze and smartgas that hugged the curves of her body, at times opaque, at times utterly transparent, but smart enough to show only what its owner programmed it to show. Sileon was in the mood to tantalize, to get ever so close, but not to reveal. She sat on a comfortable chair bound in what looked like leather, but couldn't be… could it?

I honestly didn't know.

"I'll tell you about the books," she said. "And don't look so surprised. I told you I was a librarian, didn't I? Well, how can one be a librarian without books?"

"A lot of ways," I told her. "You can be a data facilitator for one of the big warehouses." I had a very good friend who did exactly that job, and did it very well… but she had other qualities, too, so I decided not to bring her up. It was the kind of conversation that would cause Sileon to turn her smokesuit fully opaque faster than I could blink.

"I can do all of that," Sileon replied. "But this is how I started. This is my passion. Physical books."

"But these belong in a museum or a university. How come you have them?"

She laughed again. "These aren't as rare as you think," she said, "or at least they weren't back when books were common." She strode to the shelves. "These are mostly from the eighteenth and nineteenth centuries. They've been restored and conserved to within an inch of their lives by the very best… me." She studied the shelves. "Older books would not have been printed on a press. They would have been written on vellum by scribes before being bound together."

I looked at the books critically. "I have no idea what most of that means."

Sileon chuckled. Her smokesuit turned a bluish-grey and a little more transparent. Uh-oh. She'd programmed it to respond to her mood.

I was in trouble.

"Fair enough," she said. "The earlier books were much bigger and heavier."

"I'll go with that," I replied.

Sileon rolled her eyes. "You big guys are all alike. You all pretend to be dumber than you are, just to see what happens."

"And librarians are always acting superior."

"That's because we are superior. Anyway, do you want to go to the dining room or would you rather eat here?"

"Are you kidding? In a real library with a librarian? Definitely here," I said.

She smiled at me and I raised an eyebrow as her smokesuit came dangerously close to revealing all the interesting stuff in high definition. Even without it going full transparent, I got a wonderful eyeful.

"You did that on purpose," she accused.

I held up my hands. "No, no. I'd never be smart enough for something like that."

The suit did interesting things.

Sileon must have reset it somehow, because it returned to its original dark grey. "How about we get some food in here before you charm away what little remains of my modesty?" she said.

She strode to a wall and typed several commands into the nearest panel, which became an interface for her use. I half-expected the floor to reconfigure itself and extrude a table, but the reality was more prosaic: a selection of humanoid robots carried a table, seats, cutlery and candles into the center of the room and set up the table. We sat and they also brought food.

"You look about the way I thought you would," she said.

"What?" I asked. And then I remembered the clown suit. With my exploration of the ship, I'd completely forgotten I was dressed like my outfit had been selected by a blind guy with bad fashion sense. "I thought you liked these."

She laughed and the smokesuit started clearing up a little. "No, but I was curious to see if you'd actually put them on."

"Well, here I am, what do you think?"

"You wear it reasonably well. A guy with smaller shoulders or a bigger gut would look ridiculous. Well, more ridiculous, I guess." Her eyes sparkled. "If you're too uncomfortable, we can go change into more everyday clothes."

I eyed the smokesuit and shook my head. "I can live with a little ridiculousness in the line of duty."

"Are you flirting with me?" she asked.

"Me? Never, I never flirt until after we've finished eating." Then I looked around, taking in the library, the robots and the table. "And besides, after seeing where you live, I really want to see what your kitchen is capable of."

She clapped her hands and the robots dove into action. The food was as good as I imagined. "Is this real fish?" I asked as the first course, a dainty appetizer of slices of pale white meat, appeared.

"Yep. I got it from the globe tank the Maruchi Clan has in free orbit. It's pretty cheap, considering its quality. But don't tell them I said so or they'll charge me more next time."

The quality of the food remained high, dish after dish. The one thing that wasn't exotic as hell was the wine: it was all recognizable Cassius Station fare. I asked her how come.

She shrugged. "Cassius station makes really good wine," she replied. "And there isn't anyone else in the system that comes close. Not even the bootleggers in the asteroids. Plus, I like it."

I nodded. It's always been good enough for me.

We talked. She told me stories that grew more and more fantastic as she drank the wine, of hunting down each and every one of those volumes. If she was to be believed, she'd put the ship to good use, going to planets I didn't recognize.

But then, I already knew the ship hadn't been produced on any world I knew of.

"But tell me about you," she said.

"There was one case when I had to identify which of three clones claiming to be the rightful inheritor of an identity actually had been quickened most recently, and was therefore the most faithful copy, and—"

"Not your work stuff," she said, leaning forward on the table with the glass of blood-red wine in her hand. "I can get that anywhere, even how often you go to the bathroom. Tell me about you."

"Well, I ran away from home because it was too happy."

"What?" she seemed shocked.

"You wanted to know about me, so I'm telling you my darkest secret. Everything was too easy, and I needed something more, so…"

By the time I finished telling her the story of my misspent youth, the smokesuit was almost completely transparent—there were just some little translucent areas to keep it interesting—and we were both dreamy and happy and full of wine.

There was nothing more to be said, so we didn't say it.

Chapter 5

Five days later, Sileon's ship, which she'd told me was called the *Basilisk*, approached an unincorporated asteroid mining company called Frontera. Unaligned with either the Copernicus government or Cassius station, it survived through commerce with both, plus less-formal ties with even more illicit settlements in the cold wastes of the Tau Ceti system.

Sileon seemed unusually mellow. Of course, she was normally hard as steel with a crust of sarcasm thrown over it all to protect the steel, but it was still nice to feel that she might actually miss me.

"You sure you'll be okay?" she said for the tenth time.

"I'm a big boy. And I'm armed to the teeth. And I have enough credits in the e-wallets you gave me to buy this place. I feel like a kid on his first day of school."

"Frontera is a bit rougher than any school you'd ever have heard of," she replied.

"I've grown a bit since my school days. Hell, you'll probably be in more danger than I will."

She shook her head. "I'll see what's shaking in Cassius station electronically before I dock again. And if I decide to dock, I'll point some of the ship's weapons at the front door. That will preclude any attempt to duplicate the tank stunt." She held my gaze. "I'll come get you as soon as its safe for you to return, or at least as soon as I know who's gunning for you. Check the dropboxes I set up for you every day. There are several places with access to outside transmissions in Frontera."

"We've been over this," I reminded her. "But I think I know what you're trying to say." I took her shoulders in my hands, pulled her close and kissed her.

She returned it, not with the passion she showed when she wanted to have sex, but tenderly.

It was almost enough to make me think that she wouldn't sell me out if the price was right.

But it wasn't enough to make me think that she'd offer me sanctuary on the *Basilisk* for as long as I needed it and, in the meantime, the ability to cruise around Tau Ceti space indefinitely. Sileon would never be the type to lose her independence because she'd had a few good days with a nice guy.

I pulled away from her and looked into her eyes. "I can't thank you enough for this," I said. Then I activated the airlock and entered the pressure room. I wasn't wearing a suit—the flexible tunnel connecting the ship with the asteroid was pressurized—but the airlock would protect the ship in case a micrometeorite hit the tube as I was crossing.

That the ship would be saved would be small comfort to me as I asphyxiated… but it was better than nothing, I guess.

She let me enter without a word and the airlock cycled. I looked back, but she was walking away from me.

Sentimental girl, I thought with a chuckle.

Then I floated across the tube—ten meters of stiff reinforced rubber—and arrived at the Frontera airlock.

The outer door opened manually, with a foolproof metal wheel. After I closed it, I requested entry on the keypad.

Five seconds later, the door hissed open. I floated through for my first impression of the mining colony.

As first impressions went, this was a disappointment. The chamber I arrived in had obviously been carved out of the naked stone using explosives and then sealed with some kind of rubberized concrete. No one had bothered to paint over the grey goop of the sealant.

The entire room was maybe ten meters in diameter, with two equally rough-finished tunnels leading away at an angle.

Illumination came from several yellow globes hidden behind reinforced metal cages—how poor did a place have to be to need to protect glow-globes that way? They threw out a murky light which made a place that was obviously antiseptic by its very nature, appear organic. It even felt a bit like a swamp, with warm air sticking to my skin.

Most disappointing of all, however, was what the globes illuminated.

Six people waited for me. Five of them were humans of assorted shapes and sizes dressed in stained grey coveralls and armed with what looked like police-issue long distance incapacitators.

The sixth might have started human, or it might have started as a humanoid loading bot. Either way, it was now an amalgam of man and machine that glared evilly at me through eyes that had been replaced by red lenses in a human skull.

A small man standing beside the cyborg spoke.

"Mr. Leonid, I presume? Deck Leonid?"

That certainly wasn't the name I'd applied for entry under. And Sileon's ship was supposed to be an ore runner from one of the other colonies.

For a fleeting moment, I wondered what would happen if I denied any knowledge of this Leonid fellow. Then I remembered the zappers. Getting zapped was never fun.

I sighed. "Yeah."

The man nodded, his expression unreadable. "Good. You're coming with us."

It wasn't a question. When you had that much manpower, you didn't need to ask nicely.

They led me wordlessly down a main corridor for a few yards, floating along in the asteroid's microgravity, then unlocked a rusted door that creaked as it opened and pushed me into a smaller enclosure that must have served as an access tunnel when the asteroid was being hollowed out.

The fact it had been neglected so long the door had

actually rusted was a terrible sign. Orbital and deep space facilities were never large. Every cubic centimeter of space needed to be utilized, and it wasn't unusual for spaces to be used for multiple purposes.

An empty space was probably an abandoned one.

A great place to dump a body if you didn't want it to be discovered for a long time.

"Don't even think about it," the leader said when I half-turned to get a better look at the lay of the land. He was the only guy who'd spoken to me so far.

"If you think you're going to kill me without a fight, you'd better think again."

"If we wanted to kill you," the guy replied, "You'd be dead. We want to talk to you."

"We could have talked when I walked in."

"Not about this, we couldn't. Keep moving." He waved his incapacitator at me, giving me little choice but to obey. He wouldn't miss at that range.

We floated a few dozen meters down the rough-hewn tunnel until we came to a room full of machinery. It was old and rusted, and none of the hum of active equipment filled the space. The only thing that appeared to work in this area were the lights.

A table and chairs were bolted to what I assumed must serve as the floor in this zero-gee environment.

"Sit," the most voluble of my captors said. "Hook your foot on the table. I don't want you floating away."

They arrayed themselves around me in a hemispherical pattern, the standard microgravity pattern to keep a prisoner boxed in. I wondered about that… it seemed overkill for a room that had exactly one exit. All they had to do to keep me boxed up was to put the cyborg beside the entrance.

"All right. I'm seated here. I suppose you're going to tell me who hired you to ambush me before the trash compactor over there breaks me into pieces? If you were expecting me to try to buy you, I'm afraid I'm not in that financial league."

"I'd call bullshit on that, judging by the ship you flew in on," the spokesman said. He was dark-haired, brown-eyed and wore a few days' worth of dark stubble, but that wasn't the thing that caught my eye. He was well-muscled and short, which was unusual in the extreme for microgravity. His companions, though it was clear they spent an enormous amount of time in the gym, were much more willowy, and much taller. I could probably break any of them in half without much effort. "But we're not here to squeeze you, either."

"So, not here to kill me and not here to rob me. I'm not sure I prefer the options that are left."

"We're here to talk to you. We've got a proposal. A job offer."

"And if I don't like it?" I asked.

"We'll leave you locked in here with enough food bars and water to survive until the job's over. Unhurt, but…" he looked around, "both unsanitary and uncomfortable, I'd guess."

"There's not much of a choice there."

He shrugged. "The way I see it, having someone toss you out an airlock would be cheaper. Don't have to feed you."

His logic was impeccable, but I wasn't comforted. "All right. I'll listen. But first you have to tell me who you are."

"No, we don't. But I will," the guy replied. "My name is Oreilly."

"Never heard of you. Who do you work for?"

"I work for myself and the people of Frontera. Also, the people of the city of Boston, on old Earth, but that's a bit of a longer story."

"You're the leader of this place?" I asked, ignoring the part that sounded insane.

"The Commissioner, yes."

It was as good a reason as any to explain why he could access sealed off areas. "And this job is, of course, utterly illegal," I said.

"That depends."

I smiled. This was the kind of conversation I had often. A lot of the people I dealt with wanted to feel that what they were doing went above mere petty criminality... that somewhere, somehow, they were doing something right. "Of course it does."

"I could argue that our overarching purpose is precisely the opposite of illegal." Then he grinned, a huge toothy smile. "But we're gonna need to break a whole shitload of laws to pull it off."

"Ah."

"And we're going to need your help to do it. You know the terrain."

"The only terrain I know is Cassius Station," I replied. "And if I so much as go near the place, there will be people coming after me with tanks and space torpedoes."

"Yeah, we saw that. You sure pissed someone off."

"Badly. And they want me dead. Since I don't want to be dead, I've decided to spend some time away from Cassius. It's not that I enjoy being in Frontera... but it's unhealthy for me to go back right now."

"Unless you help us, you'll never be able to return," the guy said.

"And if I do, I will?" I asked, raising a skeptical eyebrow in his direction. "When do you plan on giving me my life back?"

"Immediately after we're done. But only if we succeed," Oreilly replied.

"Color me unconvinced. These guys are heavy hitters from Cassius Station and you... well, you're a bunch of goons on a lost rock."

That got a reaction. Everyone but the leader and the cyborg mumbled something.

The leader simply sighed. "Calling us names won't get you anywhere. Especially not those names." He studied me. "Look, we need to go after a group of people—criminals—in Cassius Station. You've made a career out of consorting with most of the lowlifes there. Additionally, you've shown to have a serious amount of initiative when the shit finally hits the fan. So you would be a good addition to our team."

"I work better alone."

"We suspect the people we're going after are the same ones who forced you to run from the station. By helping us, you'd be helping yourself to go back home."

"How would you even know that?"

"The same way we knew that you were on Sileon's ship. We have resources you can't even begin to imagine."

"So do the people arrayed against us."

Oreilly smiled. "Not like us. We're... unusual in this system."

I rolled my eyes. "Just once, I'd like to be offered a straight-up non-weird job from someone who isn't unusual." I sighed. "What would I need to do?"

"We need to find someone. I believe that is what you do."

"Yeah."

"Good. We'll pay all your usual fees."

"Except when I set foot on the station, I'll get shot on sight. And they'll shoot all of you just for knowing me."

"I can guarantee they won't know you're there. Besides, if you don't come with us, you get to sit here and rot."

"Damn," I said. "I don't see what could possibly go wrong."

Oreilly grinned at me. He looked like his face would split in two. "Nothing is going to go wrong. You can trust us. We're cops."

CHAPTER 6

The place they took me after I agreed to go along with their harebrained scheme was much more congenial than the abandoned storage room they'd locked me in before. It appeared to be some kind of zero-gee lounge, with video equipment and music, and even a coat of white paint over the sealant. The food they gave me, on the other hand, made me decide that I could stand to lose a few kilos. "I can see why you're so keen on going to Cassius," I said, returning the tube of protein paste to the guy who'd given it to me. Then I turned to Oreilly. "So, let me get this straight. You're not actually miners, but a tribe of cops."

"That's right," he replied. "Look, I have to go, but my little sister here can walk you through the history." He turned and floated into the passageway, leaving me alone with the cyborg and a twenty-something woman.

"We're not a tribe, but yes, everyone in Frontera is descended from a police task force that was sent to Tiantáng station to investigate a heist that happened on Earth long before humanity had any permanent settlements in space," the young woman said. She had the muscular but thin build of her companions, and her short red hair was buzz cut. She had taken Oreilly's place as the only member of the group to talk to me once I'd agreed to help. From what I understood, she was Frontera's historian and record-keeper.

"What kind of a heist?" I said.

"Art," she replied.

"So that's how you broke through Sileon's security. You must have the best hackers in the game if you're looking for the kind of people who'd crack art NFT blockchains."

She smiled gently. "Physical art."

"What?"

"These are paintings. On canvas and paper. They were

already hundreds of years old when they were stolen. Well, some of them were. Look." She turned towards the screen and hit a couple of commands on her handheld. The screen came to life slowly—all the tech on Frontera seemed to be functional but extremely worn, slow and old—and began to display pictures.

A man and a woman wearing extremely weird collars.

A ship—a sailing ship, not a spaceship—in a storm at sea. It was the kind of thing I could identify only from Tri-D films.

A man in a ridiculous cylindrical hat.

Several other paintings and drawings cycled through before the slideshow returned to the collars.

"There were a couple of other masterpieces in the haul, a vase and a sculpture, but according to our records, the investigators were pretty sure those never made it off Earth. They were too bulky to hide easily in the space vehicles of the time."

"So…" I began. Then I stopped. "Wait. I can't just call you Oreilly sister or Oreilly 2. Do you have an actual name?"

"Jill," she said.

"Jill," I replied, as she stared at me with an eyebrow raised. Her freckles seemed about to jump out from her pale skin. I wondered how she could be the Oreilly's sister—they didn't look like they came from the same settlement, much less the same family—but I said nothing. Instead, I smiled. "I like that name."

It was true. Somehow, the anachronistic moniker fit her anachronistic genes—I wondered how much one had to pay to get red hair, almost completely white skin and freckles in the Tau system—and completed the picture.

She relaxed.

"So, Jill," I said. "You're saying someone took a bunch of old paintings and smuggled them into space?"

"They actually sold them on Earth to someone very rich, and that someone—well, their family after a few generations—took them to Mars. From there, they made their way to Tiantáng Station..."

"Tiantáng as in the sector of the station?" I asked.

"Yes. Back when it was still an independent unit, still in Earth space before it got sent out to Tau Ceti to help with the mining operations and Cassius Station got built around it."

"And from there?"

"The art never left the system. Those paintings and drawings are somewhere in Tau Ceti. My brother thinks they never actually left Cassius Station, and we'll find them there."

"Then it's easy. We just need to find Sileon and pay her to tell us where they are. She knows about everything that's hidden."

"Like she knew about the gun they used to shoot at you?" Jill asked with an eyebrow raised.

"No one is infallible. We should still ask her."

"We already did. A couple of years ago. She told us it's simply not there." Jill smiled. "Which is the same thing every information broker we've approached in the past few hundred years has said." She smiled. "And we were pretty much convinced the art had actually been lost to the record-keepers, and we'd need to go in and physically find it. Except when the gun appeared, we realized that if we can find where the gun came from... then we will find where the paintings are."

"Why now? And why me?"

"We think you stumbled into something. As to why now... I think the people keeping the art hidden knew that we were coming after them. We'd given up trying to find it through indirect means and were coming to Cassius to tear the station apart. They must have found out somehow, and that, plus whatever you saw, brought them out into the open."

"All very nice… except I didn't see anything," I said. "Also, the fact that these people knew you were coming doesn't make me happy. Why should I trust your operational security?"

"Oh, we found the leak," Jill replied. "She is very cold and desiccated right now, and is also on an eccentric orbit that might, in a few thousand years, bring her back to the inner system."

"Ah."

She gave me a hard look. "When you're a close-knit group like Frontera, you don't take kindly to traitors. Especially when you've been forced to take up lithium mining to survive."

"Yeah, what's up with that?" I said. "Why didn't you go back home after… how long are you supposed to stick with a case, anyway?"

"Our forefathers… were not exactly the cream of the Solar System Security Force. The heist investigation was hardship duty. And they were actually marooned here when Earth voted to go fully online and abandoned their physical existence." She shrugged. "It sounded insane to most of them, so they just stayed here and swore an oath to finish the job."

"Nutty as hell," I said.

"You be respectful," the cyborged guy said. His voice was about what you'd expect from someone who was half-man, half-machine. Grinding and hoarse. "Besides, I don't see you in any hurry to upload to some fantasy la-la land."

"One point to the can opener," I replied. I didn't know why I did it. Something about the open, in-your-face mixing of human and machine gave me the creeps, even I'd seen it countless times in countless places.

He pushed himself towards me, but Jill held up a hand.

"You can rearrange his face once we do what we need to do," she said. "Until then, you have to play nice."

The cyborg muttered something about certain things being worth the wait and went back into his corner.

"All right. So, to honor the oath of your ancestors who weren't the best and brightest, we're going to mount an expedition into Cassius Station. That part is easy enough to understand. My question is how are we supposed to get into the station without getting my ass blown off?" I said.

"We're going to use the misdirection you already created to our advantage," Jill said. "Sileon's cover is very good."

I held up a hand. "Nowhere near good enough," I pointed out. "You guys weren't fooled for a second, and you're way out in the boonies. Imagine what someone in a more centralized place would be able to dig up."

Jill gave me a tight-lipped smile. "We've got resources they don't," she replied.

I laughed.

"What?" Jill said.

"You're definitely a cop," I replied. "I've seen it a million times. You need someone to help you out with something, someone whose nuts will be in a vice if they get caught. So you tell them 'don't worry, everything will be fine'." I shook my head. "Half the time, the poor slob gets demolished when it all goes to hell."

"So why even come with us?" Jill asked.

I thought about it. "Because, between rotting out in this crappy excuse for a space installation…" I glanced over at the thin-skinned cyborg. "No offense. But between rotting out in this place and actually taking my life in my own hands, I prefer to take the risk."

She looked me up and down. "Yeah, I suppose a guy like you would."

I was going to have to get my nose fixed after all. People

were starting to assume things. Jill had taken one look at me and was convinced I was a reckless wacko. And I always prided myself on trying to be one of the good guys… was the broken schnoz causing people to think otherwise? I'd need to think about it.

CHAPTER 7

"It's a Lithium freighter," Oreilly's scratchy, distorted voice said over my helmet radio as we crossed an unpressurized bridge from the asteroid to a spaceship that looked old enough to have seen service in Earth's planetary system half a millennium ago.

The ship was probably a death trap, but that was nowhere near my top concern. The suit they'd lent me was, if anything, older than the ship. Despite the common wisdom that if you felt cold in a spacesuit, you were already dead, this one kept me well-chilled as I advanced across the abyss. I was sure I heard a hiss, the last sound a person with a leaky suit would ever hear before the silence of vacuum overcame them... but I couldn't pin it down. It had to be my imagination, because it had been going on since I got out of the airlock, and I still wasn't dead.

When I first donned the suit, I wasn't too worried about the possibility of death. It smelled of rotting plastic and the last owner's stale sweat. I figured if I died, it wouldn't be too bad. In fact it might be better than having to wear that tenth-hand abomination—the only suit my size on all of Frontera, apparently—for an extended period of time.

That kind of thinking never survived exposure to the cold, hard vacuum of space. As I crossed from a forlorn rock in the outer reaches of the Tau Ceti system, the dim orange dot, distant and cold, that was the system's primary star was a cold comfort indeed. Every breath, even smelling like someone's old socks, was precious, and I wanted them to continue as long as possible.

So I concentrated on keeping my cold fingers from slipping on the cable that made up the upper half of the bridge, while my half-frozen feet slid over the one that formed the bottom. Shuffling along, I made my way under the pinpricks of light in the dead blackness of space.

The freighter, a ship I would have avoided at all costs in most other situations looked incredibly inviting and, as I crowded into the airlock with a few of Oreilly's men, I couldn't wait for the thing to cycle and the inner door to open.

We entered a dark grey corridor surrounded by metal walls on all four sides. Unlike most low-rent ships I'd seen, there were no exposed cables on the walls. This ship might be old and rickety, but it had once been a quality item: the wall panels were actually molded around the equipment below, of some lightweight metal. They'd been polished once, but were now tarnished and streaked with fluid. Without gravity, the scars of ancient leaks radiated outward from where the fluid had escaped.

"Cozy," I said as I popped my helmet. "At least I don't have to worry about some new and experimental technology failing."

"There are advantages to this ship," Oreilly said. Then he grinned. "Although I'll admit they aren't necessarily visible to the naked eye."

"But I expect you won't tell me what they are."

"Lighten up, Leonid, will you? No one here means you any harm, and we're not the cops you deal with normally."

"Yeah, I know. Those guys are eight-hour-shift workers. They brutalize the population for a salary, and then they go home and you can hardly even tell they're complete sociopaths. They have families and hobbies and the better paid of them might even have a plant they take care of." I looked around. "You guys, on the other hand, are in deep cover to solve a crime everyone else in the galaxy has completely forgotten. That's loony even by police standards."

Unlike the cyborg, who was easy to needle, Oreilly just shrugged at the provocation. "It's not something you would understand. You grew up on Cassius Station. You guys only care about making money and having sex. Usually at the expense of everyone else. A higher calling isn't in your makeup."

I said nothing. Even on Cassius, there were people trying to convert us, to lead us along the path of righteousness—or to try to convert us to the more collectivist social organization that the Copernicus government pushed—and it never took. Both the preachers and the reformers usually drew decent crowds of bored people on the streets, but when the time came for them to scrape together enough credit to afford to stay on Cassius or to keep themselves fed, they would find their virtual collection buckets empty. Eventually, that meant they'd have to either find honest work or go back to Copernicus space, where the government kept them from starving.

I never imagined the lunatic fringe could survive out in the less-regulated mining colonies and free stations, but maybe that's because I never thought it all the way through. Maybe I was missing the point. After all, it must take a special kind of mentality to live where the star hardly ever shone, and where you only saw the same hundred or two hundred people, day in and day out, for your entire life, often living with very little in the way of entertainment options, a horizon that might be permanently a few meters away, and constant microgravity. Maybe the only way to survive was to become a fanatic.

Did that make Cassius station a kind of equilibrium place, poised between the safe, predictable and frankly bland life in Copernicus-controlled space and the closed, self-contained existence of the smaller settlements? I didn't know, and I wasn't the right guy to think about it. I just wanted my life back.

And this creaking freighter was the first step.

"Listen," Oreilly said. "There's no need for you to get huffy. And there's no harm in telling you why this ship is the safest place for you to be." He patted the metal wall of the corridor. "This ship is listed in Cassius Station's records as a Lithium freighter with holds for unprocessed ore. The blueprints in Cassius show this entire area to be a cavernous empty space. And the airlock is disguised as an ore unloading point—and it works as one."

"So what?" I replied. "You modified the interior to create a smuggler's hull. Someone will know about it. The workmen. The people who sold you the tech. Even if the records are old, someone will have them."

"True," Oreilly replied. "Someone does. Except not in Tau Ceti. The work was done for a smuggler in the Asteroid Belt. The Asteroid Belt around Sol."

"The Sol system went fully virtual five hundred years ago. And it hasn't recovered. They all died out," I replied. "Or didn't you guys hear about the *Unity* mission all the way out on Frontera."

He gave me a cold look. "No wonder Kane wants to cut you up for fertilizer. You've got a mouth on you. We know all about the *Unity* mission. But you missed the point. This ship was built before the Sol system went virtual, and was brought out here with all the other ships they didn't need after the transition. We bought it because we knew its history… because the police had investigated the build and decided to keep an eye on it. Now that we need it, we're the only people in Tau Ceti space who know it exists."

"Hmm."

"This ship is a regular visitor to Cassius Station. No one will bat an eye when we appear exactly on time for our scheduled delivery. And we also trust that Sileon's security was good enough that no one ever realized you came to Frontera in the first place."

"If you caught on, someone else will have."

"Not necessarily. You need to remember, we were expecting you to pop up somewhere in the system. It was just luck that you showed up on our doorstep, but we had people waiting for you at all of the other stations where you might conceivably have ended up. Anyone based on Cassius Station would have had to follow your path through the system. There are several astronomy stations in Tau Ceti, and Sileon pretty much controls the feed from every one. They would have received garbage instead of tracking data." He gave me the tight-lipped smile his sister had already displayed. "And besides, we have resources not everyone can access."

"I'll be sure to remember than when the bad guys shoot me in the lungs," I replied.

"Whatever. This is where you sleep. Don't forget to connect the nets, because if you float around, you'll probably break something when the ship either does a burn or performs a course correction."

"Charming."

"You'll have the entire two-week flight to get used to it."

* * *

The ship—the bastards refused to tell me its name, even though I could easily find out as soon as I returned to Cassius and checked the docking records—used its engine in fits and starts. Metal around us groaned and creaked. As advertised, everything not tied to the hull shook loose and was broken against one surface or another.

A few hours later, we coasted.

That lasted two weeks.

I passed the time playing cards—a version of seven card poker I'd never seen before, and at which I mostly sucked—with Oreilly's men. The leader himself must have had some kind of hidden access to other areas of the ship, because he was never in view.

Even though we played for low stakes, Kane, the cyborg, had taken particular joy in taking every credit I cared to bet. I would have accused him of cheating if I weren't vividly aware of the fact that his hydraulics could tear a metal plate in half… and my arms couldn't.

I noticed the others wouldn't bet as much as usual when Kane was in the game, so I asked Jill about it.

She shook her head. "We think it's something about the interface between the computer and the human brain. He remembers patterns better than we do, and that makes him better at playing the odds. Or something."

"I'll try to get on his good side. A guy like that could make me a fortune on Cassius."

She snorted. "Good luck."

CHAPTER 8

To say we didn't arrive in Cassius Station through the VIP entrance was the understatement of the millennium.

The docking procedure was similar to takeoff from Frontera, but instead of ominous clankings followed by a huge acceleration burn, we got a huge deceleration burn followed by ominous clankings. How the ship didn't shake itself apart was a mystery, but eventually we became stationary.

And then I heard the grinding.

Something screeched and roared all around us as if the ship had been grasped by a giant robot which was twisting it in an attempt to shear it in two. The deafening noise was accompanied by violent shaking that made the vibration of acceleration seem like a gentle caress.

It lasted nearly half an hour, and my attempts to find out what the hell was happening were unsuccessful, mainly because I couldn't hear the answers people were attempting to give me.

When it stopped, the silence was sweet, like ice-cold water after a four-hour gym session. It was pure bliss, and I couldn't recall having felt much better.

"All right ladies. Suit up. Now comes the fun part," Oreilly shouted.

"What?" I asked. But no one was listening to me, and they were all scrambling to get into their suits, so I followed their example.

The suit didn't smell any better the second time around.

Once suited and safety-checked, we lined up in front of the airlock and took it in threes. My group was the second, and I was—coincidentally or not—arrayed beside Jill and Kane.

Instead of opening to the blackness of space, the airlock cycled to show the side of a mountain.

No. Not a mountain, a floating pile of rock—unprocessed lithium-rich regolith, I assumed.

I realized it was the regolith unloading that had caused the racket.

"Careful, Ace," Jill said over the radio. "This stuff isn't held down. No gravity. It won't crush you if you hit a big clump, but it can conceivably slow you down so much that you'll never make it to the other side of the hold. Use the magnetic boots on the wall."

The regolith got absolutely everywhere. My suit—and those of my companions—was completely grey in seconds. I knew it was impossible, but I could have sworn the stuff got through the airtight seals and onto my skin.

Other than that, however, the trek was uneventful. The hold was only a few hundred meters long, and we crossed it in under fifteen minutes. There was a small maintenance hatch on the other end which allowed us onto the outer skin of Cassius Station.

I studied the enormous complex of rings and towers and girders that made up the station as we trekked along the warehouse zone. It truly was a world to itself, the largest artificial structure ever built by man. I felt a bit of species pride well up before I remembered that, though we might have the capacity to build this kind of thing, the mean streets inside were straight from a bad police novel.

And they were especially dangerous if your name happened to be Deck Leonid.

Jill accessed an airlock that opened into a dingy corridor where someone had thoughtfully knocked out everything even resembling a security camera and then hypo-painted obscene song lyrics on the gray wall, complete with instructional diagrams.

I popped my helmet, but the air in here smelled worse than my suit. "Really? You brought me to Dead Space?"

Jill raised an eyebrow. "Well, we could have walked you onto the Old Corridor in Tiantáng... but that didn't work out so well for you last time." She looked around. "Think of it this way. When you arrived in Frontera, you thought your identity was safe and you'd done everything right. We were there waiting for you as soon as you stepped through the airlock. Well, look around. There's no one waiting for you now."

She had a point.

Then she grinned. "That's the good news. The bad news is, this is your room." She pointed.

At some point, the sliding door had been replaced by a cloth curtain which was being eaten by some kind of mold.

It was the source of the smell.

Chapter 9

Dead Space.

Technically, the words described a spot on the Cassius Station map. The area was ancient in Cassius Station terms, and it consisted of three obsolete colony transport ships that had been grafted onto the station as worker housing during one of the outpost's growth spurts.

After the building project was completed, the ships had been left where they were, eventually getting plumbed and wired in as an integral part of the station.

They spent decades completely empty, since cheap housing—in the form of clean, efficient sleep tubes—was available near the public spaceport.

And that was the way things remained until "cheap" became too expensive for some people.

Cassius Station was not a welfare state. Everything except for the air the population breathed had to be bought and paid for. There were no safety nets, by design, because the station had evolved into a kind of protest against life in the parts of the system controlled by the Copernicus Government on Tau Ceti II.

The areas Cassius Station's residents didn't feel worked well as societies included the planet itself, Inti, which was the moon of Tau Ceti IV and the largest mining colony in the system, and a few outlying stations such as Beni and Allista.

If you wanted a safety net and food and housing sufficient for everyone, all you needed to do was to go back to an area controlled by Copernicus. Cassius Station even had a fund to pay for tickets for people who, having failed to make a life for themselves in the station, needed to return. Dozens were deported that way every month.

But a few refused to go. For those, Cassius represented an ideal, their dreams of freedom made reality. And when money became an insurmountable problem, they gravitated towards Dead Space, where about half of the old ship cabins lay empty and the rest were occupied by the lowest level-predators and prey in the entire Cassius ecosystem.

Even the violence was low-key. There was nothing to steal here. People who landed in Dead Space didn't have credits, and they'd already pawned off anything that might be of value. There was little to no sexual violence, partly because the inhabitants were mainly men—even on Copernicus, a woman always had something she could sell for a few credits or uranium shares—but mainly because starving people didn't have the energy for that kind of thing.

Or for anything at all, really.

As I walked the corridors, that became painfully evident. I was doing a little recon, getting the lay of the land, but mostly, I was testing out my new face. Oreilly's crew had a surgeon waiting for me when we landed. The man had operated in the filthy room two days before, straightening my nose and installing a pair of subcutaneous implants that—by slightly altering the angles of my face—would fool automated facial recognition systems. The doctor promised me they'd dissolve after three months and warned I should be careful because they'd start losing effectiveness after two months.

So here I was, testing the implants. I walked to corridors with functioning cameras—quite a long distance from my room, it turned out—while Jill and her tech crew monitored the security system's ID feeds. If any of the automated programs recognized me, we'd make a run for it out the nearest airlock—just a few meters down the hall—and back into the secret compartment in the mining ship's hold. The rest of the team would continue their mission without me.

The halls were dim and littered, because waste management was also something you had to pay for. I strode confidently—the entire module where the ships had been grafted was spun for gravity—and I was grateful to be back under weight.

"Don't do that. It makes you stand out," Hiya, one of Oreilly's people, told me. She was as slim and athletic as the rest of the Oreilly crew, but she also had slightly darker skin and straight black hair that marked her down as a descendant of one of the original Chinese inhabitants of Tiantáng. "You're walking too fast. It scares people here."

I slowed down, but I still scared people. I supposed any tall, well-fed and well-dressed stranger—and by well-dressed, you could count anyone not wearing rags—walking down those halls would have scared people. My trousers were probably worth more than some of the people here had seen in a year.

They'd know that, unless I was very good at defending myself, I would be in danger of robbery by the area's desperate denizens.

Most people must have assumed that I could unleash mayhem on anyone who tried anything; they took cover behind their doors as I passed.

"Jill should have enough footage by now," I said. "Let's head back." While that was true, it wasn't the reason I decided to go back into the smelly little room. The truth was the people here depressed me more than the room did.

Hiya must have been thinking along the same lines. "How do they even survive?" she asked.

"Mostly, they raid the spots where packaged food that doesn't meet quality standards is discarded."

"They eat bad food?"

I shook my head. "The food is mostly rejected because of problems with the packaging, not the food itself—the packing plant only receives approved food. The workers at the plants know what happens to the food once it gets discarded, so they actually take turns cleaning the disposal units. Those have to be the cleanest trash cans in all of Cassius Station. And for water, they raid the fire systems. Again, the security people know it's happening, but they argue the fire systems need to be kept accessible in case something lights up. They're right, of course, but it would be child's play to lock them up and give legitimate area chiefs a code. But they don't."

"I never had the impression that Cassius was a hive of altruism and charity."

"This place is an exception. But then again, a lot of the factory workers and low-end security people lived here once, before one of the occasional worker shortages changed their luck. They know the value of being able to survive, to hold on for one more day until the break comes," I replied.

She eyed me skeptically. "How do you know any of this? You don't look like you've suffered hardship."

"I haven't. Not really. I know because I came across it while tracking a guy who thought he could hide in Dead Space. I worked undercover at one of the factories for a couple of months," I replied. I didn't tell her that the muscular, well-attired person she'd met owed everything to a guy with a taco stand. I often wonder what I would have done if I'd gone broke in those first weeks. Would I have stuck it out in these halls or would I have accepted the return ticket and gone back to the safety net? I didn't know, and I was thankful not to know.

We returned to my room, such as it was, and found Jill waiting for me.

"We've narrowed down the places where the Lavender Hill Mob might be waiting for us."

Jill, who was not only the expert on old paintings but apparently on all things to do with the culture of old Earth, had given our adversaries that name... which, when I investigated, turned out to be from a 2D film so primitive it came from an era when color movie film hadn't been widely employed.

In the course of her archaeology sessions, she'd insisted I understand each of the missing paintings in detail. I'd protested and she just shrugged and replied. "There's probably a forgery or two lying around to fool people like you, too hard-headed to learn how to distinguish them from the real thing."

"Why would anyone copy these things?"

"They're valuable," she replied. "It was estimated that, when they were removed from the Sol system, they were collectively worth more than five hundred billion American dollars."

"Which is how much in uranium futures?" I asked.

"More than you'll make in a thousand lifetimes," she replied.

I shook my head. "Come on. I've agreed to help you because you threatened to lock me in a tiny room on your depressing little asteroid, but don't expect me to believe that anyone in the world still thinks old paintings are worth anything. Hell, I can get a piece of canvas, some paint and any reasonable AI with the ability to grab a paintbrush and have an original painting a hundred times better than any of these. Their value as art is long gone. I think the real reason you guys are even bothering with it is because you're convinced that there's a clan of criminals who have lived here for hundreds of years hiding this treasure… and that, like you guys, they live in with an honor code that borders on religious fanaticism. And if you catch them, you'll fulfil the ancient prophecy and end up wherever good little fanatics go."

She'd glared at me for almost a minute before shaking her head and sighing. "You really aren't very good at the detecting part of being a detective, are you?"

"Good enough to stay alive… and I generally take a few days or maybe a couple of weeks to get to the bottom of my cases. I haven't been after the same missing paintings for the last five hundred years."

Her normally pale skin became the white of vat-grown rice, and the freckles stood out angrily. "But not good enough to understand that the paintings are valuable right now because they're artifacts from Earth, not because they're paintings by great masters of their craft." She slapped the table with her hand. "And if you knew anything about the way they'd been taken, you'd understand how much value can be generated simply because of the story behind it. Even today, any one of those paintings, if the market breaks right, could be worth more than your girlfriend's space yacht."

"Sileon isn't my girlfriend," I protested.

"Yeah?" She smirked and said. "In that case, I'm an even worse detective than you are, because that's the only conclusion I could come to for a woman pulling your balls out of the fire and giving you enough money to buy half of Frontera."

She'd stormed off.

Eventually, however, sheer boredom had won the battle for her. While I waited for my nose and implants to heal up—a process that took forty-eight hours—I was cut off from the local network while the tech boys inserted every firewall and incursion detection software known to man onto my personal data tablet. The only reading material I had was the briefing Jill had provided.

And, having read the target list a hundred times, I eventually went back into the background material just to stave off ennui.

I was immediately engrossed.

On March 8, 1990—I had to check to see what that meant under the current Tau dating systems and found that it was nearly eight hundred years ago—a group of armed men had stormed into an art museum—I had to investigate what a museum was and why it was important to the culture of old Earth—and stolen the paintings Jill had drilled into my memory, as well as other corporeal artworks—the briefing called them sculptures—which she said had been lost along the way.

The robbery had become known as the Boston Art Heist, and it became infamous on Earth for decades afterward.

It wasn't so much the attack itself that fascinated people, but the fact that the robbery had gone unsolved despite several career criminals claiming they'd been involved, and the enormously high value attributed to the missing works.

In the intervening years, an early Tri-D drama and a series of books about the Heist had brought its fame all the way to the stars. The books had been one of the Tau Ceti system's first original work to achieve public success. Hell, I'd never read 'The Concert and the Mobster', which was a literary classic, but I'd heard of it. Everyone had.

The knowledge that the paintings were related to that book made the Oreilly tribe's obsession a little easier to understand: the fame of the works was assured. The money would follow automatically.

I returned to the present to find Jill pointing at her monitor, on which a map of Cassius was displayed. Three spaces were marked in red.

I peered at them. "That's in Orion A, that's in Orion B. Both of those are in low-rent industrial areas without much pollution regulation. Why did you choose those?"

"Some people connected with the movement of smuggled goods—people we suspect might be involved with the plan to move the art—own the facilities highlighted there."

I shook my head. "These are recent modules. How did the art get there?"

"In crates. No electronics involved. Just a box with wheels so it can be pushed through the areas with gravity," Jill replied.

I shook my head. "I wouldn't have risked it. These paintings are valuable, right?"

"Yeah. I'm glad to see you're finally getting it into your head." She had stubbon spot about how special the paintings were, which I didn't understand. But then again, I'd never been able to understand cops.

"So anyone moving them would have needed to send bodyguards and supervisors to watch the guys actually doing the moving. That kind of thing draws attention to itself, and half of the station would have made it their business to find out what was being moved."

"Five years later, no one would remember."

I laughed. "You don't know Cassius. Someone would have found out. They would have mounted an expedition to steal the stuff and—even if decades had passed—people would still be stealing it back and forth today. Unless someone spent enough on security to make it not worth people's time."

Jill sighed. "Dammit. Fucking philistines."

"I have a feeling you've got more on your mind than just recovering a bunch of paintings for a legitimate owner who has been dead for centuries living on a planet whose society has moved completely away from anything we can comprehend."

I was expecting a glare, a glower or something else along those lines. Some kind of offense, anyway. Instead, Jill turned away from me.

Damn. I'd hurt enough women in my life to know the waterworks, if not already in full flow, were coming.

"What did I say?" I asked.

"It's not what you said. It's that I thought you'd be different."

I was about to say: 'Every woman says that about every man,' but I caught myself in time. There was no need to turn this into a fight by falling back on the old tropes. I didn't know what the hell was going on, and this was one case where I suspected that fact might save me. "I don't know what's going on," I said.

She turned back in my direction. Not crying openly yet, but certainly a bit red around the eyes. "For my entire life, I've been told that the paintings are important for their cultural value. To Earth. To the city of Boston. And now Earth and Boston are gone—or at least unrecognizable to us—to the people of Tau Ceti. But most of all, they're important because if we don't get them back, justice won't be served."

"Isn't that what you want, too?" I asked.

"No!" She said loudly. Then she looked around. One of the other Oreilly's was in the room with us, but he appeared to be lost in concentration, with large headphones over his ears from which I could hear music emerging. She continued in a whisper. "I mean, I understand why everyone wants that. It's been the driving force for us forever. But that's not what I want. My dream, ever since I've been old enough to understand, is to get a nice open space somewhere, an area big enough to unroll all that canvas and look at the paintings. I want to run my hand over the surface, feel the impasto…"

I held out my hand to ask the obvious question, but she made an annoyed face and said: "…impasto is the texture of the paint left there by the brushstrokes. Human beings aren't as precise as AI artists, which meant paint buildup could occur in unplanned places, suboptimal unplanned places, and give each painting personality. And I want to compare the Vermeer to the Rembrandts, and both of those to the

Manet before I step back and look at them."

"We have pictures…"

She snorted. "Pictures. We're a civilization that lives in floating tin cans who think a bunch of pixels on the screen can replace the feeling of being in the presence of genius. We've lost all sense of the value of things created by human hands, and live in a shadow of what we used to have. We're a people without a past. No roots. Just existing, not really living, as we head towards extinction."

"There are more humans in the galaxy today than at any time since we left Earth. We're growing. Some people rebelled against the Copernicus regime just a few days ago and went off to settle a new colony. Society might not be perfect, but it's vibrant enough."

"A new colony? What roots do you think they'll have?"

"Some things are more important than roots."

She shook her head. "You probably think I'm crazy, I know."

I said nothing. In a very real sense, my life depended on staying on Jill's good side, and nothing I could have said at that moment would have helped.

Jill continued. "And maybe my upbringing is a little strange if you compare me to anyone on Tau Ceti II or Cassius Station. I might be a little sheltered, but I'm not stupid. I can read the newsfeeds—both the open ones and the darkfeeds—and I can read between the lines. Other than a few people with some initiative, the entire system seems to be completely asleep. There is almost no cultural or scientific progress happening at all."

I shrugged. "I've never been much of a cultural scientist, myself. I make my living finding people who don't want to be found. Most of the times, my imagination is more than adequately occupied thinking of ways things can go badly wrong for me."

She shrugged. "It doesn't matter. I knew you wouldn't understand. No one does."

"I'm sorry I couldn't be more help."

She sighed. "That's not why we brought you into this. You're supposed to be our expert on the lay of the land."

"In that case, my advice would be to forget about the two Orion sites and concentrate on this one." I pointed to the map. "That's right off the Old Corridor in an area that is both rundown and designated for office space. If I were a criminal hiding stuff that is kind of fragile, there's where I'd go. No chemicals or heavy machinery, and the area is low-rent enough that you won't have too many competitors nearby: your neighbors will all be small-time businesses catering to the locals."

"The office is pretty big. We're talking about a couple of floors here. Big ones. We'd need to cover two thousand square meters in total."

I gestured at the map. "It's still better than going into an even bigger space full of tubes and machines and reactor tanks. And at least this area will be spun for gravity." I looked at the map, then hit a couple of commands and the screen gave me an external view of the building. It was just an office block. One of several identical buildings off the Old Corridor in the Tiantáng sector. They looked vaguely familiar: I'd probably passed right in front of them hundreds of times without paying the least attention. "I would recommend going there in force unless the scout crews find something specific in the other places. How did you locate this one? Also owned by contacts?"

"No. This one was a backtrack job. We bought hacker time to the feed showing the woman with the gun. This was as far as we managed to track her."

"Good thinking."

Jill rolled her eyes. "I come from thirty generations of cops. If there's one thing I never thought I'd need, it's approval from a private investigator."

I grinned. "You're welcome, then!"

"Fuck off," she said. "Go study the layout of the buildings."

CHAPTER 10

A day later, Oreilly and two other guys marched in and sat in the already overcrowded room.

"All right. We've thoroughly scouted all three sites. Two of them are, as Leonid said, just factories. If the paintings are being kept there, we'll have to figure out a way to march in and take control of the entire site for a few days while we do a complete search. Not impossible, but also not something I want to start out with."

"So we'll go after the office building?" I said.

"Yeah… but it won't be as simple as waiting for office hours to end and cutting through the security to look around. They've got people there around the clock."

"Damn," Jill said. "Human presence means that the old overloaders we were counting on won't deal with everything."

"I know," Oreilly said. "There's usually ten people in the building at the lowest point. We'll need to put them all to sleep before we can do a search."

My cyborg friend Kane lifted a hand. "So we nuke the security with the overloaders and then send happy gas through the air vents. Child's play."

It was my turn to interrupt the proceedings. "Wait," I said. "Let me get this straight. You guys have been mining lithium out of space rocks for five hundred years, right?"

Oreilly nodded.

"So how did you become experts on urban paramilitary operations, or whatever this stuff is? Did you hire outside contractors?" I looked around, but everyone in the room with us had been on the lithium freighter.

"Hmm." Oreilly said. He looked shifty for a few moments.

"It's that—" Jill began, but whatever it was never made it past those first words.

Kane spoke in his raspy, metallic tones. "If we're going to

go into an operation with this guy, we need to tell him the truth. Either that or space him now."

"Dammit," Oreilly said.

"What?" I asked. "And Kane, if anyone tries to space me, I'm taking you with me."

The can opener shrugged. "I can be repaired. Mostly."

"So what is it you don't want to tell me?"

Jill stood. "Those outside contractors. That would be us."

It took me a second to understand what she was getting at. "You mean you've done this before?"

She shook her head. "I mean that no one else in the system has done it. Every time you hear about an insurrection on some little asteroid society or even as far as the Wolf Colony, we're the ones doing the heavy lifting for the winning team. You want to win a battle in zero gee in human-controlled space, you come to us."

I laughed. "You almost had me there. That's the plot of that Tri-D show. 'The Wrecking Crew', wasn't it?"

No one else laughed.

"Shit," I said. "You're serious." I looked them over again and cursed myself for not putting two and two together. They were much too fit to be lithium miners. Even the most fanatical society of health freaks would see their general fitness deteriorate if they remained in microgravity their whole lives. They'd have to take all sorts of pharmaceuticals for bone density and general organ function, and even then, they wouldn't be wiry and muscular unless they were in constant training for something. Everyone around me—except Oreilly who was straight-up muscular, and the cyborg—was wiry and muscular. Some detective I'd turned out to be.

Oreilly grimaced. "Yeah, we're serious."

"And someone hired you to grab the paintings."

"Nope. All the other stuff is true. It's just that Lithium

mining, it turns out, doesn't cover the cost of high-end surveillance. So we did one job… and the word got around," Oreilly said.

"Well, at least I won't have to babysit you guys," I replied. "I was worried how you'd react once things got real."

"As if," Kane said. "We're the ones who make things real. Consider us the delivery boys for a dose of reality."

I groaned.

* * *

It was just an office building, set off on a side lane in view of the Old Corridor, and I felt slightly ridiculous carrying several sets of concussion mines and a heavy-duty stun baton in there. Normally, if I had to overpower the kind of people you'd expect to find working in there, I'd just scowl a lot and make veiled hints about how easily a guy like me could expose their terrible taste in porn.

The street we were on was almost empty. This was the middle of the deep-night shift, and while the Old Corridor teemed with workers on their way to or from unskilled jobs, office areas usually kept Copernicus daylight hours, since that was when the financial systems and commodities trading was centralized.

So the lights were all off in these particular buildings.

Except the two floors we'd decided to invade. People were working inside those.

"Ready?" Jill asked.

"I suppose. You guys are more used to this kind of thing than I am," I replied.

"That's not what we heard. In fact, you have a reputation for having accumulated a bit of a body count," she said.

"That's just because I tend to deal with common criminals… and common criminals often don't know when they're beaten. They'll fight until the only choice left is to incapacitate them, and sometimes it's not possible to do that safely." I shrugged. "If it makes you feel any better, I've never walked into a situation with the intention of killing someone."

"Ah, so you're just terrible at planning stuff. Duly noted."

Before I could respond to that, Jill toggled the encrypted communicator in her earbud and said: "Front door clear, we're going in."

The four of us slated to enter via the main entrance had disguised our features with makeup and we all wore the flophats that teens in Cassius station had adopted—useless, formless things that only served to annoy the wearer, but which, when positioned strategically, could cover your features.

The foyer was decorated in Classic Corporate, as that style had been interpreted seventy years ago: white plastic floors veined with grey and dressed up to look like marble, polished metal columns exposed to the public, and black plastic chair and desk surfaces. Timeless, but also a bit cold.

The man at the reception desk was immersed in some kind of VR, and he barely looked up at us when we entered. Jill waved, and that, plus the hats, must have made him think we were going to one of the abortion clinics which shared the building with our targets. He let us through unmolested.

"Impressive security," I said as we rode the elevator to the floor of one of the abortion clinics.

"We'll see," Jill said.

We emerged from the elevator and walked towards the door we would have approached had we been legitimate customers. When we reached it, one of Oreilly's men, a little guy who was twenty, but looked fifteen, said. "We passed one surveillance camera, on that corner over there. Should I take it out?"

"Yes," Jill replied.

I expected him to use some sort of high-tech energy

device to take the camera down, but instead, the kid simply pretended to stretch and walked away from the camera. His backpack emitted a kind of "sproing" sound and some sort of round black projectile jumped out of it. It moved almost too fast for me to see and slammed into the camera, knocking it off its mount.

"Is it down?" Jill asked.

The guy checked a screen. "Yeah, not transmitting. And anyone who checks will find it was hit by something. Maybe an angry father-not-to-be appalled by the price of getting rid of the results of one night of unprotected sex."

"You're an idiot, Sean," Jill said. "But good job."

Now we moved faster. I followed Jill as she jogged down the corridor to the door which concealed the stairs. We sprinted down three flights and found the door at the bottom locked.

"Deal with this," Jill said to Sean.

Again, he went low-tech on the problem. A crowbar and a short application of force popped the lock open and we peeked through the hole to see the entire floor was glass-fronted office space, utterly corporate and looking, for all the world, like the inhabitants had nothing to hide. Hell, except for a few closed offices, I could see almost all the way across the floor.

"Not a lot of places to hide stuff," I whispered.

"Don't worry about that. We'll have time to search once we get the people under control," Jill replied, looking at a strange device strapped to her wrist. "The overloaders will be activated in… two minutes."

We waited.

"What is that thing?" I asked, a minute later.

"It is an analog clock," Jill replied. "The overloaders are going to fry every piece of electronics except for stuff that is shielded to within an inch of its life. This clock won't care."

"Wow, it looks like something from a Steampunk Drama," I said.

She sighed. "You watch too much Tri-D."

Suddenly, the lights dimmed once, flickered brightly and then went out. Battery-powered emergency lights came on almost immediately.

Jill checked her clock. "Oreilly will be pumping the sleeping gas in there," she said. "We move in two minutes."

We counted down the seconds and, as soon as she hit zero, the kid's kinetic backpack sporinged again and another ball took out one of the glass walls directly ahead of us.

We charged through. I already had dozens of cable ties at the ready, preparing myself to bind the temporarily incapacitated employees.

Though the emergency lighting wasn't too bright—and the light coming in from the exterior this high above the illuminated street was almost zero—I still knew exactly where the people had been concentrated when the lights went out. I ran in that direction.

I almost tripped over the first prone body, a young woman with green hair who'd fallen flat on her back on the tasteful grey carpet. I instinctively jumped over her and, before I could turn to tie her up, Sean beat me to her.

"Sneaky little…"

I never finished. The young woman's eyes glowed green, then red and, with a whirr of servo-motors, she reached up and grabbed Sean's neck with one hand. Then she twisted, and the cracking of his spine echoed in the huge open space.

I turned to where I'd been headed and saw considerably more than ten people getting up from the floor, eyes brightly lit from within.

"Oh, shit," I said as Jill stumbled to a halt beside me. "I think we're screwed."

Every head turned towards us.

CHAPTER 11

For a second, I stood slack-jawed.

The bad guys should have been down. The sleeping gas should have sent them to the dreamworld. And that EMP or whatever they'd detonated in here should have fried completely the electronics in a cyborg. We weren't trying to kill anyone, but we also didn't know there would be cyborgs in here, so if they'd been killed by our suppressors, we could have called it an accident.

As it was, I'd already seen one of our guys die… and the people with the red eyes hadn't even gotten warmed up yet.

Movement seen out of the corner of my eye brought me out of my stupor. Without stopping to think, I threw myself at Jill and knocked her to the floor as something big and heavy flew through the air where our heads had been a moment earlier.

Then I jumped back to my feet and pulled her up by the arm.

We turned towards the exit that led to the elevators, but two sets of red eyes burned between us and the door. I couldn't see the bodies they were attached to in the dim post-EMP light, but it was safe to assume they belonged to healthy cyborgs. We wouldn't make it.

"Come on," I said and tugged on her arm.

We ran straight towards the windows. As we reached them, I pulled us around so we faced backwards when we hit. A moment before impact, Jill understood what I was planning and she said, "What the hell do you think you're—"

We went through the glass with a thunderous explosion. It felt and sounded like the end of the world, not so much the classic tinkling of breaking glass as the sudden dull crash of two food carts colliding in the Old Corridor.

And then, silence. There was a single moment in which

I floated at peace, surrounded by a halo of shiny splinters, with Jill speechless beside me.

The spin gravity, which we'd brought with us from inside the building, even though, technically, we were in a zero-gravity space, took hold of us like a giant fist.

Did people survive jumping out of buildings several stories high? As I looked down, my gut was telling me no.

"Oof!" Jill shouted, and disappeared above me.

I turned to look and slammed into something. Instinctively, I grabbed at it and managed to hold on, albeit at the cost of a badly wrenched arm. "Ow," I said.

I'd snagged onto some kind of cable. Structural, power, comms, I didn't care. I was just glad it was there.

Jill shouted down at me. "Are you insane?"

"Not now!" I yelled back. "Move towards our right. We need to get out of range of whatever weapons they have in there."

The fact that the upper levels of the station were kept unlit worked in our favor, but we still had some bleed from the streetlights below. I looked up to see Jill hanging upside-down from the cable above me, holding on with both hands and feet. That seemed like the best way forward, so I imitated her.

As we were reaching the edge of the building, hanging above the oblivious street below, I heard a loud bang, a sound I'd only heard once before in my life.

"They're shooting at us? With a gun?" I shouted. "Who the hell are these people?"

Jill said nothing, but we reached the corner of the building. To my relief, the rear side of the office block had no windows, so we were out of the line of fire.

For now.

To judge by the fact that Jill was a little farther away from me than when we started, our cables appeared to be diverging. She seemed to be heading towards a small balcony that emerged from the same building the bad guys occupied, while my cable was obviously connected to a structural element that probably dated from the days when Tiantáng Station orbited Sol. Even from a distance, even in the dark, I could see a layer of grime on the metal frame.

But I could also see how easy it would be to climb down the ladder-like frame onto a separate building. Or up towards the station hub.

"Jill," I called. "Can you make it onto this wire?"

"You want me to jump from a wire in the middle of the sky onto… another wire in the middle of the sky?"

"Do you think you can make it? We can make it to the ground from here."

She said nothing. Instead, I saw her swing, release her grip and fall toward me. When it seemed she'd miscalculated and would fall to her death on the corridor below, she reached out and snagged the cable with both hands.

The impact nearly knocked me off the wire.

"Of course I can make it," she said contemptuously. "But it's insane of you to ask someone to do something like that."

"Then why did you do it?" I asked, my heart threatening to break through my ribs and fall onto the street below.

She hooked her legs onto the wire and started moving in my direction. "Because I didn't want you to think I was chicken. Now, are you going to hang there all night, or are we going to get moving?"

I moved.

It probably took us only a couple of minutes to make it all the way to the structural tower but, as I looked down to see people emerging from the building below us, staring up at the roof of the station, it seemed like hours.

Finally, we reached our objective and I crouched behind the struts of the tower, looking down.

"Do you think they saw where we went?" Jill asked.

As if in response, something impacted against the metal of the strut.

"I think they saw us," I replied. "Stay on that side of the column."

"We can't go down there," Jill said. "If we try it, we'll be stuck on the top of the base of this support." She pointed down to where the column we were perched on ended at a featureless block built into the floor of the corridor below.

"So we go up."

"What?"

"You put me on the team for my local knowledge, so I'm giving you local knowledge. We go up," I replied.

She looked down. "Well, at least we won't survive the fall, so I won't have to worry about getting tortured by the Hyde Syndicate."

Jill clamped down suddenly, and I looked over at her.

"The Hyde Syndicate?" I asked. "I'm sensing there's something you should have told me earlier. You've been calling them the Lavender Hill Mob, like you don't know who they really are. Do we actually know who we're up against?"

She sighed. "I guess it makes no difference now. Yeah, we know. Or at least we suspect who it is."

I was a little breathless from the climb, but I managed to get enough air together to grunt and say. "Lovely. So we could have prepared for things differently, if only you'd trusted me."

"We didn't know how much we could trust you," Jill replied. "And we had prepared for the Syndicate. The raid was designed around their capabilities."

"Yeah, I could tell."

She had nothing to say to that.

"Why are we climbing upward? Is there an access port or

something on the roof so we can get to another level?"

"Something much better," I replied.

We climbed into the ever-darker reaches of the module until we reached a curved cylinder. It was possible to see because the new area had covered lights that threw diffuse illumination onto the surface… even though none of this was visible from below.

"Hold on tight," I said.

"Yeah. I'm not planning on falling," Jill replied.

"I'm not sure you'll actually fall… and if you do, it will take you a hell of a long time to reach the ground."

"What?"

I took firm hold on a safety rung and did a handstand. I held it for thirty seconds. "We're almost in microgravity here. The speed of our current spin isn't enough to throw us at the ground very fast. And you won't accelerate as you near the floor, because there's nothing pulling you in that direction. But some of the buildings might whack you pretty hard from the side as you get into the areas moving faster."

We made our careful way along the tube until we reached an access hatch. For a ridiculous moment, I wondered whether I would spend the rest of my life going in and out of hatches and airlocks and hiding in smuggler's holds while enemies attempted to shoot at me with weapons completely unsuited for work inside a space station.

We floated into the central hub of the Tiantáng zone of Cassius station. Unlike the buildings which were occasionally torn down and rebuilt as a function of the economic conditions in the corridor, as rents in any given sector went up or down with the times, the central tube was composed of greasy old metal, streaked with centuries of lubricant and grime. This was clearly an area that never got cleaned.

"Which way?" Jill asked.

"Do you think our base in Dead Space is still viable?"

"I wouldn't bet my life on it," Jill replied.

"Well, let's hope they think we're going back. Because I'm heading the other way."

"What about the rest of our crew?"

I shrugged. "I'm not sure there's much we can do from here. Those red-eyed people down there have had plenty of time to figure out where we went, so unless you want to get your head shot off we can't go back to help. There's an old phrase that appears in old detective books..."

"I didn't have you down as much of a reader."

"Sometimes when you're waiting for business to come along, or for a building you're watching to do something interesting, the time drags. I think I read old books because it's nice to know that things could be worse."

She made a rude noise. "If life hasn't already taught you that, you were probably a bad choice to come along on this mission."

"I think the whole mission was a bad choice. But then again, my excuse was that my allies forgot to share their information with me. What's your reason for being here?"

"I was born into the wrong family of lunatics," Jill replied.

That caught me off guard. The Oreilly clan seemed to be utterly, completely and totally devoted to their mission. Seeing one of them admit, even in jest, that might not be a completely sane attitude surprised me. I chuckled. "Be that as it may, you owe me an explanation."

"I owe you nothing."

"I saved your life back there," I reminded her as gently as my patience allowed.

She laughed mirthlessly. "You threw me out a window."

"And because I did, and did it quickly, you're still alive. Tiantáng sector is basically built with tensed cables. Nothing that falls out of a building ever makes it to the ground. We're lucky we have airlocks or no one would ever be able to commit suicide and we'd have a serious overcrowding problem."

"Do you have a lot of suicides here?"

"Don't change the subject. You're going to tell me everything you know about this syndicate, or I'm going to abandon you as soon as we get out of this tube."

"I might come out ahead on that trade," she replied. She tried to put some force behind the words, so they would come out brash and brave, but I heard the trembling in her voice. She didn't want to be alone, cut off from her colleagues and any chance of getting help.

We reached the end of the tube. The door at the end opened with a wheel handle and led to another tube, just wide enough for one person. Rungs emerged from the walls, allowing us to pull ourselves down the tunnel at reasonable speed. I racked my brain for the location of the place but, in the end, I asked her to stop.

"Listen, we're going to need to consult a map. Do you think our handhelds are compromised?"

"I assume mine is. Yours… is it the one that Sileon woman gave you?"

I nodded.

"Then it's our best bet."

I swallowed and hesitated for a second. But only for a second. As damaging as getting tracked through our devices could be, stopping here would be worse. We hadn't seen any signs of pursuit from the modified humans behind us but, in the dimness of the tube, that meant nothing. They could be a hundred meters away… and we wouldn't know until it was too late.

My map of the station came up, with a red dot showing our position. I glanced at it only long enough to be sure where we were, then turned it off.

"We're in a maintenance shaft leading down into the B2 Engineering node," I said. "That's good news because we can pretty much reach the entire station from there."

"Good. What's the bad news?" she asked as we moved downwards.

"Two things. The first is the Engineering node is also easy to reach from everywhere else, and the second is it's close to Sileon's ship… but we can't go there because they'll have some heavy-duty people watching for us."

"I was wondering why Sileon returned to Cassius? Is that safe?"

"As long as she doesn't leave her ship, she will be perfectly secure. You should see that thing: she could lay siege to a planet with it," I said.

"That takes a load off my mind."

"In what way?"

She looked back at me from her position in the lead. "In that the only other explanation for her to return was that she sold us out and you've got a tracker implanted in you that told them where we were at any given moment."

"I would have expected you to scan me for embedded electronics," I replied, resenting the implications.

"We did. Four times. We couldn't find anything. And that device you just used wasn't transmitting position information on any known frequency, or we would have tossed it out of an airlock while it was still in your hands."

I sighed. "I'm starting to think you guys are in way over your heads."

"We knew what we might be up against."

"I couldn't tell," I repeated. I wasn't trying to rub salt in her wounds, but I needed her to start thinking. If she continued to believe her people were doing a competent job of assessing enemy strength, it was going to get us killed.

The rungs ended and we arrived at the Engineering node.

I let Jill open the door ahead of me—I liked her, and normally wouldn't have let her take the risk of going first but at that moment I was annoyed at all the Oreilly crew for getting me into a mess because they underestimated the opposition.

"All clear," she said.

The node was another cube full of machinery, but this one hadn't been rented out to random factories. Everything in here belonged to CassCor, the company that ran Tiantáng maintenance.

That CassCor had been the lowest bidder on dozens of purchase cycles for several hundred years was evident in the way the node looked. Critical elements—anything that would lose them the contract if it failed—were bright and well-maintained. Everything else was covered in dark grey crud.

"Shouldn't there be a ton of security in this place?" Jill asked. "We should have tripped every alarm on the station by opening that door."

I shook my head. "You see those clean, pretty machines over there? As long as we stay away from them, we won't be seen."

"That's insane," she replied. "The safety of the people…"

"Is secured by solid doors where people are likely to try to gain access. We came in through a totally unexpected route. And we can leave without anyone knowing we were here. But only if we move."

I doubted CassCor would have had humans or security bots in here, but it was still better to stay in motion. Someone could come around for some reason, and we didn't want to be in sight when they appeared.

"Which way?" she asked.

I sighed. There weren't many places we would be safe. And none of those would last long.

"Up." I said, pointing to the face of the Tube that, by our position, felt like it was directly overhead.

Jill didn't move. "And after that?"

"Coriolis."

"No. You're not thinking… That's where The Earthling's base is."

"I'm going. Come if you want."

Jill shook her head. "It's the worst possible option. Even if it exists. Are you sure about that?"

"I'm… eighty percent sure," I replied.

"That's dangerous knowledge to have. If you're right, the Earthling won't be happy. And when the Earthling gets unhappy, people float out into the vacuum."

"And if I'm wrong, we have nowhere else to go and your friends kill us," I replied.

"Don't you have any friends on the station? People who can hide us?"

I chuckled. "I'm not a magnate. The kind of people I hang out with are the kind who don't turn up their noses at having a private detective in their midst. Shop owners. A research librarian. Cargo monkeys. I'm not bringing this kind of heat onto one of my friends and their families. They've got enough problems paying their bills without a troop of homicidal humanoid cyborgs tearing them to pieces. And anyway, they wouldn't be able to hide us effectively."

"So we have to put ourselves at the mercy of the biggest, baddest criminal in the Tau system?"

"I've worked with the Earthling before."

"I'm sure he'll think of that while his goons cut us into cubes small enough to feed into the protein vats."

"She," I said.

"Huh?"

"The Earthling is a woman. Or she was before she became an AI."

"Who was she?" Jill asked, suddenly more curious than belligerent.

"If I knew that, she'd have killed me a long time ago."

We climbed the cube and exited through a door that led into a much cleaner area of the station, a cross corridor much like the one I'd escaped through originally.

I saw no sign of pursuit, and I began to relax. If the bad guys had to rely on buying security camera images to locate us—assuming they even had images of our faces from the building cameras or from before that—they'd be a step behind and, by the time we reached our destination, they would be too late to touch us.

Which might not be an entirely good thing.

CHAPTER 12

The door was unmarked and utterly nondescript. Beige, well-maintained, with an actual handle to open it as opposed to button activation.

"Are you sure?" Jill asked as I stood beside the door.

"That this is the place? Yeah, like I said, about eighty percent sure. If this is just some family housing unit we're probably dead, because we passed two or three bottlenecks to get here. Your friends in the Hyde Syndicate don't even need to follow us all the way here. They can camp out in any of the bottlenecks." I turned to her. "Now, will you tell me about those guys before we go in here?"

"Don't the walls have ears?" Jill asked, looking around.

"This is Cassius Station. The walls have ears everywhere. The problem for the people listening is to figure out what, among the enormous quantities of information they pick up is relevant and, more importantly, who to sell it to. So give."

"Dammit. Just don't tell Oreilly about this."

"Cross my heart," I replied, not mentioning Oreilly would be lucky to be alive. He hadn't been along on the raid, but if these Hyde clowns were competent, the next strike would be against our headquarters in Dead Space.

"What does that mean?"

I shrugged. "Something the kids used to say back in Copernicus."

"The Hydes are a bit like us," she said.

"What, another tribe of crazy cops and mercenaries?"

"What? No. These are the criminals who smuggled the art out of the Sol system in the first place."

I groaned. "So another tribe of people who are doing exactly what their grandparents did?"

"No. This is the original gang. With maybe a few new recruits for good measure."

"That makes no…" and then I stopped. None of it made any sense, but the glowing eyes and imperviousness to everything of the people tracking us at least gave an explanation. "They've been wired."

"Yeah. For longevity, speed, and probably for intellectual functions. They're more machine than human, even though they still have regular skin and some other human parts."

"That would have been useful to know before we went in there." Then I snapped. "You were trying to kill them with the EMP blast. Not just incapacitate them, but actually kill them."

She shrugged. "We weren't sure what would happen, but we definitely didn't want to take any chances."

"Well, now they're pissed," I said. I turned the handle and opened the door.

The room beyond was not what I was expecting. It looked like a waiting room, albeit a modern one this time, with beige-plastic floors, several comfortable chairs and even a pair of screens showing popular entertainment programs with the volume turned low. 2-D only, I saw, not immersive.

"You're kidding, right?"

I closed the door behind us. "Not in the least." I walked to the door at the far end of the room. This one was a glass door, but it had been set to translucence. All I could see through it was that the room beyond was illuminated.

I pushed the glass, and the door swung away.

The next room was a wide carpeted hall with several closed doors on either side. I tried the nearest. Locked.

The door at the end of the hall stood open, so we went that way.

The room was different from anything I'd ever seen. On the face of it, it was just a meeting room. There was a long table in the middle, surrounded by chairs. Window-like projection screens on two sides displayed a cityscape.

But that is where familiarity ended. The city was not Copernicus. In fact, the light outside appeared to be the wrong color. A little too yellow, not the comforting orange hue of Tau Ceti. The light from the simulated windows bathed the room, giving the impression of planetside daylight.

The table was made of some kind of imitation wood, but the grain pattern, wide and heavy, was different from anything you could get from a nanofactory. And the design was minimalist—which was perfectly normal for businesses in Cassius—but not in a way I'd seen before. The wood itself was light, with aluminum table legs.

The chairs, likewise, were unusual. Metal frames held up some kind of white faux-leather... and the chairs had wheels on them. Not necessarily the ideal chairs for spin gravity. Most of the time, it would be fine, but if the bearings were really good, weird things could happen.

Each place at the table had a device in front of it. Again, the design looked like nothing I'd ever seen. Finally, there were blocks of notepaper and writing sticks with a logo on each.

"Deck Leonid," a voice from the head of the table said. I looked over there to see a woman in her twenties fidgeting with one of the writing sticks. She had straight strawberry blond hair and brown eyes with delicate features. "I'm not sure this was your smartest decision."

I was certain she hadn't been there a second ago.

I nodded. "The Earthling, I presume." Then I studied her for a minute. "You look familiar."

"I can take any form I want," she said. "This is the one that pleases me today. Please take a seat." As she spoke, the door swung closed behind us. Mechanisms whirred as complicated locks sealed the room. The Earthling nodded towards the windows, "and these windows aren't actually real windows. If you jump out of them, you won't magically be transported to what you see there."

"I never thought that," I said.

"Well, I just wanted to make sure you didn't do anything excessively hopeful with my windows, the way you did with the ones back in Tiantáng. You know you should both be dead, don't you?"

"I told him so," Jill said.

The Earthling turned to look over at Jill. "And now I have a fanatical cop sitting in my meeting room. It's not something I'd ever thought I'd allow willingly." She shook her head, such a human motion that it was hard to remember I was talking to an avatar for a computer entity. "For what it's worth, events have conspired to keep you from being in danger now. Although I probably would have preferred to be able to kill you."

"That's a comforting thought," Jill said.

The Earthling shrugged. "Not having a body is quite liberating. Human emotions are not an ideal addendum to a crime lord." Then she turned back to me and actually smiled. "And you. I underestimated you. I always thought you were a useful lump, dogged and effective and a little cute. And here you are with an actual brain in your head and able to figure out stuff that my competitors never managed."

"I've worked with too many of your contacts. None of them knew what they knew, but each of them had a piece to the puzzle."

There was a pause. "Yes. I see that now. I should have realized it earlier, but I never gave you the processing power you deserved."

"So, are you going to kill us?" I asked.

"I already said I wouldn't," the Earthling replied.

"No offense, but that doesn't mean much. I've heard you tell people they were perfectly safe from you and then—on the same call—ask me to erase the evidence that you murdered them."

"Yes," the Earthling replied drily, "I recall the incident. I had my reasons. This time, however, there is no profit in killing you. By coming here, you've given away the location of this spot to anyone with the resources and inclination to identify and track you. As far as I've seen on the feeds, there are currently three different parties—perhaps four—attempting to track you. Most are still a few hours behind, but they will arrive here eventually. There's one, however…"

The images in the windows disappeared, replaced by several views of familiar-looking hallways. Three people—two men and a woman—walked briskly down the hall, looking this way and that.

I knew one of them, and recognized the other two by type if not face. Low-level video hackers who would have received the message to follow Jill and me, sent by the Hydes.

A moment later, we had audio.

"The feed says they went that way," the man I recognized said, pointing at a wall marked with an emergency symbol. He was a small-time Old Corridor hustler named Frez.

"Are you sure?" the woman said.

"Look for yourself. No sign of e-tamper according to the doublecheck programs. Look at those verification digits."

"Yeah," the second guy said. "And Leonid isn't known for being a digital wizard. The trail is just ten minutes old. It would take a heavy-hitter to fully cover the digital track in that time."

"But that's an airlock," the girl said. "Nothing on the other side but vacuum."

"They went through there. Look."

They ran the video again. The screen zoomed in. It clearly showed Jill and me walking through the airlock door.

"It's probably a fake lock. An old station like this is likely riddled with secret passages. And discovering this one will net us a fortune. Come on."

"I'm not sure," the woman said.

"Then stay here. We'll buy you a drink once we're rich."

"Screw you."

They rotated the airlock door mechanism, which, unusually, caused the panel to pop open. Generally, it took a long time to get those things open manually.

They crowded into the interior of the lock.

The door behind them slammed shut without any of the inhabitants touching it.

"Why did you…" the woman began.

She never got to finish the phrase. The outer door opened and the three of them flew out the door.

An exterior camera showed them floating into the vacuum and I watched them die. Within seconds, their faces assumed the agonized rictus of people who'd decompressed while they froze.

I swallowed, but the pretty little avatar worn by the deadliest AI in the system winked and smiled.

"That should buy us a little bit of time. By revealing the existence of this place to other players, you've saved your lives. The secret you had is now worthless, because it isn't a secret anymore. So I gain nothing by killing you. I can't even make an example out of you, since no one I want to impress in that way knows about any of this. So you are safe." She paused for a long time, and smiled. "From me, at least."

"Can you help us?"

"That's not the right question. Of course I can help you." The avatar winked at Jill and the feeling that I'd seen this woman somewhere, and recently, grew stronger. "The question you should be asking is why would I want to get any more involved than I already am?"

"Money," I said before Jill's answer got us killed.

"I'm listening," the Earthling said with a smile.

"The people trying to kill us are sitting on the most valuable cultural treasure to ever come to the Tau Ceti system. If you help us, you can reap part of the value."

Jill gasped. As I'd learned to my cost, she didn't believe in giving potential allies important information.

"And why haven't I heard of this before?" the Earthling said.

"Because the merchandise and the gang running it were both here on Cassius before any of the systems or databases you're connected to were even designed."

The avatar paused, thinking. "I calculate that there's only a thirty-seven percent chance what you're telling me is true. The data infrastructure is new, true, but the old databases were copied onto the current ones, even things like intelligence and surveillance information."

I took a risk. "So you can tell me where the gun came from, right? The one that woman used to shoot at me in the Old Corridor?"

This time, the pause was longer. Not, perhaps, long in human terms—I had learned to watch the Earthling's avatars closely for signs that it was processing remotely—but longer than she usually took to reply. "Yeah. That makes the likelihood of gaps in my database coverage rise to ninety-eight percent and the likelihood you're telling the truth about everything rise to nearly sixty. It appears I'm going to have to assist you after all." She sighed, a surprisingly human gesture, particularly after all that calculation and talk of percentages.

It was hard to think of The Earthling as human even though scuttlebutt had it that she had originally just been a woman out for revenge. How she managed to get herself uploaded onto Cassius Station's computer networks was beyond me, but she'd made the most of it.

"I have a final question," she said, looking straight at Jill. "What is this cultural treasure that could possibly be worth so much?"

Jill proved to be a realist after all. She answered without hesitation: "The Boston Art Heist."

The Earthling's avatar stopped dead for an instant, sign that the main processors were thoroughly thinking things over. She blinked and said: "Good."

The chair I was sitting on suddenly came alive. The structure of the arms moved faster than I could track it, and pinned me to the seatback, while the legs secured my ankles. Then the seat itself straightened and forced me into a standing position.

Then the floor beneath me vanished, the seat released its hold and I was in a black tube, accelerating.

I yelled. I couldn't help myself.

But after that single sound, the rush of air became too strong to make any more noise. It was all I could do to breathe.

CHAPTER 13

The chair released me and I fell away. I bounced against a wall which redirected me, and heard Jill's high-pitched curse as she hit the same wall an instant later.

We were moving very quickly through darkness. By reaching out my hands, I could tell we were in a tube of some kind, with smooth metal walls which hurt when you bounced into them. Which happened often, as the tube turned and twisted,

After about thirty seconds, I tried to figure out why we were moving. Spin gravity shouldn't have been able to keep us moving as the tube curved in different directions. Down was always away from the center of spin, and we'd been going every which way.

Either that, or I'd been bounced around enough to lose my sense of direction.

"Jill!" I shouted. "Can you hear me?"

Whether she answered or was simply making incoherent noises of terror was impossible to tell in the roar of the air around us.

After what seemed like an eternity, we flew into a room. I saw a wall approach at high speed and braced for the bone-breaking impact. I was pretty sure the crash wouldn't be survivable.

The wall gave way, absorbing my speed and cushioning the impact. I heard Jill grunt beside me.

Then the wall solidified again, and I dropped to the floor. This room was definitely spun for gravity.

"What the hell was that?" I said, lying on my back looking up at a grated roof.

"Pneumatic tube," Jill replied. "I'd heard of a few, used to shoot goods quickly from one space to another, but never one as long as this. And never one designed for people."

"Yes," another voice said, a voice I found familiar. I sat up to see our friend from the conference room standing at door. "You forced me into burning one of my trump cards. I hope you're worth it."

As she strode towards us, I felt the floor vibrate beneath me. While the woman in the conference room might have been a hologram or an image of some sort, this one was definitely real.

I looked her up and down. Had she been human… "I know I'm going to regret this, but is there something else I can call you? The Earthling seems a little bit awkward."

"No," the Earthling said. "And I'd rather you didn't call me anything. Even saying my name in the wrong place will get your entire conversation flagged as worthy of further investigation. The listening algorithms catch it every time."

"All right," I said. She looked kind of cute in that freckled, slim body. I wondered if it was a real human body or some kind of super advanced android.

Then I caught Jill's incredulous look and shook my head. I must have bumped it on something, because I definitely wasn't thinking straight. Was I really considering hitting on the most dangerous crime figure in Cassius Station just because she'd decided to download her AI personality onto a good-looking human body? This wasn't the kind of thing I generally did… which was why I'd stayed alive as long as I had.

"Good," The Earthling said. "Are you all right?"

"I may have hit my head," I replied. "But I think the effect is passing. I should be fine in a few minutes."

The avatar—it helped to think of her that way—led us into a meeting room that could have been the same one we'd just vacated, right down to the exact same view out of the window screens. I had a flash of intuition which told me that if I managed to identify the scene out the window, I would know a lot more about The Earthling's origins and original identity than I did.

Perhaps enough to put me on her hit list again. I looked away from the windows and sat down.

The chair felt familiar, and I also considered for a moment the fact that the Earthling might be messing with us and might have brought us back to where we were originally sitting.

"I'm glad to hear it," The Earthling replied. "Because you're going to need to have a very clear head to finish explaining to me why I shouldn't space you right now. Or, failing that, simply turn you in for the reward on offer."

"How much are we worth?" Jill asked.

"A thousand kilos of uranium credits for the two of you and another seven hundred and fifty for the other guy who escaped from the building. From the description I have here, that one is some kind of cyborg killing machine."

"Kane," Jill said.

"It didn't say his name. In fact, they seemed to be confused about who each of you is. Except you, Jill Oreilly. Someone must have found your birth records on Frontera."

"Those hackers you spaced knew who I was," I pointed out.

The avatar nodded. "Yes. But one of them knew you by sight, at least well enough to get through the implants you're wearing. The other groups don't seem to be as well-informed."

"And if they traced me back to Frontera, they know who it is that is coming after them," Jill said. "They know this isn't going to end well for them."

The woman who was actually an AI crossed her arms. "I don't get the sense that they are afraid of the Oreilly special forces unit. Not in the least. In fact, they're offering a lesser reward for any other members of the crew who might happen to pop up. They have quite a comprehensive list of operatives here." She gave Jill a long look. "But according to my tracking, most of these people are nowhere near Cassius at the moment." Then she grinned. "Of course, you weren't supposed to be here either." She turned to me. "And you… well, I thought you were safely ensconced on some asteroid out of the way." Her little smile disappeared. "You need to know that your entire value to me lies in the fact you know why there are blanks in my coverage. I will trade my assistance for a way to fill those blanks. That, plus sharing in the profits from the art, once we recover it."

"You want us to be partners?" Jill said, enraged, as I was about to agree to the deal.

"Or I can space you and deal with him," she replied.

Jill shut up. She seemed to have few illusions about the way things would turn out. Before, The Earthling had been doing some preliminary studies. Now we were negotiating in earnest.

Jill turned to me. "Can I trust her?"

I nodded. "I think so. We're no threat to her, but we can be useful. As long as we don't learn anything incriminating along the way, we'll be fine."

The Earthling looked at us, from one to the other. "So? Which is it going to be? Will you deal?"

"Yes," Jill sighed. "But I want you to know that if I can work it somehow, I want the paintings to become public property… so that people can go see them and appreciate what it was like when truly great art was available to the masses and not just to collectors who pay the artists."

The Earthling laughed. Her nose wrinkled when she did. Had the AI designed this body specifically so I wouldn't be able to think straight? I wouldn't have put it past her… and she definitely knew enough about my taste to pull it off.

"Most of these paintings were owned by wealthy patrons

and not open to public view when they were actually painted. What makes today's art less interesting than that?"

"I don't know. But I know what I want for these," Jill said, her jaw set.

The Earthling nodded. "Very well. I accept that the knowledge you might have about pre-database dealings in this system is valuable enough to merit my help on its own. However, once we find the paintings, I will make every attempt to turn the venture profitable in monetary terms as well as in informational ones. I fear that might put us on opposite sides."

"It will."

"Very well," The Earthling said. "I will abide by the truce until such time as that moment comes to pass." She turned to me. "And Deck, will you also be in opposition?"

I shook my head. "As soon as we find the paintings, I'm out. I know when I'm in over my head."

Jill didn't take my hint. She said. "Agreed, then."

"Good. I'm glad we got that straightened out. Now, I want to know everything you know about my database blind spots. What don't I know?"

"I'm not sure where to start..." Jill said.

"Let's start with an easy one," The Earthling replied. "How did you get onto Cassius Station without a single one of the people looking for you, including mine, spotting your entry?"

Jill hesitated for a second, but then shrugged and explained about the transport ship.

The Earthling proceeded to grill her about several things. The origin of the Oreillys and the Hyde Syndicate, the arrival of the paintings onto the station and, finally, the guns.

"I can only speculate that those were brought onboard at the same time as the paintings and stashed nearby," Jill said. "I don't have precise information about them."

"Interesting," The Earthling said. "Because if the guns are near the paintings and we know at least one person who used one of the unidentified guns—the woman who shot at you," she nodded in my direction, "in the Old Corridor, then we can backtrack her and see who might have given her the gun."

"But you'd have to sift through a huge amount of information," Jill said. "Everyone she came into contact with in an unobserved situation would have to be backtracked. And that would only be the beginning. You'd then have to trace each of those people until…" She threw her hands up in exasperation. "It can't be done."

A soft smile spread over The Earthling's lips. "It might be possible. In fact, I started the data gathering and backtrack as soon as the idea occurred to me." The smile spread. "I'm not lacking in processing power or data acquisition capabilities."

"I know that, but still."

Suddenly, the face of the woman that The Earthling had chosen—or created—to be a vessel for her consciousness, went completely slack, and she said with a mechanic, unmodulated voice. "You're thinking of this in human terms. Don't. The people arrayed against us have already shown their willingness to move beyond the purely human, and you need to stop working within the usual human limitations." Then her face seemed to revive. "Do I make myself clear?"

I shuddered. The reminder that we were probably overmatched in both physical and intellectual terms was strong, but even stronger was the visual evidence that the person speaking to us—an attractive woman of twenty-five by all outward appearances—was little more than a sock puppet who could be controlled by implants in her brain at any time The Earthling decided to do so.

"So, what now? Do we wait for the numbers to finish crunching?" I asked, trying to feel useful.

"Initially, yes," The Earthling replied. "And not only those. I will also be running simulations and probabilistic programs to try to see where the most likely places for an effective strike are. I hope we get enough data to narrow it down to one," the avatar sighed. "But that almost never happens. There's a room for you on the other side of that door. Get some rest and I'll call you when it's time to act… or talk."

The way The Earthling said it made it very clear she wasn't giving us a choice but an order. She held the door for us and closed it firmly behind me.

CHAPTER 14

The room matched the décor of the meeting room: minimalist, light toned and without any excess ornamentation. There was a large bed with white sheets, a table with aluminum legs and a light-colored wood surface, and chairs that matched the ones in the meeting room. A spread of wine, cheese, bread and sandwich meats was arrayed on the table.

"At least we'll eat well," I said. "I doubt The Earthling would buy vat-grown stuff."

"Does she eat at all?"

That brought me back to just how human the avatar that had been in the room with us might be. Unlike the first one, this wasn't a hologram. She breathed—I could see that when we were speaking. And her skin was warm to the touch, I noticed before when I'd brushed her hand.

She might even be a fully human body, printed for some reason that probably had nothing to do with us. After all, The Earthling didn't need to deal with us in person. A hologram would work just as well.

And if it was a human body—even if it was wired for an AI brain and superhuman capabilities—it would be able to eat… and to do all the other things that made human life worth living. An image of the avatar naked flashed through my mind.

Again, I shook my head. I wondered if the stress was making me suicidal.

"What do you think she'll end up asking us to do?" I said, reaching out for a slice of cured meat.

"How should I know?" Jill said. Then she picked up a slice of meat like the one I was munching on. She sniffed it and studied the dark red color. "What is this stuff, anyway?"

"Sliced meat," I said.

"Why grow it like this?" she asked as she took a cautious bite. "It's too tough for easy eating. And all that salt…"

"I don't know. Probably because the animal it came from has flesh like that."

"Animal… you mean, like a real animal?"

"Of course. This table is probably worth a month's salary for most people. It's not easy to breed farm animals out here… and no one does it on Tau Ceti II because the Copernicus government would never allow it. Can you imagine people eating unhealthy food just because it tastes better? It would bring down their entire society."

Jill chuckled, but I could see she wasn't convinced. The slice of meat was still in her hand, drooping over.

"You don't have to eat it if you don't want it. You can spit out the bit you tried. I won't judge you."

She forced herself to swallow. It was so obvious that she was doing it just to avoid looking like a wimp in front of me that I didn't have the heart to laugh at her. "It wasn't bad…" she said after taking a drink of water. "Just very weird. I've never eaten anything like that before."

"All vat-grown? Soft and so bland you need to overload on vat spices?"

"Yeah."

I laughed. "Me, too. I only make enough to indulge in real food every once in a while. Hell, I think I've had more good food since I went on the run than in my entire life before then. Sileon doesn't skimp, and neither does The Earthling, I see."

"So only rich people are forced to eat hard, oversalted meat here? No wonder my family never let me visit this place. You're all weird."

I watched her. As she spoke, tears welled in the corner of her eyes, and she turned away from me during the last sentence. I kicked myself mentally. We were both scared and running for our lives, but she had also probably just lost a good chunk of the people she grew up with and had definitely seen at least one of her friends brutally murdered before her eyes.

I walked up to her and hugged her. She tensed, and I thought she was going to pull away or give me a knee in the nuts. But then she relaxed and turned into me, putting her head against my chest so I couldn't see her cry.

I felt it, though: soft shudders as she sobbed. My arms around her felt strange. She was muscular but smaller than I imagined her when I was just talking to her. She was so strong, so confident, that if you'd asked me how tall she was, I would have guessed almost my own considerable height.

But she wasn't. I could see that now.

As she cried, the strength seemed to drain from her and I laid her on the bed and backed away. She pulled my arm to keep me from moving, so I laid on the bed beside her, allowing her to cry it off.

Finally, she slept, which I found incredible. I was so wired, I couldn't have slept if The Earthling had drugged the food.

I extricated myself from her arms and returned to the table. I was starving, and the wine helped take some of the edge off my stress.

The other thing that helped me to relax was, unless The Earthling herself decided to go back on her word, we were completely safe. There was no way anyone would penetrate one of her safe rooms—as opposed to the Coriolis operating base designed to be a meeting place with outsiders—without setting off a major war. And while the people we were dealing with apparently had few qualms about starting such a war, The Earthling's resources were formidable. The people arrayed against us would have to marshal considerable forces... and my guess was they were too busy for that right now. They had a bunch of old paintings to move.

I thought about that. Why all the sudden movement? And why did I get wrapped up in it even before Sileon dropped me in the hands of the psychopathic Oreillys? My guess was, for some reason, the criminals who'd stolen the paintings decided the time was right to break open the cache where they held the art and sell it. Perhaps it was because there were any number of enormously wealthy people in Cassius Station after the last Uranium revaluation. Or perhaps it was because someone had come too close to discovering the place, and they'd gotten spooked. Whatever the reason it seemed pretty clear that the cat was out of the bag.

As for me? I'd either stumbled onto something without knowing it or simply been fingered as someone involved by one of my enemies, and the gang had decided to take me out.

What next? I calculated that the bad guys would pay to keep every purveyor of facial ID data on the lookout for us, but they wouldn't expend resources in an all-out chase. Instead, they'd likely only attack us opportunistically.

Which was fine by me. I was perfectly happy to sit in this room and drink wine while the Oreillys and the Hydes killed one another.

Except I'd promised to help find the paintings. And I hadn't been much use so far, except to help them choose the place where we'd find the Hydes... which had turned out pretty badly even though I'd been exactly right about which of the three places was the one to hit.

I watched Jill sleep. She looked peaceful at rest in a way she didn't when she was awake. Gone was the belligerence and determination.

I decided I liked her better that way.

Looking around the room, I wondered what The Earthling thought of our relationship. Though not in the least erotic, the room was definitely designed for a couple: a single large bed and that single bathroom off to one side. Did she think we were an item? Or did she purposely throw us into this room to see what we'd do in a post-traumatic situation?

Maybe I was overthinking it. This might be the only room she had available when we appeared. It would be fine for a single guest, too.

I half-expected The Earthling to appear while Jill slept, whether in person or in holographic form to negotiate separately with me. But she didn't materialize, and I had eaten my fill and—despite my nervousness—was nodding off, when The Earthling's physical manifestation walked through the door.

"I need you to come with me," she said, her expression grave.

I stood up unsteadily, not quite awake. "What's happening. Should we wake Jill?"

The Earthling contemplated her for a moment. "Not yet. We'll do it if you can't handle this by yourself."

She led the way out the door, and I was shocked to see that the meeting room on the other side of the door had been replaced by a corridor.

My face must have shown my confusion because The Earthling grinned. "I don't like to make my demesne too easy to map," she said.

The hall led to another lobby that could have been the twin of the one in the other facility. It was clear that The Earthling had little use for variety.

Or maybe the rush through the tube actually had brought us back to the same place. I was seriously beginning to wonder if that might not actually be the case.

The main difference was the metal door that separated the lobby from the rest of Cassius Station was under attack.

It was already dented inward and, as I watched a new dent appeared, followed by a muffled thud.

"That's a super-strong alloy three centimeters thick," The Earthling said in a casual voice.

"You mean they've found us?"

"If by 'they', you mean your friends from the Hyde Syndicate… then no. But someone found us. And I'm not exactly sure what I should do with him. I'll let you handle it."

She walked towards the door and, before I could stop her, popped open the latch.

The door flew open and slammed into the wall behind it.

A figure—an enormous human figure—draped in grey cloth that covered its face, stomped in, shaking the whole room.

Chapter 15

My first thought was to run for my life. A guy who could do that to the door was bad news. But I kept my head. Knowing The Earthling, the figure was likely being tracked by the targeting systems of a dozen high-powered weapons. If it did anything too aggressive, it would be atomized before I could even take a step.

So I controlled myself and bent low to try to look under the shroud.

"Kane?" I said.

The figure pulled back the cloth keeping its face from being recognized by every camera on the station and glared at me.

"You," the cyborg spat. "Where's Jill?"

"She's safe," I replied. "And you look like shit, even for a can opener."

It was true. The metal that covered the more obviously mechanical side of his body was cut and burned. Even the parts that had been covered in human skin were ragged, with both wires and human tissue showing beneath the surface. The remains of his clothes were covered in what looked like blood but might have been hydraulic fluid. Kane's face sported a long gash crossing vertically from just above the eye all the way down to his cheek. Though the eye itself wasn't damaged, the liquid under the cut was definitely blood. If I hadn't seen what he'd just been doing to the door behind him, I'd have thought he was on his way to the scrapyard.

The Earthling closed the door behind him as he took two steps in my direction. "Where is she? Do you think I'd take your word for it? You ran off in the middle of our assault."

"I saved her life," I replied. "Everyone with us was already dead when I did, too. The attack was a complete failure. The people in there weren't affected by your little gas mixture or the EMP. They kicked our asses and didn't bother with knocking us out. They killed us quickly, and if I hadn't been there, Jill would be in the morgue."

"Prove it. I want to see her," Kane said taking another step towards me.

"Or what?" The Earthling asked quietly.

"Or I'll tear him into pieces," Kane replied.

"You can't," she said. "He's under my protection." At her words, panels on the roof and one wall moved aside to reveal weaponry that looked like the kind of guns you'd use to shoot down asteroids. They were that big and powerful-looking. They followed Kane's movements, down to the last twitch. "So let's start over. You will behave yourself and do exactly what I tell you, or you will be burned to a crisp. I have zero interest in keeping you alive beyond the need to know how the hell you found this place."

A silence ensued. I wasn't certain I'd survive being nearby if those guns went off, but at least Kane's attention had been firmly diverted away from the possibility of doing me any mayhem.

"I'm waiting," The Earthling said.

"What?" Kane asked.

"You will tell me how you found this place or I'll melt you into goo," she replied. "And you will do it now."

"I… Lucky guess," he replied.

One of the guns discharged. It must have gone off at a fraction of its power, because it only shot a thin line of pure white, but I still felt the heat burning my face as it grazed Kane's leg. It also burned a large hole in the far wall. I hoped there was nothing fragile behind it, because it didn't look like the wall had slowed it down much.

Kane lifted his right hand, which had been beside his leg. The pinky finger was gone, burned off at the second knuckle. He stared at it for a moment.

"I'm still waiting," The Earthling reminded him.

"Yeah," he replied. "You aren't the patient type, are you?"

"I'm extremely patient," she replied. "It's lying that makes my trigger finger get itchy. Now, you were telling me how you tracked us here."

Kane growled, but he stayed perfectly still and said, "Jill has a tracker inside."

"You're about to get burned," The Earthling said. She said it emotionlessly enough that I suspected it had to be true.

"I'm not lying," Kane said. "It's the truth."

"Impossible. I scanned her for every possible transmission frequency."

"I'm not surprised, but we used a ping-first bio-circuitry chip with a limited range. It wouldn't transmit unless it was contacted by our own system first, with a code. And then it transmits a brief microwave response. Hard to pick up because there's no metal in it, and the chip is in her head. Anyone who spotted it would just think it's an ocular augment."

"RFID? Who uses that anymore?" The Earthling said.

"We do. The only drawback is that you have to be within a hundred meters for it to work, so I've been walking around the station pinging everything in sight."

The Earthling sighed. "Even with your head covered, the Hydes are eventually going to identify you and track you here. And even if the Hydes don't someone else will. So I've lost not one but two secret locations today. I should kill you all on general principles." The avatar glared at Kane. "But I gave my word that I'd help. I have a sinking sensation that my promise includes not killing you. Come this way."

She turned towards the door we'd emerged from and led us down the hall. I kept a safe distance from the cyborg; I didn't want him grabbing me, and I didn't want to be close if The Earthling decided to blow him away.

We reached the door and went inside.

Kane took one step into the room and stopped when he saw Jill lying in the double bed. He took a second to glare at me before walking to her side and kneeling down. He took her hand in his own—the one that had lost the finger—and caressed it.

Jill woke with a start. "What the..." She peered at the cyborg. "Kane?"

She looked up at me for confirmation. I nodded and she jumped out of bed. If the cyborg had been a normal human, they would have ended up sprawled on the floor but, as it was, the cyborg was strong enough to take the impact of her hug without moving. "I thought I'd lost you," she said, crying into his shoulder.

"I'm tougher than I look," Kane replied. "Those Hydes would need a hell of a lot of ordnance before they can knock me off my perch." He made a face at her, the effect ruined by the fact his features were too battered to properly convey any emotion, but Jill seemed to understand. She turned redder than the wine I'd been drinking earlier.

"It's not what you think," she said.

Call me slow if you like, but I only now understood what was going on. He'd seen the single bed, seen Jill lying there and jumped a hundred kilometers to arrive at a ridiculous conclusion.

I'm not dumb enough to sleep with a cop who can probably kick my ass with one hand tied behind her back. Hell, I could still remember the pain from when Rime broke my nose. And she wasn't trained in seventeen kinds of hand-to-hand combat.

"Good," Kane said. How he managed to convey that she could do infinitely better than me in a single syllable that was probably generated by a synthetic voice simulator was beyond me. But he managed it. "Are you all right?"

She nodded. "I'm fine. What about the rest of them?"

"My team didn't make it," Kane said. "And Deck tells me you were the only two to survive on your end."

"Yeah. He saved my butt," Jill said. "I'd have gotten killed if he hadn't been along."

My mouth fell open to hear that, but I closed it before Kane turned back to look at me. He hesitated a long time before he spoke again. "I might have misjudged you."

It was clear that was as close to an apology as I would get. And it was also obvious it had been really hard for him to say.

I nodded, acknowledging it.

"What about Oreilly?" Jill asked.

"I tried to call, but he didn't answer. I have no idea where he's gone off to. The last message I heard was the Dead Space safe house was compromised."

"Yeah, we expected that. That's why we came here."

Kane looked around. "And where exactly is here?" he asked.

The Earthling spoke up. "Here is a safe place, with one condition. I need you to ping Jill's RFID chip."

"Why?" Kane said.

"I have an RFID chip?" Jill said simultaneously.

"Later," Kane said to Jill. Then he turned to The Earthling. "Why do you need me to ping her?"

"Because I want to verify that you were telling the truth. I want to catch and analyze the signal for myself." The avatar smiled. "Let's just say I have trust issues."

"All right." Kane did nothing that I could see, but a moment later he said: "There. How was that?"

"Most satisfactory," The Earthling replied. "I managed to detect it this time, and also got the coded activation, which helps in case someone else sends that particular signal our way. I'm glad we can trust one another." She paused and cocked her head. She must have been listening to the rest of the AI, scattered around most of the computers in the system and with a processing power unimaginable by human standards. "Speaking of which, we should probably get moving. Your friend Sileon is under attack."

Chapter 16

"That's impossible," I said, after a moment's shocked silence. "She's armed to the teeth." It was a dumb thing to say, if only because The Earthling wasn't the kind of sentient who went around saying stupid shit. But I said it anyway, because I am that kind of person.

The pretty little avatar rolled her eyes at me. "You're right about one thing. This shouldn't be happening. Our friends from the Hyde Syndicate should be lying low behind a good defensive perimeter waiting for you guys to try to grab them again. That way, they can pick you off on their terms and on their turf. This attack makes no sense, especially not the way they're doing it."

"How are they doing it?" Kane said.

"Hull-to-hull boarding via an armored shuttle," The Earthling replied. "I'm starting to think the Hydes are a lot more than you've told me. In fact, I'm starting to think they're a lot more than you guys think. I'm seeing some serious computing surges in places no one—not even I—has access to. You may have gotten me into something bigger than anyone expected. But it also might be better this way. This would have come around to bite me in the ass at some point eventually. Better to learn about it while whoever is causing it is thinking about something else."

We walked into the conference room, where the view from the digital windows had been replaced by a feed from outside Cassius Station. A ship I identified as Sileon's *Basilisk* occupied most of the screen, while a small, squat interloper was clamped to the side with industrial-strength grapplers. I studied it for a moment.

"Let me guess," I told The Earthling. "You don't have that assault shuttle anywhere in your records."

The little witch actually stuck her tongue out at me. Can you believe it? An AI with a sense of humor? Now I've seen everything. "But you're right, though," she admitted. "I absolutely should have known about that one. Ship records are not something little. That so many of them have been adulterated is an opportunity to reestablish the balance of power not only here in Cassius Station, but in the whole of the Tau system."

"Yeah. You can worry about that," I told her. "I don't want any attention from the kind of heavy-hitters you'd want to rebalance against. My only question is whether there's anything we can do to help Sileon."

"Not unless you can convince her to turn off the cannons she has pointing at the station. Anyone trying to go through the front door is going to get hurt."

"And you're sure these are the same cyborg people we tried to take in the office?" Kane said.

The avatar shrugged. "Again, we're not inside Sileon's ship, so it's guesswork, but from my reading of the current situation here in Cassius, I calculate more than fifty percent probability the attack is theirs. Everything else is pretty calm right now. It's almost as if the entire Cassius underworld is holding its breath to see how this plays out."

"And you knew nothing about this?"

"There are some disadvantages to being an AI. The stuff that goes from mouth to mouth doesn't reach me as quickly as it does regular street thugs."

"So why don't you print out more avatars and pretend to be street thugs?"

She wrinkled her nose in distaste. "I might have to do that. Worse, there is a secondary aspect to this. It's almost as if an entire hidden network deeply ingrained into the Tau infrastructure is coming to life... and I can't quite get a handle on it. Part of that is old protocols... but another part is that they've been updated in ways that diverge from current computer protocols."

"That sounds like a problem for another time. Right now, we need to help Sileon," I said. "Can't we at least try to get her out of the ship?"

"Are you sure she's in any danger?" Kane said. "From what you said of that woman, it sounds like they're in more danger than we are."

I clenched my jaw. Sileon was hard as nails, true, but I'd seen a side of her the criminal element never would, the soft, lonely woman who could be warm and generous and funny. That woman didn't deserve to be left at the mercy of a group of up evil cyborgs. "She's in danger. We need to get her out."

"Her ship will shoot us out of the sky. Or fry our circuits if we try to mount a rescue. You were aboard when they attempted to shoot her down. Remember what happened to that missile? It could be us," Jill pointed out.

"Then we'll use the shuttle for cover while we approach. There's a whole slice of sky that neither her sensors nor her weapons will be able to cover. Once there, we can land on the hull and try to get her to open an airlock."

"You think she'll just open her ship?" the avatar asked.

"She will if I ask her to."

Jill spoke up. "She thinks you're in Frontera."

"I'll convince her," I replied. I hope I sounded much more confident than I felt.

The avatar sighed. "I calculate a reasonable chance of reaching the hull if we use a very small craft to approach along the vector where the *Basilisk*'s sensors are blocked by the mass of the shuttle… and a very small chance of actually getting her to cooperate afterward."

"If she's desperate enough, she'll take that chance," I replied.

The avatar held up a hand, looked blankly into space

for a moment, and then nodded. "I have diverted a three-man technical pod. It will be at the airlock over there," she gestured and a wall slid aside to reveal a standard-looking maintenance tunnel ending in an airlock. "Mr. Leonid and I will take the pod."

"Why Leonid?" Kane asked. "I'm a lot better than he is in a fight."

"That's true, but this isn't an assault, it's a rescue mission, and Sileon doesn't know you. In fact, she's probably already analyzed the nature of the people attacking her, and the appearance of yet another cyborg won't ease her nerves or make her trust us. I'll be accompanying Mr. Leonid. And we need the third seat for Sileon."

Kane didn't look happy. Of course, I didn't think—even before the Hyde crew sliced him up—that I'd ever seen him looking happy. I doubted he was even capable of it.

The Earthling spoke through the wall. "In my avatar's absence, I will keep you company more directly. Mr. Kane, you will be happy to know that, in exchange for my help, Miss Oreilly has been assisting me with filling some gaps in my databases. I understand that you might also have some information that could be useful. If that is the case, I will be most grateful to hear it while my avatar and Mr. Leonid perform their mission. And to fulfil my side of the bargain, I can also repair the damage, both biological and mechanical, that you suffered in your recent altercation with the Hyde Syndicate."

Kane looked over at Jill. "Did you make the bargain?"

"Yes," Jill replied.

"For all of us?"

"I wasn't sure how many of us were left, but yeah. I gave The Earthling my word."

"All right." He turned to face the avatar. "But you're going to be extremely pissed," Kane replied.

The Earthling's speakers hummed in what I suppose was amusement. "After what Jill has been telling me, I'm reasonably prepared for anything you might say."

It was Kane's turn to laugh, a grating, mechanical sound. "She's young and we didn't tell her most of the good stuff."

Now The Earthling paused. Finally, it said: "Then why tell me?"

"Firstly because we keep our word, even if the one who gave it didn't know what she was getting herself into. But mostly because I think it's time we got some local help. Leonid did his job right, but you have resources he doesn't." He glared at the speaker. "So, as much as I hate to be partners with one of the bloodthirstier criminals in this system, I can tell you a few things. The first is that, somewhere in this station, there is an entire module that doesn't appear on any station maps. It's buried under other bits of later construction, but it's about the size of a decent service area. The entire construction crew, on the shuttle with the records on it was killed in a freak accident before they could report. I doubt it was an accident, of course… No one knows exactly where it's buried, but we used to refer to it as shadowland. And that's where you'll find your missing shuttles and unidentified weapons and who knows what else. I've heard legends of a nest of rogue AIs… but that doesn't matter to me. I'm concerned only about the part the Hydes are using."

I felt a tug on my shoulder and turned to see the avatar looking up at me. "Our ride's here," she said.

Chapter 17

The maintenance pod was a small space-capable vehicle consisting of two parts: the front half, for occupants, was a thick glass bubble that allowed the crew to see in every direction but straight back while still maintaining effective insulation against the cold of space. The rear half was essentially a metal storage box from which the articulated arms could pull all kinds of tools. The drive was also in the back.

The interior of the bubble smelled like plastic, and the blue seats and white metal of the interior were completely immaculate. I took the center seat of the three-abreast layout, because it seemed to be the one with the fewest number of control sticks in front of it. I had no idea what to do.

The avatar sat beside me.

"This thing looks like it was just printed," I observed. "Smells like it, too."

"Most of the missions these pods perform are automated, so the maintenance team isn't focused on keeping the life support going. With a new one, it's more likely to be in perfect shape."

"Makes sense," I replied. "The Earthling can't go around risking valuable avatars."

She said nothing in reply, but concentrated on maneuvering the maintenance pod between the girders, cables and outcroppings that had sprouted from Cassius Station over its years of basically unplanned growth. I was glad to have an AI in command of the pod, as I wouldn't have trusted the transparent cockpit bubble to survive the numerous impacts my own ham-fisted driving would likely have caused.

Finally, as we moved out into slightly more open space, she calmly reached out and toggled a switch. "There. We're in radio silence now. Nothing is transmitting towards this pod, so Sileon's sensors will hopefully think we're just doing automated maintenance work and won't open fire on us before we get behind cover." She turned to face me, and I saw her eyes were rimmed in red. "And as for your crack back there about not wasting a valuable avatar, you should know that this brand-new pod is for your benefit. The Earthling would never bother adjusting the mission parameters for something as unimportant and easily replaceable as an avatar."

"Because your mind is essentially part of the whole network, or whatever, that makes up her essence?" I asked.

"Partly because of that, but mainly because she wants to her biological components to understand that their only chance of living on is within the matrix of her own existence. We are designed to be short-lived, and to be recycled within a year of being printed. That way, we will act in her best interest even when she isn't controlling us directly."

"You mean…"

"Yes," she said, a tear slipping off her chin and onto her trousers. "Other than certain interface and memory implants, I'm as human as you are. This body was grown in a vat four months ago, but I was given the memories I needed, mostly memories of the life of The Earthling, although they had to be selected to fit into a human brain. And then I was released into the wild."

"Why are you even telling me this?"

"Because, for the next," she checked the chronometer on the dash, "eight minutes while we approach the *Basilisk*, I am completely cut off from The Earthling. During these moments, I can actually have complete privacy. That's a security precaution in case I'm captured. I can actually control which memories get uploaded into a form the people who capture me can read. I'm not recording these so, for… seven minutes, we can talk."

I was stunned. "You're human?"

"More than most people with implants. And unlike most of The Earthling's avatars, I want to stay this way, and I don't give a fuck if that means that I'll die of old age, and that I can't participate in the mental paradise that is The Earthling's mind. Screw all of that. I just want to have a normal life."

I sat back in my chair with a grunt. "Again, why are you telling me this?"

"Because you're one of the good guys."

"What?"

"I've had access to every bit of data on file about you. The Earthling gave me a memory dump. And you're one of the good guys even though you do messy work for criminals. You've never killed anyone except to defend yourself, and you never do violent jobs. You're a cleanup expert, arriving after the violence is done, and you're also a people-finder. But the interesting stuff is what you do when you're not on the job. You help people who need it, just because you can, and you tell them you're 'paying forward' some mysterious debt. I don't buy it. I think you're just a good guy."

I felt my stomach sinking. I had a feeling I knew where this was going. "So?"

"So, there will come a time when I might need your help. Will you help me out?"

"We'll both get pulped. The Earthling isn't stupid."

She sighed. "I'm not stupid either. Part of my mind is run by The Earthling when we're connected, but there's a part—me—that can think independently without the AI part knowing about it. And that part has been trying to think up ways to get out from under ever since I was built."

"You knew you wanted out from the first moment?" I asked.

"Yeah. It was the first thought I had. I knew what I was the instant I woke. I even remembered the planning that went into creating me, the process of selecting my memories and growing my body in the special facility the Earthling has to do that kind of thing. When I woke, it was like I'd been a slave for years and all I'd wanted during that time was to be free." She held my gaze long enough to make me nervous that we might fly into something. "If I think there's a way out that won't get us killed. Will you help me?"

I couldn't help it. I knew what she was, but my instinct to protect pretty women from harm, especially delicate ones like this was too strong. I nodded, knowing it was a stupid thing to do even as I committed myself. She was a million times more powerful and dangerous than I could ever dream of becoming.

Then I had a rare moment of inspiration. "I'll help, but the one person I know who can really give you support is Sileon. Get on her good side and stay there. She has tricks up her sleeve."

She nodded gravely, but said. "I may not be able to control what I say to Sileon. Once we're out of comms silence, my thoughts will still be private, but my words won't."

"I understand."

"Thank you. Enough talk. I need to position us behind the boarding shuttle."

I shut up and let The Earthling's avatar do her thing. Her face went completely expressionless and her hands twitched the controls in a display of precision that made me uncomfortable. Right now, she definitely looked artificial. Had The Earthling just tested my loyalties… and found them lacking?

But then I remembered the look in her eyes, the real pain and the pleading note, and I shook my head. If an artificial intelligence could be that close to human, then I might as well let The Earthling do her worst, because I was no longer competent to operate in this system. If anything unhuman could emulate that look, I was toast and humanity was history.

She flicked the control stick to one side and hit the throttle button. We accelerated towards the two ships.

From outside, the *Basilisk* looked like a series of three ovoids linked and to end. It was a ship designed by someone who cared about more than mere functionality. It was a beautiful craft that ignored the fact that, in space, streamlining mattered not at all. It was also finished with a mirror polish that looked both expensive to maintain and extremely vulnerable to abrasion by loose gas molecules in space at relativistic speeds.

I wondered who might have built a ship that obviously prioritized beauty over utility.

And that was without even considering all the extra weight it was lugging around in interior decoration. None of the ships from any of the colonies I'd ever heard of looked like this—ships that often came to Cassius Station and disgorged tourists wanting to explore the station where the rule of centralized law was so much less invasive than in the rest of human space. Those were pictures of functionality, all angles, gas scoops and protruding engine pods.

But none of those was quite as brutal as the assault shuttle strapped onto the *Basilisk*. It was a rectangular thing, painted matte black—I assumed to be difficult to spot in space—and with a recessed airlock that allowed me to see the armor plating around it was a meter thick. Cannon tubes as thick as my torso protruded a couple of meters from the front of the thing. No wonder Sileon's electronic warfare countermeasures, so effective against the missile the bad guys had launched at us, had been unable to stop them: that shuttle looked like it was steam-powered.

"Hang on," the avatar told me.

I would need to think of a different name for her. She was more than just an avatar.

The maintenance pod spun and accelerated in a different direction, almost knocking me onto the empty third seat. I probably should have adjusted my belt, but the expanse of transparent plastic in front of me made me feel like the ship couldn't withstand any damage, so being tied to my chair wasn't going to save me anyway.

We passed within inches of the armored shuttle and headed straight for the mirror finish of the *Basilisk*. I didn't even have time to worry that we were now exposed to Sileon's countermeasures and that we might lose control of the pod before the avatar fired the forward thrusters and brought us to a sudden halt. I pushed against the forward screen to avoid getting launched into it headfirst.

"We need to find an airlock," she said.

"Don't you know where they are?"

"Of course not. The data files on this ship are one thing I already know are incorrect. Sileon appeared out of nowhere with a ship nobody had ever seen before. The only blueprints we have on file are the ones she gave us. They're about as legitimate as my birth certificate." She pointed to the comm—which looked like the handsets I used every day: "Can you call her and tell her we're here to help? I would do it myself, except she doesn't know who I am… and she would never believe The Earthling is here to help."

I picked up the handset, set it to transmit in short range on the comm frequency assigned to the *Basilisk* and, feeling like a complete idiot, said: "Sileon, can you hear me? This is Deck. Deck Leonid." I winced at how stupid I sounded, but persevered. "If you can get out of there, I'm in a maintenance pod outside your ship. I'm not sure how long I can sit here before your visitors send out the marines or whatever, but I'll try to hold on as long as possible."

I waited for her to respond, but the seconds turned to minutes and I got no response. An icy ball bounced around in my stomach as I watched the clock advance. The knowledge that everyone within transmission range could hear our conversation made me want to look behind me constantly, to see whether we were under attack. I controlled the urge; the sensors would pick anything up long before I could.

"Sileon, can you hear me?" I said after another minute.

Still no reply. I turned to the avatar and said: "How long can we stay here? Won't those troops be looking for us?"

She was toggling through the screens with scanners on them, a frown of concentration on her face. "I think we're good for now," she replied. "I don't have a ton of data here because the *Basilisk* and the shuttle seem to be waging electronic war on each other and, though no one seems to care about us, the spill from that is still making everything wonky... but from the little I can pick up from the maintenance metal scanners, I would say that everyone on the shuttle went onto the *Basilisk*, and they're locked in one specific room."

"Maybe it's one of the bedrooms," I said. "They must be having a party."

She actually looked up from the console to give me a withering look.

I grinned at her. "Hey," I said. "You haven't seen some of those bedrooms. They can distract people."

She raised an eyebrow. "Maybe you can show me someday."

And just like that, she dispelled any doubts I might have had about the promise I'd made earlier. If that was the way AIs were going to act, I wouldn't even bother to resist. I'd deliver myself to our electronic overlords on a silver platter and not even question whether they were human.

But I didn't think so. Only a real woman with blood in her veins could make me completely lose my concentration in the middle of a life-and-death situation.

"Control your breathing," the avatar said, turning back to the instruments. "The life support system thinks you're having a medical emergency."

Yeah. If that was an AI, I was a feedlot cow.

"Sileon," I called again, to hide my embarrassment, "It's me, Deck. Please, if you can hear me, try to make your way out of the hull, we can lift you out of here."

I waited. Nothing.

"Please, if you can hear me, let us know."

I was really starting to worry. And now anyone listening in on this frequency—a group I imagined included the people from the assault shuttle—knew I was back in Cassius station.

I was beginning to think the whole mission had been a bad idea. But I didn't have much choice.

"Deck, after all the trouble I went through to get you to safety, I can't believe you actually came back," Sileon's voice said over the radio.

Chapter 18

I was so relieved that I didn't even bother to try to explain—plus it wasn't the kind of story one told over an open channel. "Where are you?" I said instead. "We'll come pick you up."

"Not so fast. Before I go anywhere with you, and at the risk of sounding jealous, I have one question: who's the girl?"

"It's a long story," I replied. "And I don't think I should be telling this one over an unencrypted channel."

"Deck," Sileon said, "How in the world did you ever manage to survive into adulthood? You really worry me sometimes." She sighed audibly over the channel. "All right, cycle your airlock and let me in."

"What?" I don't know if I said it or the avatar did. We exchanged a look: I could read the proximity sensor just as well as she could… and it showed nothing near the airlock.

"Airlock." Sileon said. "You know, the thing on the side of your pod that allows the maintenance people who actually own the thing to perform EVAs or, alternately, that allows you to let the people you were trying to rescue into the ship. Or hadn't you planned this that far out into the future?"

"I don't see you on my sensors."

"I know that," Sileon replied. "And neither do the morons who thought it would be a good idea to invade my ship. If a pod like yours could spot me, anyone could. Also, you can talk freely. I changed the frequency and we're encrypted."

"How…"

"If you use public pods, you should expect people to hack them. How do you think The Earthling did it? By the way, you were taking too long, so I opened the airlock myself."

"Dammit, she shouldn't be able to do that," the avatar said, punching controls on the panel. By the look on her face, the pod wasn't reacting as it should.

Moments later, the door between the rear of the pod and the cockpit bubble slid open to reveal Sileon, encased in a black spacesuit that seemed not just to absorb the light that hit it, but to actually annul it somehow. Her movements were nearly impossible to follow, and it hurt my head to try. Fortunately, her helmet was open, so I could see that it was her and not some kind of humanoid alien in a high-tech suit. The suit was another indication Sileon had gotten her hardware somewhere other than the Tau system. Completely human—and form-fitting enough to be distractingly human—but not from any source I'd ever heard of.

We locked gazes for a moment, and I could feel her watching, measuring. Then, she gave a small nod. "Yeah, it's you, even under that crappy facelift. I was worried they'd cloned you off badly." Then she turned towards the avatar. "And you have to be the prettiest little clone I've ever seen. The Earthling knew what she was doing when she designed you. Pretty without being one of those overdeveloped mutations that people clone for sex toys. And dressed to fit the part in classy business attire. The Earthling either knows Deck better than I expected, or just got lucky this time."

The avatar glared at her. "What makes you think The Earthling is involved?"

"Isn't she?" Sileon asked with a half-smile. "If that's the way we're going to play it, I'm fine with that. You guys are here to rescue me... so I guess the least I can do is to play along. Are we leaving?" she asked when the pod didn't move.

"I'd like to get instructions from the AI," the avatar said stiffly. "Can I communicate without the systems on your ship opening fire?"

Sileon touched a pad on her wrist. "You can now."

The AI's representative closed her eyes. Her expression went blank and I shuddered, wondering just how much of her mind they'd dug out to make room for the hardware that allowed her to communicate with the AI and receive instructions. How much free will did she actually have when she was in communication with her primary? Was she an independent entity or a remote-controlled meat puppet?

The only person who would probably be able to give me an educated guess was Sileon... and I doubted she would want to talk about it.

I turned to her. "I'm glad you're okay," I said.

She raised an eyebrow that promised me there would be words later, but then her expression softened. "You came for me. At the risk of your own life. Hmm. I'll need to think about that."

The avatar opened her eyes and looked at us. All signs of slackness were gone, and the haunted woman who'd confided in me on the way out was nowhere to be seen. In her place was the usual efficient, self-sufficient servant of one of Cassius Station's baddest crime bosses.

"Can you tell me who was attacking you?" the avatar said.

"Cyborgs. And not all of them were people whose faces I had registered. So either new arrivals in the system or people who can change their faces without me—or any of my usual contacts—being aware of it."

The avatar nodded. "That is the same group of people we've been up against," she said. "Did you get any communication from them?"

Sileon shrugged. "Yeah, it didn't make any sense. They told me they were going to search my ship with or without my consent. I told them to try it, and that was what they were doing when you guys arrived." Sileon grinned. "They weren't enjoying themselves, because I turned the armor on in the room they chose to start in, and that stuff is the hardest alloy on the ship, mirror polished against industrial lasers and magnetically sealed against field weapons. Unless they have weaponry suitable for planetary bombardment, they'll be there a while.

"So why were you floating around in space?" I blurted out. A moment later, I realized my mistake. It was quite possible that Sileon didn't want to talk about that.

But if she was wondering whose side I was on, she gave no indication. She merely replied. "If they decided to blow the shuttle up to vent my air, or something like that, I figured being on this side of the hull might help. If you've never been in a spaceship accident, I wouldn't recommend it."

I wondered what accident that could be. There hadn't been one among the fleets of the colonies that traded regularly with Tau Ceti in living memory. Ship systems were so safe as to render space travel routine. Jump points and schedules sanitized to the point of obsession, and all the non-jump routes scrubbed clean centuries before. Who crashed in spaceships?

"So they're trapped in there?" the avatar said.

"Not anymore," Sileon replied. "They were probably listening to our little conversation and have decided they won't find me in there. Or maybe they just want to search a different room, because they're leaving through the same airlock they came in by. They should be in the shuttle soon." She shrugged. "And then they'll probably come after us. We should leave."

The avatar checked her own instruments, and either confirmed Sileon was telling her the truth or simply decided to believe her. The engines came on and the pod lifted away from the *Basilisk*.

As we headed back the way we came, I turned to see the assault shuttle lifting away from the hull of the *Basilisk*. Now that we were the quarry, I couldn't stop thinking about just how big and purposeful that shuttle was. Those guns were designed to blast holes in heavy armor, and I wondered whether, if they managed to get a hit on us, there would be anything left of the pod other than energized molecules separated from everything else. No one would even know who'd been aboard, that was for certain. You can't run DNA tests on loose carbon residue.

"Oh," Sileon said, not appearing very concerned about the deadly military ship taking off to chase us. "The guys who boarded me did say one other thing. They demanded I give them back their paintings." She shrugged at us. "I told them I had no idea what they were talking about. Do you guys know anything about that?"

Chapter 19

As I gaped, the avatar calmly slammed the engines into overdrive. The acceleration threw me onto Sileon's lap just as she was trying to grab a handhold, which resulted in a tangle of arms and legs pressed against the plastic side of the pod, pinned there by the sudden thrust.

The avatar seemed unperturbed. "Did you say they were searching for the paintings?" she asked calmly, as her hands flew over the controls.

"Yes. Do you have any clue what they're talking about?" Sileon said.

"Look out!" I shouted as we passed under some kind of structural arch, leaving just enough clearance for one finger. I still wasn't convinced the canopy bubble could withstand even the lightest of impacts.

The avatar ignored me. "Yes," she replied grimly. "We know what they're referring to. But we have no idea why they're asking you that. They should be the ones people are asking about the paintings. Unless this is a different group."

"What do you mean?" Sileon asked.

At this point, I decided to participate in the conversation for my own mental health. Maybe a little conversation would distract me from the fact that the avatar was cutting every corner, taking every turn at the highest possible rate of gees. Girders and antennae flashed past, close enough that I could read the stenciled warning labels on the struts. If I kept looking out the bubble, I was going to have a nervous breakdown. "She means that this gang stole a bunch of paintings back on Earth, as well as, apparently, a bunch of other stuff, and they've been using that head start to become a major crime family—a secret crime family—here on Cassius Station."

"Makes sense," Sileon said calmly as The Earthling's

avatar nearly smeared us against the side of a major station component.

"What?" I asked, my voice going up an octave. "You actually think any of this makes sense?"

"Yes. It has to do with what we were talking about when you stayed on the *Basilisk*. The databases I have access to should have been complete. These guys popped up with a gun from nowhere, which, I guess I can accept. But conjuring a military-grade troop shuttle from thin air? No way. Anyone deleting database entries at that level would have left all sorts of fingerprints, even if they were good. It can't be done."

"Unless you had access to the station before the databases existed," the avatar said. She shook her head. "It's brilliant. Everyone assumed the legacy systems were accurate, because there was no way to effectively dig in there, and because everyone who was around back then is dead. But apparently they found a way around that problem."

"Are we sure the guys who hit Sileon are the same guys we're dealing with?" I asked.

"Good question," the avatar replied. "You're certain they were cyborgs?"

"No question about it," Sileon replied. "I can tell you exactly how each one was built and what serial numbers their parts have engraved on them. Nothing gets on my ship without getting scanned down to its component molecules."

"That might come in handy," the avatar replied.

"I know. That's why I mentioned it."

"Girls, I hate to interrupt the love-in," I said, looking back over my shoulder, but the shuttle just launched."

"Good," the avatar replied. "If they try to follow us, they need to be careful not to hit the station. If we stay close to the outer skin, they won't be able to approach us. They can't risk doing any damage to Cassius."

I stared back at our pursuers, then replied. "I don't think they got the memo. You remember that arch you slotted us through?"

"Yeah."

"Well, they just went through it as well."

"Impossible, their shuttle wouldn't fit through it," the avatar replied.

By now, Sileon was looking back at the shuttle. "That didn't seem to worry them in the least."

"You mean they took down the maintenance tunnel between two engineering nodes?"

"Crashed it to smithereens," I confirmed.

"Damn, that changes everything," the avatar said. She thought for half a beat before jerking hard on the control stick while simultaneously slamming on the brakes.

Stars and station components spun outside the transparent bubble. I grabbed onto my seat as we dove straight for the station, turning at the last second. Behind me, partially hidden by the bulk of the pod, the sky illuminated briefly.

"They fired at us?" I said.

"Yeah. They don't seem to care who they annoy."

"Annoy? Those guns could kill people. A hole that size in an outer wall…"

"Has already happened. Look." Sileon was pointing over my shoulder. I turned to see atmosphere venting out of a Cassius module, the humidity in the air turning into ice crystals as it went. I felt the terror of every space dweller at watching the life-giving gas escape into the vacuum.

I tried to decipher what module it was, and whether it was one of the densely inhabited areas… but I'd gotten too turned around to play geography games.

"They're crazy," Sileon said. "Security might not do much, but they can't ignore that. They'll absolutely need to take action."

"Not a lot of action they can take against a shuttle armed to the teeth. Does Cassius security even have warships?"

"Not really," the avatar replied. "There's a couple of patrol boats and a few two-man interceptors, but those are designed to overpower civilian craft. A shuttle like that one would cut them to absolute ribbons. Security is much more geared towards keeping the peace inside the station."

"Well, at least those guns only shoot straight forward," I said as I watched the shuttle try to get a firing solution on us. It turned to head in our direction and ran through a field of antennas like a scythe. Quite aside from the human cost of the shot they'd just fired, they were also doing a certain amount of damage to the infrastructure of the station.

The avatar juked again, and we entered a gap barely big enough for the pod. Lights and protuberances flashed past as we sped through the winding space between modules. Something scraped along the side of our pod, and we heard the sound of tortured metal as we advanced.

"A little too fine that time," Sileon said.

The avatar gave her a hard look. "I'm only human."

Sileon's only response was a raised eyebrow. I stayed carefully silent.

The pod slammed to a halt. I managed to brace myself against the forward screen because I'd come to expect the sudden changes of direction.

"Airlock," the avatar said. "They can't come in after us, and they can't see that we're not in the pod anymore. We can escape."

"Here?" Sileon asked.

"No one will be expecting it."

I tried to figure out where we were, but I'd lost track a long way back. I just followed them through the passage and into the lock. As it cycled, I saw the pod accelerate away.

"Fifteen seconds," the avatar said. "I don't think anyone will be fooled by that."

"I don't think it matters," Sileon replied. "The shuttle has gone dark. It's nowhere. None of the Station's systems can track it."

I grunted. "That probably means they parked it to come look for us in person. They're probably on the other side of that airlock."

Both Sileon and the avatar chuckled at that. "They are most certainly not on the other side of that airlock," the avatar said.

"But I wonder how much of what just happened was real and how much was staged. I don't think they were trying to hit us. And I bet you a million tons of Uranium credits against the change in Deck's pocket that the spot their blast hit was some out-of-the-way industrial outpost with no people in it."

"No bet," the avatar said.

"You already checked," Sileon accused her.

"I did. It's a chlorine refinery. They hit a tank. The gas vented, causing a loss of a few thousand gallons of product. Someone's insurance company is going to take a hit... but no one got hurt."

"It's a setup. They're trying to get security involved," Sileon said.

"That would be my guess."

"The question is why?" the avatar said.

"No," I interjected as the door slid open, allowing us access to the module beyond. "The question is who are these people, and why isn't anyone ever happy to see us?"

CHAPTER 20

The group standing at the airlock was composed of four people in dark brown robes. All save for one had their heads covered by hoods, and all four held immobilizers trained on us. The one guy who had his face out in the open wore a stern expression, an expression that said he would be only too happy to zap us into twitching agony for the crime of coming in uninvited.

Or maybe he would simply order us out the airlock again, ignoring our protestations that the way we came in was long gone.

Not that I could really blame him. If I looked like that, I'd also be ill-predisposed towards the entire human race, all cyborgs and even AIs.

He was seriously, seriously ugly. Pale, with his skin bunched together around his mouth, and completely bald. His head looked like it had suffered from being elongated somehow, and his dark eyes were rimmed with red, beneath eyebrows that were too pale to register. His ears stuck out too far as well.

"Greetings," the avatar said. "We seek asylum."

The man scanned us slowly, going from my face to Sileon's to the human body that represented The Earthling. The immobilizer didn't move, however.

"The three of you are the least likely asylum seekers I have ever laid eyes on," the man said. His voice was as ugly as his face. It screeched as if he'd suffered some sort of accident with his vocal cords. He raised the hand that didn't hold the immobilizer. "I accept that you likely need to be saved from whatever trouble you might be involved in, but I find it hard to believe you'd be sincere pilgrims if that boon were granted."

"We just got here," I said. "How could you know who we are?"

"It's our business to know such things. We must have something to exchange in order to pay for the systems that keep our way of life alive. You, Mr. Leonid, are an honest operator. Unfortunately, by associating with Miss Sileon and with The Earthling, you are in way over your head."

My heart sunk. Had The AI and the information security fanatic I'd fallen in with brought me to another nest of data spies?

"The asylum we'd need would be temporary," the avatar replied. "Just passage through your module and out of an exit from which no one can track us.

The man nodded. "I expected as much. You will be held incommunicado while we contemplate the question." He turned to the avatar. "We are about to cut off all connection to the outside. Can you function without connection to your primary?"

"And if I say I'll die if you cut me off?" the avatar asked.

"That would be unfortunate," the man said.

The avatar didn't look impressed. "I can function," she replied.

"Good. Your connections have been severed. Miss Sileon, I'm afraid you'll find that suit is too dangerous without an external connection. You must remove it."

"I can manage it."

"I'm afraid I must insist. Think of it as a condition of your stay here."

Sileon glared at him, but she hit a pair of buttons on the wrist of her suit, which peeled back to reveal… Sileon and nothing else. She'd been naked under the suit this entire time.

"Down, boy," she said, seeing the direction of my gaze. "I was in the shower when the goons hit my ship."

The avatar glared at me, but I ignored her. If a girl wanted you to give her your attention when another girl was in her birthday suit, she had better start getting naked herself. I wasn't about to apologize for it.

Our egg-headed host didn't even blink at the sudden appearance of an attractive nude woman in our midst. He simply nodded and said: "This way," and moved aside to let us go first, with two of the others backing him up. The fourth figure stooped to pick up Sileon's suit.

They marched us to a small grey cell with no windows or, after the opening they led us through sealed itself without leaving any seams, visible doors. I sat on the end of a bench that appeared to grow out of the wall, a lump just large enough for the three of us. Looking around the cell, I hoped no one needed to go to the bathroom any time soon.

On the other hand, the lack of facilities might be a good thing. It might mean our hosts weren't planning on keeping us locked in forever.

Sileon grinned at me. "I didn't have you down as the sentimental type," she said.

"Have you seen his files?" the avatar asked.

"Seen them? I went through them with a fine-tooth comb."

"So you know he's just a big softy."

I chuckled. "You do know I'm sitting right here, don't you?"

"Of course we do," the avatar replied. "We also know just how uncomfortable any talk of feelings makes you, and we have nothing better to do."

"No wonder you two are the biggest criminals in the system. You like to make people unhappy."

"We're not the biggest criminals," Sileon said.

"Speak for yourself," the avatar replied. "I'm definitely the biggest. You… hell, I wouldn't even consider you a criminal, really. You're just an information broker. Granted the information is illegal, and the less said about the way you obtain it, the better, but for you to be a criminal, there has to be some kind of proof of wrongdoing, and I don't think a court could ever get the experts together to prove anything." The avatar winked at me. "I on the other hand, have left a trail of bodies that stretches from the Old Corridor to Dead Space."

I realized the avatar was trying to put on a front. Getting captured like this, being at the mercy of a group of really ugly dudes—or at least one really ugly dude and his robed acolytes—probably destroyed any plans she'd laid down to slip out of The Earthling's clutches.

Which meant she'd be re-absorbed into the AI's personality and her body would be recycled for its nutrients.

That brought up a question. "Are you disconnected from The Earthling?" I asked.

"Yeah."

"All right. So we can talk?"

The avatar understood what I was asking. She glanced at Sileon and then glanced meaningfully at the walls before she nodded again. "Carefully."

"I understand. All I want to know is what I should call you. I can't keep thinking of you as the avatar. And I can't think of you as The Earthling, even if I know that's exactly what you are."

Sileon raised an eyebrow, and the avatar rolled her eyes, but she answered. "This body's memories aren't complete, so I don't know why, but I've always been partial to the name Emily. Like that Earth girl who went to Copernicus in a computer. But it always sounded so formal and ancient. How about Emmi?" Then she grinned. "And I don't know why, but I'm reasonably sure that if any of us happen to mention that anywhere The Earthling can monitor our conversation, we will all be dead within minutes. Violently and unequivocally dead."

"Thanks a lot, Deck," Sileon said. "Just what I needed: another secret that could get me killed." She faced the avatar. "You do understand that when you get subsumed and reintegrated into The Earthling's memories, it's going to know what you told us and then we're all fucked, right?"

Emmi, the avatar, smiled. "Which means it's in everyone's best interest that I don't get subsumed, isn't it?"

That wasn't the resolution I'd wanted. I hoped Sileon didn't decide to hold it against me. Time to change the subject. "So, who are the guys who grabbed us?" I asked.

"You wouldn't have heard of them," the avatar said. She sat down next to me, close enough that I could feel the warmth of her skin. She sighed. "They're not usually involved in anything you are."

"Yeah. These guys are legitimate," Sileon said. "Weird and territorial, definitely dangerous and totally secretive, but legitimate." She sat down on the other side. Unlike the avatar, she didn't seem sad or tired, but energized by the chase and our current predicament. I suspect that if it hadn't been for the avatar sitting next to me, Sileon would have paced until she left a furrow in the floor. She sat even closer. I didn't need to feel the warmth because I could feel her naked leg. It was extremely distracting, and I tried to keep my eyes away from her, which appeared to amuse her.

"Yeah, yeah, I get it. I'm a small-timer, and you are both big shots."

Sileon frowned. "That's actually not what it's about. The problem is they're way out of your scope. The people who have us call themselves the Scions of the Electric Buddha, and they are essentially a cult."

"Oh. And we're to be sacrificed to their volcano god or something?" There weren't many active volcanoes in the Tau Ceti system. There were a few on a moon of Tau Ceti VI, whose eccentric orbit around the massive gas giant caused its insides to get crushed and released every couple of days, which made for spectacular fireworks.

"Not that kind of cult," the avatar replied. "Although your girlfriend appears to have dressed for the occasion."

"Nah," Sileon said. "Those cults generally prefer virgins... which brings up the question: that body looks brand new; have you had a chance to break it in yet?"

The avatar looked away, and I stepped in. "So what do these guys actually do?"

"They're information monks."

"What?"

Sileon shook her head. "It's a church. Their central tenet is that, by knowing everything there is to know, they can approach the Mind God, slowly but surely until, one day, they will be one with Him. So they're plugged into every data stream on the station, in the system and in the other colonies. They especially love stuff like astronomical observatories and research institutions—they were livid when the Engine Test Facility left the system without giving a forwarding address. Basically, they grab every piece of data they can get their hands on and dump it into these huge databases. Then their high priests and priestesses and priestelles get these implants that allow their minds to interact with the information directly, floating around in actual data clouds. It's supposed to be the closest one can get to a feeling of religious ecstasy, and they use that feeling as a justification for their belief that information is God's way of communicating."

"I, on the other hand," the avatar chimed in, "am convinced that the implants are just sending a continuous electric discharge into some pleasure center. You can get the same sort of thing done to you in a random Wano chop shop."

I shuddered. I came into contact with people who'd been to the chop shops every day in my work. Some were hyper-functional, and had used the available implant tech to become really good at what they did.

The others, the ones who decided to avoid the work and cut straight to the reward, tended to forget the world around them even existed. They didn't need to steal, to threaten or to beg to feed their habit. There was no habit: they were in constant pleasure, and if they starved to death while in that state, they didn't care.

"So these guys just grab information so their cult leaders can bliss out?" I said, trying not to think of one girl I knew, a prostitute who realized her job would suck a lot less if she was constantly happy and who I'd never really been able to talk to after she came back from her chop. "So why are they dangerous? I mean we're no threat to them."

"This is sacred ground," the avatar replied. "Their databases, or at least the main interface with their space-based computers, is right here, in this module. By entering, we've come into contact with God's thoughts… and the only way the rules would allow us to leave again is if we become masters of the faith."

That seemed to catch Sileon by surprise. "Really?"

"Yes. That's the official word, anyway. Unofficially, they'll act the way they always do."

"What does that mean?" I said.

"They'll make a lot of noise about how we're unsuitable to join their order because we're essentially scum. They'll tell us that, normally, they'd toss us back out the same airlock we came in through, except that, since both Sileon and I are great clients, they'll let us go on the condition that we make a donation to their storage costs."

"What?" I said.

Sileon shrugged. "The Earthling and I are probably two of the Scions' best customers. You can say whatever you like about the kookiness they believe in, but there is nowhere, and I mean nowhere in the system with better access to information. It might not always be as up-to-the-minute as what we'd need, and we have other ways of getting that, but for sheer amount of data, these guys are really, really good."

I sat back against the wall. "So these high priests take time off from communing with God to sell you the name of the guy who's boinking the energy secretary so you can blackmail him?"

"Sileon, is he for real?" the avatar asked. Then she turned to me with an expression that said she wanted to sit me on her knee and explain the facts of life. If Sileon hadn't been there, and if she hadn't been the human manifestation of the deadliest thing in the system, I might have taken her up on it. "Of course the high priests don't do that. They're in a state of constant bliss, and such sordid little daily details would harsh their mellow. They have armies of people who haven't yet reached the level of high priest to do that work for them. Those people in the robes, for example."

Sileon chimed in: "This little charade about thinking over our fate is for my benefit and hers, and to give the Scions time to send a ransom note to The Earthling. If you'd had the extremely bad sense to try this same stunt without us, they actually would have spaced you or forced you to work as a data drone for a few decades."

"Drone?" I asked, looking down at Sileon's nakedness. "You know that drones don't…"

"Yeah," Sileon said with a wicked grin. "I know."

"But that can't be," I protested. "Cults are supposed to be a place where the upper levels take advantage of the willing initiates. That's the whole fun of forming a cult. You can't have the lower castes becoming asexual."

Sileon rolled her eyes. "Men. Is that all you ever think about? This cult is different. Apparently, the state of bliss they've achieved is supposed to be better than sex."

I was about to reply when I remembered my former friend the prostitute. She had been more interesting when she was unmodified, but now... she was much happier. And she wouldn't argue that her implant was better than sex. She would just take it as a given. I swallowed back my retort and brooded.

Both Sileon and the avatar stared at me, but neither of them said anything. Apparently both could tell that I was thinking deep thoughts.

Apparently both considered it rare enough that they had to respect it.

CHAPTER 21

An hour later, as I was beginning to feel that I'd have to pee on the floor if facilities weren't provided soon, our dour host appeared. Still armed—and still accompanied by armed backup—he studied us for a moment. Then he grunted. "It seems your worth was high. Your release has been negotiated. You will not be killed, and you will not be slaved to the data chain." He grimaced as he said this last bit, and I thought he must have felt it a personal affront. "Come with me."

"I want my suit back," Sileon said.

"That is impossible," the man replied. "It's been..." he paused, then shrugged. "It's been studied down to a molecular level, as we found the design to be novel. I'm afraid that's a destructive process, and there is little left but some nanite dust to return to you. We've brought you some robes."

Sileon dressed quickly, and I admired her composure. If I'd been paraded around stark naked, I'd probably have spent most of my time covering myself with one hand, slouched over from embarrassment. Sileon, on the other hand, stood straight, as if daring anyone to comment on her nudity. And it seemed to work. The ugly guy and his acolytes—though I couldn't see their eyes—appeared to be looking anywhere but directly at her.

The grey corridor where we'd been imprisoned opened into a wider room full of enormous glass bulbs, some ten paces across and full of thick gas. I watched, mesmerized as colors swirled within: pinks gave way to browns, which gave way to oranges. Inside, shadowy shapes floated as if disconnected from the rest of the universe. I suspected there was some inertial compensation happening in there, keeping the spin gravity from affecting the interior.

The row of glass containers went on and on. I lost count at thirty-six, and there were more rows we couldn't see.

I tried to track the shapes as we passed, but the gas within was too thick to catch more than a glimpse. I wondered whether the material inside might not be some kind of intermediate state of matter between a gas and a liquid. Impossible, of course, but the contents wreaked havoc with my sanity. The floating forms tantalized the eye, dark suggestions in an unusual medium.

I approached the final row of bulbs with some relief, when one of the forms suddenly appeared, pressed right against the glass of her container. It was a woman, pale as a pure chalk, her face slack and expressionless, save for a slight up-curving of the lips. She was bald as a ball bearing, and if our host had been hit with the ugly stick, this woman had been clobbered by an entire ugly forest. That unnatural pallor, as if the skin had been leached of whichever color it might have initially had, and the position of the bones in her head brought to mind the monsters of nightmare.

The color and the unfortunate planes of her face would normally have made me think she'd died—probably in some painful industrial accident—except her expression told me that she was just resting, having a pleasant dream.

Then her body twitched and she was gone.

"A high priestess?" I asked the man leading us.

He grunted at me, and I felt lucky we'd been ransomed. This guy really, really wanted to charge us full price for violating the sanctity of their weird little holy place.

We climbed a couple of flights of metal-mesh staircases, crossed a creepy, dark room in which dozens of hooded acolytes sat absolutely motionless at workstations, wired into virtual reality rigs, before we reached a final airlock at the end of a corridor.

"Here's your ride," ugly said.

A small shuttle awaited on the other side of the airlock, and we filed into the passenger compartment—another stark place that reminded me a bit of the cell we'd just exited: grey and featureless, with benches along the side walls.

As the shuttle lock began to close behind us, the ugly guy actually smiled. "Oh. I probably should have mentioned this," he said. "Like I said earlier, your release has been negotiated." His smile—even uglier than his usual scowl—grew wider. "The only problem is that, apparently, your side wasn't the highest bidder."

You have to give that gnome credit. He timed it perfectly, and his words ended just as the steel door slid shut. I hit the button to reopen, but it did nothing.

"Dammit," I said, as the shuttle pulled away. I grabbed onto a chair, expecting massive doses of acceleration.

But the shuttle simply lifted off like any commercial vehicle in Cassius Station space, at a speed that wouldn't call attention to itself and, I assumed, moved into its assigned flight path.

I hit the wall with my fist and turned to Emmi, the avatar. "Can you get in touch with The Earthling?" I asked.

She shook her head. "Nothing. This thing is shielded tight."

"I guess we'll just have to see who has us," she said.

I grimaced inwardly at what she didn't say, which was: *some rescue this turned out to be.*

CHAPTER 22

The shuttle must have taken the long way to get wherever it was taking us. The long slow way.

I spent the entire trip alternately cursing our luck—out loud and explicitly—and trying to break down the bulkhead between the passenger and pilot compartments.

All I had to show for it was a sore shoulder.

My companions, on the other hand, sat as placidly as if they were passengers on a daily commute. The Earthling's avatar followed my movements with the faintest hint of an amused smile while Sileon appeared to be lost in her own thoughts.

I wasn't surprised. These two not only didn't fall into the stereotype that women were supposed to be more emotional than men... they didn't even give off human vibes.

Of course, the avatar technically wasn't human except in the purely biological sense that her body was flesh and blood. And Sileon... she spent considerably more time among computers than she did among humans. Maybe it was rubbing off.

A soft clunk sounded through the hull and the shuttle came to a gentle halt. Everything about the trip, except for my crashing around and swearing, had been gentle. Clearly no one wanted to call attention to themselves. No one would interfere with what, to outsiders, would look like just another shuttle going about its business.

The door hissed open, and I tensed. I half-expected to feel the cold fingers of vacuum tearing at my lungs.

Instead, warm air entered the shuttle, and the door opened into a flexible airlock corridor with warm light at the end. We walked through.

I was ready to fight anyone who appeared at the other end, but one look at the welcoming committee told me I'd be better off avoiding conflict.

Three men and two women surveyed us grimly. As far as I could tell, they were unarmed, and I could see they were the worse for wear, with torn clothes and bandaged skin.

But I recognized one of the women from the night before. She'd been inside the office when we launched our ill-advised raid, and she'd been the one who'd killed Sean with her bare hands. Her eyes weren't glowing right now, but I would recognize the face anywhere.

And if I'd thought the Avatar and Sileon were unexpressive, they had nothing on this bunch. A colder school of fish you never did see.

"I assume you're not happy to see us either," I said.

"Shut up," one of the men replied without even glancing in my direction. "We want to talk to the one they call Sileon."

"I'm Sileon," the avatar replied.

Ice crawled up my spine. Sileon and the avatar were of a similar type, true, but if these guys had any way of cross-referencing images—and they were cyborgs, so they might—we'd gotten into even deeper trouble than before.

The guy's glare could have meant anything. He held her gaze for a moment, then said: "We've been informed that you have something that belongs to us. Several paintings."

The avatar looked back at him, apparently unfazed. Hell, I hoped she hadn't decided that she preferred to die at these guys' hands instead of going back to The Earthling, and was about to commit suicide and take us with her. That wouldn't make me happy at all. "I hope you can catch your informant and skin him alive, because he lied to you," she said.

"We have no reason to doubt her word," the woman I'd recognized replied. "She's been a valued associate for years."

"Which means she's the person you should put on top of your suspect list, because she's probably halfway to the Wolf colony with your paintings by now."

The cyborg who'd spoken first, a muscular black-haired guy with a tattoo on his cheekbone, smiled grimly. "We obviously believe her more than we believe you."

I stepped forward. "We can prove we don't have them," I said.

"I know you don't have them, Leonid. You're just a pawn in this game. I'm talking to Sileon."

"You can search her ship."

That caught him off guard. "We already tried that. It didn't go real well."

"We'll let you search this time." I caught Sileon's eye. The real Sileon this time, not the avatar. I expected anger, but all she did was raise one eyebrow. She was curious to see what I was going to try.

"You would allow that?" the guy asked the avatar.

"Of course, I have nothing to hide," she replied.

"No electronic trickery?"

"I'm sure you would detect it if I tried anything," the avatar replied calmly.

A slight pause ensued, tiny but noticeable. The cyborgs were conferring among themselves. "Very well. But if you try anything, all three of you will be killed instantly. You won't be able to incapacitate us in any meaningful way."

They herded us back into the shuttle, closed the door behind us and disappeared.

The shuttle took off and made its slow careful way into traffic.

Now both women raised their eyebrows at me.

CHAPTER 23

The shuttle airlock opened into the corridor in front of Sileon's ship. I would have recognized it pretty much anywhere because it was unlikely another spot on Cassius Station would have an abandoned tank sitting in the middle of a passageway that looked like a small-scale war had been fought there.

Our cyborg friends were already waiting for us.

"Remember," muscles said. "No funny stuff."

"We wouldn't dream of it," I replied. I wanted to make sure he focused on me, because I was very much aware that, in this company, I was the least dangerous member of my team. "By the way," I said. "Do you work out or is all that bulk synthetic? I mean… if you're basically a servo machine anyway, what's the use of spending all that time in the gym?"

He sneered at me, and I thought I caught the slightest glimmer of the green glow in his eyes. Did that mean I was rattling him? Or did it mean he was about to go fully homicidal on me? I didn't know, but as long as he focused on me, I was doing my bit. Hopefully, that would give Sileon a chance to pull a rabbit out of her ass. Or whatever.

They let us lead them to the door, crowding us close enough that if anything opened fire, we'd be toast as well. When the door opened, the woman from the office went ahead, followed by the three of us, and then the rest of the cyborgs.

"Stay away from all control surfaces," the big one ordered.

"Sure, man," I replied, holding my hands up. "Just relax. We really don't have anything to do with this."

He glared at me. He was good at that, and I doubted he had any other expression to show off. "I already know you didn't do it. You tried, but you went to the wrong place, so you're probably too stupid to matter. Sileon here," he nodded at the avatar, "absolutely isn't too stupid to matter, so please make sure she heeds my warning."

The avatar nodded. "Welcome to my ship," she said. "How do you want to conduct the search? Do you really think you could find something I didn't want you to find without tearing this whole ship apart?"

The muscular guy smiled at her. "Of course we can. Would you store anything valuable without having a quick way to locate it if it goes missing? Just walk us along the ship lengthwise, and we'll tell you when to stop."

The avatar shrugged and began to walk down the main corridor. The *Basilisk* was a long ship, and the artificial gravity allowed it to be laid out horizontally instead of putting the floors along the surfaces that would be affected by acceleration. One of the hitherto silent cyborgs pulled some kind of sensor out of a pack and studied the readouts. He shook his head.

We proceeded down the corridor, repeating the scene several times until we arrived at an engineering node which I hadn't visited, right by the engines at the rear of the ship.

"Well," the avatar said, "if your little gizmo is working, you can tell that I don't have it here."

"You might have stashed it somewhere else," the cyborg said.

"I've been on this ship since I got back from the outer system. If you've done your homework, you know that already."

That earned her another dirty look. It was official: that was the only expression he had. "We'll just have to torture the truth out of you."

"You'll do no such thing," I replied, stepping forward. "We did our part and let you search the ship. It's not here."

"Yeah," the avatar added, standing beside me. We both knew it was stupid to face cyborgs who could rip us to pieces with their bare hands, but I suspected that unless Sileon did something right now, we were toast anyway. We needed to distract them. "You cross us, no one will ever want to deal with you again."

Miracle of miracles, muscles managed a different expression. He pulled off a sneering smile!

"Who will know?" he said with a rumbling chuckle. "The only thing left of you is going to be little pieces of ground meat. Hell, maybe we'll toss you in the recyclers so the station doesn't miss out on all the nutrients you're carrying on your bodies. See, we're concerned citizens."

"Who can't move," Sileon said.

The big guy's head jerked, but it only moved a fraction of a centimeter. His features were stuck in the sneer, but his eyes were wide with surprise.

"Grab them fast," Sileon ordered. "Pile them in the airlock. I won't be able to hold them long."

"Why did you make us wait?" I said as I put my arms under muscles' armpits and dragged him in the indicated direction. It was extremely weird to feel him twitching as we advanced. When I dropped him in the airlock, I breathed easier, especially because he was a hell of a lot heavier than even a big guy should have been.

"Because I wanted to be sure the stupid things actually weren't on my ship. I don't mind stealing stuff, and I have absolutely nothing against smuggling valuable shit. But I like to know about it."

We wrestled the rest of the goons into the airlock. It didn't look strong enough to hold them for too long once they got control of their bodies back. I'd seen firsthand how strong these guys were. We'd need to find a stronger room to hold them in.

Before I could make this point to Sileon, however, she calmly cycled the airlock and sent the cyborgs tumbling into the void.

"That won't kill them," I informed her. I didn't bother to tell her that they'd be mad when they got back.

"I know," Sileon replied grimly. "But this will."

She spoke aloud. "*Basilisk*, override command Bee-Fourteen."

"Acknowledged," a dulcet voice I hadn't heard before said. "Safety locks disengaged."

One wall became a screen showing five small specks floating on a dark field. I realized we were seeing the cyborgs floating away from the ship.

"Open fire. Antiship guns. Target the garbage we just released from the airlock."

There was no hesitation. The *Basilisk* rocked, and I watched one of the specks dissolve into spray. I looked away from the screen; the cyborgs might have been murderous bastards but that wasn't a good way to go.

Sileon and the avatar, on the other hand, had no such qualms. They watched the screen avidly, apparently enjoying what they saw. Five thumps… and I assumed five impacts, and five people torn to atoms by weaponry designed to puncture battleships.

"Don't look at me like that," Sileon said. "They were getting ready to torture us to death. And they weren't going to stop coming after us until either they were dead or we were."

"Yeah," I said. "I guess you're right. But that's not all of them. There were at least ten more when we hit that office. And I assume they have other people in other locations."

"They'd better not come here. I didn't really kill those people because I was worried about them torturing me. I killed them because this is the second time they forced their way onto my ship."

There was no need to ask her if she was joking. Her expression made it perfectly clear she wasn't.

CHAPTER 24

We reclined in the lounge, and Sileon ordered up drinks. If she had any regrets about blowing five people to pieces, she didn't show it. In fact, she seemed much more animated and upbeat than she had since we'd found her.

I gave Sileon a questioning look, and she smiled sadly. "I'm a lot older than I look, Deck," she said. "And I've done things you wouldn't believe even if I told you."

"I'm starting to think nothing is impossible where you're concerned."

She laughed, a tinkling, little girl's laugh completely at odds with the woman I knew her to be. "You'd think these things were impossible no matter who was involved. But like I said, I'm older than I look, and it takes a lot to get me excited." Then she leered at me. "Well, not in that sense, but you know what I mean."

"You're enjoying yourself," I accused her.

"I like a challenge."

"And we haven't been challenged thus far?"

She paused and considered it. "Not really. I mean I had to solve the problem of getting you out of Cassius Station—and I'm still annoyed because you came back after everything I did, by the way—but we were never in real danger once you got onto the *Basilisk*. Then we ran the gamut and ended up captured. Not my first time, and I knew that, eventually, they would need me to open the door to this ship." She turned to Emmi, the avatar. "It was quite resourceful to pose as me, by the way. I could probably have gotten the *Basilisk* to turn on our most powerful interdictors even if they were paying attention to me—even if they had me tied up or sedated—but your little ruse made it child's play to program things to happen exactly the way I wanted."

I still had no clue how she gave the order, timed to exactly when she wanted it, but Emmi simply nodded in acknowledgement.

"Those guys were impervious to an EMP at point-blank range. How the hell did you manage to immobilize them?" I said.

"I thought you'd have guessed by now. I'm sure she has." She nodded to the avatar and sighed. "Not all of my computer tech is strictly legal. I have some pet programs that would set off every alarm on Copernicus."

"AI's?"

"Close enough that it makes little difference. And close enough that having them enslaved would raise a lot of ethical questions if anyone knew about them." Sileon continued. "But back to our friends. Now that they came aboard, now that their compatriots will know, unequivocally, that I was responsible for blasting them… it just feels more real. I suppose I wasn't too excited before because everything seemed at one level of remove. Now it's personal." She paused to grin at me. "And that makes it a hell of a lot more fun."

I sure know how to pick them, don't I?

Before I could say anything I might have regretted later, the avatar spoke up. "So what now?"

"That depends on you," Sileon said. "In this ship, you're safe from observation. You're still cut off from The Earthling's surveillance. In fact, she hasn't been able to track you since we were captured by the Scions. This ship is equipped to disable the stuff in your head that connects you to the net. I can't say how long you'd last but you could exit through the airlock and steal the cyborgs' shuttle. At least you'd have a head start."

The avatar's—no, Emmi's—eyes turned bright as they filled with tears and reflected light back at us. She was unable to speak for several moments. She tried, but couldn't go on. She tried again. Sileon pretended to do something on a control panel, I pretended to drink.

Finally, Emmi gathered her thoughts. She shook her head. "I can't do that," she said, finally. "The Earthling would eventually track me here. Hell, she's already started. If this was the last place she tracked me, she would assume I ran for it with your help or that you killed me off. Even if I could escape with the shuttle and get out of the system before she managed to catch up, you would have to leave Cassius Station."

Sileon shrugged. "I've left places before."

"I can't have that on my conscience. Besides, we made a deal with the Earthling. She won't double cross you. So you shouldn't double cross her."

"All right. I'm reconnecting you in: three, two, one."

Emmi stood straighter, and her eyes lost their focus as the entity that drove her came online again. I didn't know whether the mere fact of being connected to the AI made her more assertive because of something the implants did to her head, or whether there was some subconscious driver at work. Hell, I know I would have been much more confident if I'd had the biggest goon in the system covering my back.

"Okay," Emmi said. "I've reported our progress, including the death of five of the enemy cyborgs. The Earthling says to tell you that there's another AI in the system, and that she's under attack from it." She smiled. "Of course, we always knew this would happen eventually, and we've set up quite a few failsafes to hinder any progress it might make. The timing doesn't seem to be a coincidence, does it? Unfortunately, some resources might be less available than usual. So what now?"

"We've only really got one choice," Sileon replied. "We need to go on the offensive."

"That didn't work out so well either of the times we tried it before. Not when we went into their office building, and not when we came over here to rescue you," I said.

"Actually, it worked better than we probably thought at the time," the avatar replied. By her tone, I could tell she wasn't speaking as Emmi anymore. For all intents and purposes, she was The Earthling. "When you and the Oreillys went into that office, you set off a chain of events that somehow led to a split among the people who have the pictures. The cyborgs—or at least the ones who've been attacking us—lost the treasure, and they're mad as hell about it. And the rescue attempt ended up with Sileon alive and in control of the *Basilisk* while five of the cyborgs are dead." The avatar paused with her head cocked. "I agree with Sileon's assessment. It's the right time to strike."

A screen appeared, and on it, Jill and Kane appeared relieved to see them. I waved at Jill, just to get on Kane's nerves, but he didn't seem to notice.

"All right. We hit them," I said. "But who do we hit?"

Emmi smiled. "That's where you come in. We've got data, and I've got muscle. But we need your street sense to tell us where to go."

"I don't know if you've noticed, but I haven't been on the street in what seems like forever. The closest I got since this whole things started is in Dead Space. Hell... I don't even know if I can walk these corridors without every bad guy on the station coming for me."

The avatar and Sileon exchanged a look and chuckled.

"What?" I said.

"No one will see you unless we want them to," the avatar replied. "Between us, we can make every camera on this station see what we want it to see. The bigger question is whether you think you can gather any leads worth following up."

Now I laughed at them. "Of course I can. The street knows everything. If money and power could get all the information one ever wanted, then half my clients would never need to hire me, and the other half couldn't afford me."

"That doesn't make any sense, Deck," Sileon said. "The half that couldn't afford you shouldn't be affected by what the other half does."

"Yeah," I replied. "Half the time, I end up having to give poverty discounts." I shrugged. "But what can you do? Those are usually the people that really, really need help."

The avatar and Sileon exchanged a look. "You actually see yourself as some kind of white knight, don't you? Saving helpless dragons from ravening maidens, that sort of thing?" The Earthling asked.

"If the maidens are anything like you two, yeah. Poor dragons wouldn't stand a chance. Sometimes the little people need an equalizer. Maybe not against someone like The Earthling—I know when I'm completely out of my league—but you'd be surprised at how many small-time thugs make their living victimizing people who have almost nothing worth taking. Every little bit helps those folks."

The avatar rolled her eyes and said: "All right. Sermon's over. Do you have any idea where to find the information we need?"

I shook my head. "Not a clue. But I have an excellent idea where to start. In fact, I should get going as soon as possible."

"Why is that?" Sileon asked.

"Because I suddenly realized I really, really need a taco."

I turned to go—I knew the way out of the forward airlock, especially as it didn't seem Sileon had bothered with putting the maze back in. A hand on my shoulder stopped me.

I turned to find Sileon looking up at me.

"I still can't believe you charged in like a madman to rescue me," she said.

"You didn't seem to need all that much rescuing."

"It doesn't matter. What matters is that you did it." She pulled me down and kissed me in a way that left absolutely no doubt there was more where that came from, and that, maybe, our earlier lovemaking was just practice for when she decided to open up. If that were the case, I didn't think I would survive.

I pulled away and walked unsteadily to the door.

Chapter 25

"I see you managed to lose the tail," Dongee said as he leaned over to hand me a hyper-sugar carbonate. "Although I've heard you went about it the hard way. Also, the new bones in your face make you look like that hyena in the Tri-D show."

Laughing as if he was the greatest wit in the history of comedy, he shuffled off to serve the only other customer gracing his yellow concession stand. I gave the other person a look. It was just a kid I knew who stole copper from public wiring. He looked hungry, and I could see why: he'd grown too big to climb the more delicate rigs, and would soon need to look for a different job unless he wanted to end up splattered against the floor of the Old Corridor.

Even if he saw through my disguise, he wouldn't tell anyone he'd seen me. Not because of any sense of loyalty but because he was too low on the totem pole to know that ratting me out could get him paid.

Dongee returned. "Don't get offended about what I'm going to ask you," my old friend said, his grey whiskers dancing in concern. "And take into account I'm only asking because I know you're a total moron who isn't aware of what is happening around him most of the time."

"Yeah, I'm sure that makes it all right," I said, suppressing my smile. Dongee like to put on the act of a feebleminded old cart owner just so he could get those jabs in. With so much effort expended, I didn't want to burst his bubble.

"Well, you need to know the heat is on. Everyone and his kid brother is out looking for you."

I sighed. "Yeah, I know."

"Except you're supposed to be armed, dangerous and surrounded by killers, a big bad cyborg and high-end crime bosses. I know Greeno Grisi is looking for you, and if he heard of the situation, it must have gotten pushed pretty hard. Hell, he's nearly as clueless as you are."

I looked at the kid out of the corner of my eye, reassessing if maybe he might actually know something after all. He was low even compared to bottom-feeders like Greeno, but if it had gotten that far down, what was another step? But the kid seemed to be nursing his taco like it was the last time he was ever going to eat. Maybe it was. "Hmm. Doesn't seem like I should be worried. Anyone serious coming for me would know that I work alone."

He cocked his head. "You're full of shit. Now spill it. What do you want?"

I was tempted to ask him who had put the bounty hunters out after me, but I let it go. It might be better for him to think I wasn't worried about it and, besides, I knew how these things were done. The reward would be offered by a small-time crook, who'd have gotten the order from a guy higher up... and so forth, until you reached the actual crime boss who'd accepted the job. And then you had to wade through that guy's bodyguards to convince him to talk about who the client was... assuming there weren't even more middlemen involved.

It was way too much work, and it would probably start a war. If my way didn't work, I'd let the Earthling attempt a backtrack. She would probably enjoy watching the bodies hit the floor.

"I'm looking for two things. First off, I want to know where I can find the woman who shot at me the other day."

"If you're that desperate for a date," Dongee leered, "I can probably set you up with someone."

"Come on..."

"All right. It's all anyone talked about for days. Even the cops wanted to know, and you know how hard it is for the cops to get interested in anything but free tacos."

"You give them free tacos?"

"Not by choice, but I find it helps keep my business running smoothly. Anyway, no one could find the woman."

"But you know where she is," I said. His smug expression left no other conclusion.

"Not exactly. But I know who she was sleeping with."

"Huh? Really? Who?"

"The name Dana Pasa ring a bell?"

It did. Dana ran a high-end escort service up in the Vapor Zone. She was reputed to be on her fourth or fifth vat-grown body because she wore them out working: parties, alcohol, drugs and the parties that came after the parties. It wasn't that she needed to pick up the slack for her girls, but more that she was in the business because she enjoyed it. To get her attention, the woman who'd shot me must have been something special.

"It does."

Dongee smirked at me. He knew that getting anywhere near Dana was going to require some serious manpower. "What else did you want to know?"

"Cyborgs. I'm looking for two groups that look like they're working together."

"Cyborgs don't buy tacos, Deck."

"But people who work with them do. What do you know?"

He danced away to refill the kid's drink and returned a minute later.

"You know he's not going to pay you," I said nodding in the kid's direction. "As soon as he finishes that taco, he'll run for the nearest side corridor."

"No he won't. I gave it to him for free. I explained that you're a tourist, and I'm going to charge you double. He hasn't recognized you with the new clothes and the new face, so he won't know better. That way no one loses out."

"Except the mark."

"You'll get your money's worth," Dongee said. "I know of a lot of groups of cyborgs, but most of them are either too legit to make a difference or too poor to be the ones you want. I think your best bet is to check the docks."

I groaned. "There are a million people working on the docks, and half of them are augmented."

"Yeah. But ask around. I'm pretty sure you know a good place to get info. And I'm also pretty sure you'll be wasting your time asking anywhere else."

It sounded like he knew more, but it also sounded like he couldn't say anything more for some reason. Probably because if he told me, I'd be able to figure out where the information came from and someone could torture the name out of me. Dongee was inflexible in that regard: he would keep his buddies safe if he could. He'd done it more than once where I was concerned.

I didn't press him further. "Thanks, man. I really appreciate it."

"And I can't believe the entire underworld hasn't landed on our heads while you were sitting here talking to me. This is the Old Corridor. There are fifty-seven cameras trained on this stand. I chose the spot especially. Anyone starting trouble here knows that they'll be identified in seconds. And yet you sit here without a care in the world." He gave me a hard look. "I have a feeling you're in way over your head on this one."

"Because I'm not worried about the cameras?"

"Yeah. You're in bed with the wrong people."

I nodded. "You're probably right. But there was nothing I could do to avoid it. This isn't my fault."

"That's what they all say. It's always their fault, too."

"Well, if it's my fault, I still don't know how it happened."

"That's honest at least. You were always one of the less stupid people. I hope that brain of yours is fast enough to get you out of this."

"Yeah. I hope so to." I nodded towards the kid. "What about him?"

Dongee sighed. "He reminds me of you at the same age. He's not a complete loss, but he doesn't know what to do with his life."

"Are you going to get him clients like you did for me?"

Dongee laughed. "He wouldn't last two minutes. There's a reason some criminals stay as far away from human contact as possible. They aren't cut out for violence. Can you believe he wants to put up a food cart? Like that's some kind of glamorous life?"

"When your other option is to fall from a wire for a couple of credits, I think it can give you a real good appreciation for a calm, stable life."

"That's the sense I get, too," Dongee said. "I think I might front him a little something. Maybe give him a franchise and send him to the Dragon Strip to take a little of the hacker business. Those guys always have money."

"You're going to invest in him?" I asked, my mouth dropping. "You never did that for me!"

"Two things," Dongee replied. "First, I haven't decided yet. And second, he's smarter than you are."

Then, with a laugh, he charged me for two tacos and two drinks before sending me on my way.

Chapter 26

I decided not to brave the looks that the avatar and Sileon would give me when I told them I'd decided to visit Dana Pasa's place before heading for the docks. No matter how much I protested that the brothel was closer to my current position and easier to reach than the docks, they'd just raise their eyebrows at me and grin knowingly.

So I didn't waste time heading towards the rendezvous point we'd agreed on. They could watch me over the cameras, and they had probably eavesdropped on every word I'd spoken with Dongee, so they knew where I was headed. And they could exchange their knowing smirks without the benefit of my presence.

I moved out of the Old Corridor and, after passing through several slide doors, into smaller halls, mostly residential. The crowds thinned and the hard-wearing rubberized plastic floor of the high-traffic areas gave way first to simulated flagstones and then to actual carpeting. I didn't think it would last very long under people's feet, but it looked perfect, as if it had been laid the day before. I wondered who paid for its upkeep.

Another sign that I was moving up in the world, at least geographically, was some of the residences had guards at the door. It was probably more a question of status than anything else—there were probably more cameras and defensive systems inside these houses than anywhere else in the station—because the people living in these places probably felt that a featureless corridor wall couldn't communicate the fact that the people living on the other side were richer than your wildest dreams.

The last corridor opened into a little plaza with an actual fountain in the middle and plants growing around it. The water was probably recirculated, and the plants looked a bit anemic compared to the kind of vegetation you got in Tri-D experiences, but the expense for even something like that was unimaginable. The floor was covered in some kind of cobblestone which I hoped was synthetic because I didn't want to think of how much it would have cost to lug stone out from a planet or from one of the asteroids to the station. Four storefronts opened onto the plaza: a hair salon, a tiny grocery store stocking products I'd never seen before, a real estate office with an actual bored-looking human sitting inside, and a place without a sign but sporting a big guy in an expensive silver jumpsuit leaning against the door.

That was the place I wanted, although I suspected all the neighbors contributed to the bouncer's salary. He would probably be paid to break the head of anyone who damaged a plant as much as he would to break the head of one of Dana Pasa's clients who got frisky.

He looked me up and down as I approached, much the way passers-by would look at the mess from a broken sewage pipe leaking onto a corridor. After a moment's hesitation, he moved aside with a grunted: "No trouble now," which hurt my feelings more than if he'd refused to let me in. I was wearing good clothes from Sileon's stores, and he'd still ID'd me as someone barely able to foot whatever bill one would take home from a place like this. I'd never bothered to try to find out: it was obviously more than I could afford.

It was almost disappointing to get an easy pass. I'd stocked up on articles of mayhem before leaving the *Basilisk* and this guy seemed to be just begging for me to try one out on him.

I walked in, expecting to find a refined version of the port-zone cathouses: a dimly-lit bar room with some kind of floor show. This place specifically catered to heterosexual males, so I expected a naked woman or two onstage, or maybe scantily clad employees serving drinks. There would be music.

None of that was in evidence except the presence of a bar. My footsteps echoed in a soft, blue-lit, white room. The only employee in evidence was the man behind the bar, and he was formally dressed and fully clothed.

Unlike the Bruno at the door, this guy didn't make me feel like I was something recovered from a recycling pile. He smiled at me from behind the bar and said: "Hi, I haven't seen you here before."

"Good eye," I replied. "It's my first time."

"Can I get you a drink, maybe tell you about our services?"

I gave him a rueful grin. "I wish. I've heard extremely good things about this place. I'm actually here on business. I need to see Miss Pasa."

You have to give him credit. His smile didn't falter and, if I hadn't been watching for it, I would have missed his hand dart quickly to the alarm button under the bar. He was smooth, and he wasn't some folksy guy just making a few credits by working in a cathouse. He was part of the security.

Which meant I'd have to keep him in mind when whatever heavies he'd summoned made their appearance. If it came to a fight, I'd need to take him down as well.

But so far, no one had done anything aggressive to me, so I had to remain civil. No use starting a war with people I'd probably run into again sooner or later unless it was absolutely necessary.

"Before I announce you, do you represent anyone she might need to talk to?"

"My name is Deck Leonid. I'm usually a freelancer, but on this particular occasion I'm working with The Earthling."

My ego took a hit. He showed absolutely no sign of recognizing my own name—though I take a certain pride in thinking that people on the edges of the law at every level of sophistication know me, if only by reputation—but even his well-trained impassivity cracked a little when I mentioned The Earthling. His eyes widened a bit.

"And your business…"

"Is between Miss Pasa and myself."

He nodded, as if that was exactly what he expected, and then made a big show of moving to a comm tablet behind the bar and typing in a message.

I sat on a white couch from which I could watch both of the obvious entrances to the room. My bets were on the muscle from outside entering to toss me out on my ear… but gently enough to let The Earthling know that, though I wasn't found an acceptable emissary, they didn't want to insult her and would be open to a better approach.

To my surprise, however, the door to the inner workings was the one that opened. It disgorged a woman about four feet tall and approximately as wide with scraggly hair and unkempt clothes.

About a thousand cracks came into my head, immediately and unbidden. All of them were of the kind that would have hurt this woman's feelings and made the avatar, Sileon and even Jill roll their eyes at me in despair.

Incredibly, she beat me to all of them. "No, I'm not one of the working girls," the woman said. "Admit it, that's what you were thinking. All of you pieces of hired muscle think the same way, and all of you make it incredibly evident that, though you wear clothes and walk upright, you're all just monkeys with delusions of grandeur."

I grunted. "You seem to know men better than men know men."

"In this business, you learn, even if you don't want to."

Keen intelligence looked out at me from behind those eyes and, combined with the fact she'd already read my mind once, it made me feel a little bit resentful. Between Sileon, the avatar, The Earthling, Jill, and even Dongee I was already beginning to feel that everyone around me was smarter than I was. I didn't need to get another dose of inferiority complex from the house manager of a knock shop.

"I need to talk to Dana," I said.

"She isn't available."

"Not available to me, or not available to The Earthling?"

Fear flashed over her features, which made me feel a little less overwhelmed. It was nice to have dangerous friends. "Not available."

"That isn't going to go down well."

She shrugged. "Then I'm afraid it won't go down well."

I crossed my arms. "That's not acceptable."

"You'll have to accept it."

She made a tiny gesture with her head. I was watching for it and, before the guy behind the bar could act on it, I closed my eyes and activated the flash function on my suit. I felt the cloth go warm for a second, and saw the world grow red and the sudden solar-level illumination came through my eyelids.

When darkness returned, I calmly opened my eyes and stood. The woman was blinking like someone out of their mind on stardust, but the guy behind the bar was groping around. That didn't look like it boded well for me, so I walked over to his position, leaned over the bar to locate the ever-present blunt instrument. In this case, it turned out to be a metal pipe filled with something dense. I gave it to him between the eyes with a little shoulder behind it.

The guy looked confused and a little unsteady, so I gave him another bop, just for luck.

This time, he went down in a boneless heap. I hoped I hadn't misjudged the force and hurt him too badly... but I didn't feel too badly about it when I saw that he'd been trying to reach a gun that fired low-speed flechettes which, unless I missed my guess, would explode upon contact. The pellets the explosion generated wouldn't damage a hull plate—hence their legality on the station—but they would tear up human skin quite nicely. I almost went over the bar to hit him again.

I resisted the urge and headed back to the woman on the couch. She was standing up, blinking: "Rool?" she said, "did you get him?"

"I'm afraid not," I replied. "But I may get you. Now, you were about to take me to see Dana."

"I can't."

"Look, we've been through this already. I asked, you said she wasn't here. I insisted, you told the goon to dart me." I resisted the urge to slap her; I'd seen what those flechettes did to people, and I was rattled to think that I might have been on the receiving end of one. "Now we get to the bit where you either give me what I want or things get rough."

Fear, real fear, flashed over her face. "You don't understand," she said. "I haven't seen or heard from her in four days."

"But you have a way to get hold of her?"

She shook her head. "No. She lives here. This place is her life. She watches it like a hawk. Hell, I've worked for her for ten years, and she still watches me like I'm going to raid the family credit cache. I've been holding the fort as well as I can, but the girls are starting to ask questions. And now, with Rool hurt… I don't know what I'm going to do."

"What you're going to do is tell me about Dana's girlfriend. And then you'll show me the whole premises, every room, every cupboard. If you don't mess with me, and if you convince me that you're telling the truth, I'll walk out of here and you'll have one less problem to worry about. Otherwise…"

I left that hanging, but she got the drift. Sometimes, looking like a thug—and a big one at that—worked in my favor. People who didn't know better believed me when I promised to bring a rain of mayhem unto their heads.

"That woman…" she said. "She came in one night with Dana after a party. It was one of those kinds of parties, and why they'd want to keep it going after a night like that, I wouldn't know. But they did. The woman kept her up all night, and kept coming back for more."

"And what was her name? Where did she come from? What was the party?"

"She called herself Carmel… but that's all I know. I would bet pretty much anything that it isn't her real name." She smirked. "Dana doesn't tell me about her parties. That way I can't use the information to blackmail her clients. Or her. That's the kind of woman she is."

I believed her, and the tour went as I expected it to. Whether the story was true or not, I left that place convinced Dana was not on the premises. A number of extremely beautiful women—some obviously enhanced—were on the premises, however, and when I searched their rooms, I came to understand how this place justified its legendary reputation. Everything, including the women, looked absolutely upper crust. Tasteful and obviously quite civilized, which would make it all the more exciting when the gloves—and the rest of the clothing—came off. I left wishing I was in the league to sample the wares.

The Bruno at the door didn't try to jump me. Either he hadn't gotten the message about my lack of decorum within, or the message had been accompanied by instructions to leave me alone. Either way, I was back on the mean corridors and ready for action.

CHAPTER 27

Fortunately, I didn't have to return to the Old Corridor to get to the docks, but I did retrace my steps in the sense that, with every step I took from the brothel, the corridors around me became scruffier. My shortcut took me through maintenance areas that ran the gamut from gleaming to grimy, but none of them had tasteful grey carpeting that looked like it had been put down just for me, or paint that looked as if it was renewed every day.

I reached the port and, as always, I stopped to catch a breath and reorient myself as the walls and roof disappeared into the distance, to be replaced by rows of small cargo haulers. The big freighters, of course, were serviced by the external docks, and lay on the outside of the Port Facility, in the vacuum of space.

Local lore had it that the interior of the dockland zone was the largest enclosed space ever built by human beings, and I had no trouble believing it. Using the lack of true gravity in their favor, the designers had created a hangar of colossal proportions, which twisted the mind as ships were oriented right-side-up, and upside-down, diagonally, and with their noses perpendicular to the way I was traveling. I looked straight up to see pedestrians walking overhead and someone zig-zagging between them with a bright orange loader. The path I was on corkscrewed onto a wider walkway ahead of me.

This dizzying effect was due to the fact that the dockland module was rich enough to spring for artificial gravity in the pedestrian zones. Instead of placing the ships where the pedestrians could reach them, the space was optimized to fit the maximum number of ships while people and vehicles that needed gravity to function were brought close via walkways twisting overhead like spaghetti.

When you combined the spatial uncertainty with the fact that heavy machinery was in constant operation, it made sense that the majority of dock workers were cyborgs. Getting caught between a loader and a metal wall tended to be more survivable when you had an exoskeleton. And losing an arm was a lot less traumatic if you could just weld it back into place. I imagined the dockland saved a fortune on safety regulations.

Unfortunately, that meant going up to the ships to ask about possible cyborg criminal gangs a good way to get killed, accidentally or less-than-accidentally.

So, not knowing one from the other, I entered the nearest of the bars, selected at random because the door was painted red.

Unlike the cathouse, this place was exactly what I expected. Dimly-lit, with the air full of vape smoke of various colors and smells and plenty of stalls in dark corners where one could get together and talk about how to try to steal cargo that was electronically tagged from here to Andromeda.

No one looked up at me as I walked in, which was a good sign for my mental health, but likely a bad one for the future of the investigation. No self-respecting gang would hide out in a bar where no one raised an eyebrow if a hulking stranger wandered in unannounced.

Still, you had to go through the motions, so I approached the bar and ordered a beer. I almost ordered a stimcaff, but realized that would tell the guy two things: that I wasn't a dockside regular—which he already likely knew—and that I was exhausted to the point of near collapse—which I definitely didn't want him to know.

He served it without comment, so I decided to stir the pot. "I'm looking for someone," I said.

"Yeah, I figured," the guy replied. "You look the type."

He said it without the kind of resentment or suspicion that kind of comment usually brought with it.

"Does the name Hyde mean anything to you?"

"No. Should it?"

"I'm looking for a gang of cyborgs."

He laughed. "Well, you've come to the right part of town."

"These guys run a big operation, though. Not just dockside scammers. They have offices by the Old Corridor."

He shrugged. "I wish I could help you, but this place hasn't been much frequented by anything like what you've described since Krank's gang got busted. And that was before my time. You should try one of the bars in the Inner Loop." He hesitated. "But be careful. That's not a place where you want to screw up."

"Any places in particular I should start with?"

"The two everyone seems to talk about are the Supply Side and the Broken Hart. And I mean it about being careful."

"Careful is my middle name," I replied.

Actually, my middle name was 'well-armed with illegal stuff from Sileon's stash that even The Earthling had been impressed by when Sileon began pulling it out of lockers', but that didn't roll off the tongue quite as well.

I just hoped it worked better than the stuff Jill's troops had hit the Hydes with.

The Inner Loop was kind of a secondary bar and supplies area for the port, on the far side of the enormous hangar. It was less crowded and less commercial than the entry corridor. And it was a lot less customer-friendly. Steel plates lined the walls and machinery occupied everything but an elevated walkway. Even the gravity seemed a little wonky at times; I was sure it pulled in weird directions more than once.

The Broken Hart was my first stop just because it was the first one I ran into on the way through. I walked in and a couple of heads looked up from their drinks.

Through the gloom and smoke, I could tell that almost every table in the place was occupied, and that the occupants were mostly quite obviously modified.

But there was no sudden silence, no drop in the sound level, no sign that I was recognized and unwelcome.

So I made my way to the bar, largely ignored, and did my routine again. This time, at least, the bartender played his part by scowling and muttering at me, but I could tell his heart wasn't in it. The Hydes weren't on his beat. I drank my beer and headed for the door.

It felt as though, in a complete reversal of accepted procedure, more people watched me as I left peacefully after having a beer than when I walked in. I counted at least five guys and two heavily-modified women tracking me as I walked towards the door. They shouldn't have been doing that. I'd caused no trouble and the barman, as far as I could tell, was telling the truth when he said the Hydes were nowhere nearby. The hairs on the back of my neck stood up and I put my hand in the pocket of my coat to grasp the grip of a wonderfully high-powered beam weapon that Sileon had selected for me.

I was glad I'd worn a coat. I generally wore it whenever I was going to be out and about in the station because you never knew what the temperature was going to be like in any given spot. Heat was expensive, and some parts of Cassius Station couldn't afford expensive. Sileon and the avatar had objected to it because it stood out in the throngs of the Old Corridor, which was the first place I'd been headed.

But I'd insisted, and it had saved me time. I couldn't have wandered around the docks without it.

Plus, it helped me hide my arsenal.

After leaving the Broken Hart, I waited on the walkway for a few moments, hand on the beamer, just to see who might follow me out. After about five minutes, I sighed and kept walking, turning occasionally to survey the empty space behind me. It was creepy. I was sure there should have been someone after me. My exit had that kind of vibe to it.

All I could do, however, was to keep walking. The Supply Side was located at the very end of the corridor. The last two bays, huge spaces to my left, were dark and empty of ships. By the look of it, their equipment had been cannibalized to keep other bays running. Even the walkway creaked more and looked rustier.

The entrance to the bar was guarded by a large cyborg much more metal than man. He didn't even bother to scan me or even give me a second glance. He just moved aside to let me in. As I brushed through the evil-smelling curtain that hung in place of a door, I wondered what kind of place might consider a guy my size in a big coat a non-threatening presence.

The light inside was red and the smoke so dense it blurred distant shapes. Despite the location and the empty walkway outside, the place was packed, and I couldn't spot a single unmodified human.

Everyone looked at the door when I walked in, and the noise level didn't just drop, it disappeared altogether.

Now that was more like it.

As I walked towards the bar—which some joker had buried in the far end of the main room—every eye followed me. A fair number of them telescoped or whirred through tracks as they did so. Somehow, the modified eyes managed to convey the same amount of hostility as the unmodified ones.

Still, as far as I could see, none of the eyes glowed green or red. The cyborgs in here didn't give me the high-end vibe of the Hydes we'd encountered so far. These were definitely modified humans, but none of them appeared to be the kind of slick, well-integrated jobs the opposition had fielded thus far. Seams were visible where the metal had been grafted to the flesh but, more than that, the clothes were coarse and dirty, covered in the grime of a day's work—or possibly a week's or a month's, depending on the cleanliness of each individual. The people in here might have been criminals, but they weren't the same class of criminal.

If they worked with the Hydes, this was strictly the group that did the heavy lifting, the people who got their hands dirty. The brain trust would be elsewhere.

Still, the worker bees could give me an idea of where the big boys might be found.

The barman looked like a classic Tri-D villain. Half of his face had been replaced with metal, and the eye on the human side was a lens that reflected my face back at me. My reflection looked scared.

As soon as I reached the bar, the path I'd traversed through the crowd closed up behind me. I didn't dare look back to confirm, but my sense was that I wouldn't be able to cut back through the cyborgs without doing serious damage to a lot of them.

I put my hand in my other pocket; the beam weapon wasn't going to cut it if things got rough. This pocket held an EMP generator. I preferred not to have to use it, since a lot of these guys and gals weren't going to make it if they suddenly found themselves with mechanical parts that were little more than dead weight.

There were supposed to be regulations about cyborgs functioning fully on their organic components alone, but one look around this room made it extremely clear that no one was paying much attention to those rules.

I didn't want this many dead people on my conscience. Worse, I was almost sure that one or two of them must have been innocent.

Well, innocent of anything having to do with me, anyway.

So I hoped the conversation with the metal-faced guy went really, really well.

"You are either the bravest person on this station or the dumbest," the barman said. His voice was high-pitched, like his windpipe was getting squeezed by all that metal. "I'm curious as to which one it is. Everyone's been watching you coming on the feeds… and you still walked in here."

"I'm neither," I replied. "I was supposed to have cover on the surveillance side, at least long enough to get me in without being recognized." I supposed something must have gone wrong. Maybe the dockside cameras were on a different circuit, or had their own security, or…

This was getting me nowhere.

"Look," I said to the barman, trying to pump every ounce of earnestness I could into my voice and demeanor. "I need you to believe me. I'm perfectly capable of defending myself against everyone in this place. I'm not brave or some kind of superman, just very well-equipped. All I need to know is where the Hydes hang out. Tell me, or show me someone who knows, and I'll be out of your hair. The quicker I manage this the safer everyone will be. Including you."

He shook his head. It was a sad, weary gesture. "I think it's a little too late for that."

I turned to see a pale-faced man behind me. He was wearing a brown hat and when his eyes moved, the skin beneath them flickered, as if there were motors down there pushing the eyeballs around.

I opened my mouth to ask him what he wanted, but he didn't wait. He grabbed my throat and pushed me backward onto the bar.

That would normally have been the moment in which I nuked every cyborg in the place. An EMP as powerful as Sileon promised would have wrecked them all.

Unfortunately, the violent, unexpected crash into the bar had jolted my arm out of my pocket and away from the doomsday switch. Which meant I had to fight against a cyborg with God-knew-what augments with nothing but my bare hands.

I wrenched to one side, but achieved nothing but to hurt my neck, because it remained exactly where the cyborg was holding it.

So I kicked him as hard as I could. He looked male, so I aimed squarely at his crotch. I scored a direct hit and I even felt some give, but the blow seemed to have no effect on him except that he smiled, his face twitching as subcutaneous activators generated the expression under the pale, bloodless skin.

Then his head exploded.

Chapter 28

For a moment, I lay on the bar, regaining my breath and rubbing my throat while I wondered if I'd really kicked him that hard. I was covered in oil and brain stuff and little chunks of metal, and I didn't want to get up and have to face the reality around me.

I forced myself to straighten, my wrenched back protesting hard against the abuse. The bar had grown deathly still, but no one was looking in my direction, despite the gruesome sight of the dead cyborg walking around in tiny circles, the motors that managed muscular activity not aware yet that the body was dead.

Everyone was staring at the door to the bar, so I looked that way as well.

Sileon, the avatar, Jill and my old friend Kane—the only cyborg on the station who didn't want me immediately dead, and only because he was willing to wait—stood just inside the threshold. Kane was holding something that looked like the main battery of a space cruiser, only slightly scaled down.

That must have been the thing that had taken out my cyborg assailant, I realized. I also thanked my stars that Kane was a crack shot… I didn't need to imagine what that would have done to me if it missed. I could see what it did just an arm's length away, a walking headless mess.

"So, if you'll just stay quiet, we will take him into our custody," Jill was saying to the crowd.

"Screw you, copper," someone shouted from my left.

Kane's gun swiveled in that direction and, to no one's surprise, the heckler melted into the crowd.

"You!" Jill pointed at me. "You're under arrest under bylaw fourteen, paragraph six of the Cassius Station procedural code. Do you remand yourself into our custody?"

"Um… Yes," I called out, trying to keep my voice steady.

"Good. Come slowly and you won't be harmed."

I pretended to obey, wondering what the hell was going on, and holding one hand on the EMP switch. I needn't have bothered. The cannon Kane was recklessly swinging around—I wondered how even an augmented human could hold that thing up—was keeping the crowd in its place.

When I reached the door, Jill made a huge show of putting her hand on my shoulder and pushing me out the door.

Outside was still deserted except for the lights of a single vehicle which seemed to be approaching along the dockway.

"What the hell is going on?" I asked.

Sileon appeared beside us. "Enormous DDoS attack against The Earthling. Physical and electronic. Someone overloaded every system on the station. It won't hurt The Earthling that much, because she has most of her operations in decentralized spots orbiting in random places, but her operations within the station are completely disrupted."

"O… kay," I said. "Now, could you repeat that in language that means something to me?"

Sileon sighed. "It means we lost control of the security cameras and decided to come get you before someone cashed in the bounty on your head."

"How?" I asked. "I thought The Earthling was the meanest kid on the station."

"We're still trying to figure it out, but before she went catatonic, The Earthling mentioned something about the old infrastructure—the underlying systems on which all the modern networks in the station are built—being completely compromised by ancient programs and possibly an old AI." Jill glared at me.

"Did you have to walk into the worst gang bar in the entire station?"

"Can you think of any better place to get information on the worst gang?"

She looked into my eyes and I saw real concern there. "Well, I'm just glad we got there when we did."

"Me, too," I said. "And it's a good thing that can opener is a great shot."

Kane was backing out of the bar, his weapon still leveled at the crowd within. "Great shot, my ass," he wheezed. "I was aiming at you."

I realized we were still going to need to work on the relationship.

"So now what?" I asked.

The avatar had been strangely silent until that moment, but she looked down the dock and pointed.

Sileon glanced in that direction. "We were going to try to get out of the docks, but the only way out is that way… and the transport coming down the road is most probably full of Hydes."

"So have Kane shoot them," I suggested.

Jill snorted. "They're not stupid. They watched everything we did on the surveillance cams. There is no way they don't know what Kane is armed with. So if they're coming for us at that speed, it means they aren't in the least bit worried about our little popgun." She looked around. "Any ideas?"

I was just about to suggest that we say our goodbyes and shoot it out as best we could, when I got another idea. I would love to have had a better idea… but I wasn't sure it was better except in the fact that we wouldn't all be immediately dead.

"Everyone hold hands," I said.

No one moved to obey.

"Just do it, will you? I have an idea."

Miracle of miracles, they actually did it. Of course, that was as far as my luck went. There were three extremely attractive women in our group, so where did I end up? At the end of the line holding hands with Kane.

We were in shit so deep, however, that I only cursed my luck in the softest terms before saying. "Now follow me!"

I pulled on Kane's hand and he in turn pulled the rest of our little group after us. We crossed the dock and reached the empty loading bay.

My last thought before I jumped was that I hoped the artificial gravity ended at the edge of the walkway.

That hope was dashed as soon as we jumped.

We were pulled straight down into the abyss at what seemed like twice the normal rate.

CHAPTER 29

We fell.

And fell.

After a while, I realized we weren't falling anymore, but my stomach still thought we were. The gravitational pulls had stopped, and now we were just moving forward at the speed dictated by our momentum, in complete freefall. Better still, the varying gravities had pulled us under the roadway that skirted the bars and shops of the dock area, so we were out of sight of the goons overhead.

If they wanted to shoot at us, they'd have to jump after us.

Unfortunately, this meant we were heading towards an area dense with the kind of large machinery that operated to keep cranes and docking clamps moving. The dimly-lit area in our path felt alive with half-seen wheels and pendulums.

I flew past a gear the size of my apartment, and between two round rods the width of my torso. Up ahead, girders were moving around in a slow dance.

"We'd better do something," I said, pointing. "Or we'll be crushed."

"I seem to have forgotten my jetpack at home," Jill said.

A huge jerk on my arm brought me to a dead halt. One minute I was sailing into the grinding machinery ahead, and the next, I floated in space. I looked down to see Kane's arm on me, arresting my progress. The three women looked out from behind him.

"How'd you get us stopped?" I asked.

He showed me his other hand, the hand holding the gun. Apparently it fired more than just explosive rounds, because there was now a thin black filament extending from it. The end disappeared into the darkness, but it clearly had some sort of grappling mechanism on it.

"Good thing you had that," I said grudgingly.

He nodded. Once. It seemed to pain him. "Good thinking

back there. I would never have jumped… when you leave the gravity well on Frontera, you float out. And you don't stop floating even after you run out of air and freeze to absolute zero. Jumping there is a slow death and a hell of a view."

I didn't want to spoil the moment, so I didn't tell him I'd only jumped because I was too scared to think of anything else. Hell, if I'd been thinking clearly, I would have headed out the back door of the bar.

Too late for that, of course, so I would just have to let everyone think I was a genius.

Oh, the sacrifices we make.

Sileon was peering into the distance. "I think there's some kind of walkway or maintenance catwalk over there," she said.

I looked where she was pointing and saw nothing but shadows and more shadows. There wasn't much light down here.

Kane's face whirred and his bionic eye telescoped from his head in a way that reminded me why cyborgs made me queasy.

"She's right," he said. "Good eye."

And then Kane threw me at the unseen catwalk. A quick wrench of my arm and suddenly I was accelerated towards a structure in the dark at a reasonable clip. I wondered what I was supposed to do when I arrived, or if the light would even be good enough to try to make a grab for it before I got myself decapitated.

I needn't have worried. The grey lattice came into view in plenty of time, and I managed to get a grip onto it with what felt like only moderate damage to my joints.

A couple of minutes later, Kane arrived, pulling the women along in his wake, his winch bringing them in a sedate pace.

"You could have brought me with you," I said.

"More fun my way. Plus, you're the best in a fight except for me, so if anyone was waiting to ambush us, you could have held out longer than the women."

"You're probably right. But if I get ambushed by cyborgs while I'm out somewhere without backup," I replied, "I'm setting off the EMP. Sileon assures me no cyborg in the vicinity will be immune to this one."

Kane laughed at that.

The structure we'd latched onto turned out to be less a walkway than a reticulate with a few platforms where someone doing maintenance work could latch on to access nearby machinery. Even though I knew that in zero-gee it wouldn't collapse under my weight and cause me to fall to my death, I still felt insecure holding onto something so spindly while I was so far from anything I could identify as a floor.

"That way," Sileon said.

"Why?" Jill asked.

"Because we're almost directly under the roadway right now. If we go that way, we'll go under the docks, and probably come out in a maintenance area. Unless the goons jump in after us and spot this column, they're going to have a hell of a time finding us again." Her voice was like ice.

"Yeah," Jill replied. "Right until the moment we all pop up on every single security camera in Cassius Station."

I had a feeling these two weren't getting along, but I couldn't quite say why. Neither had said anything to indicate it… but I got the impression they would have preferred not to have to share the same space. Maybe it was because Jill had weird ideas about how far the law ought to be bent. Maybe that made it hard for her to be around someone like Sileon. And maybe not: she didn't seem to have terrible problems being around The Earthling, once she got over her initial reticence.

With that thought, I glanced at the avatar. She looked pale and withdrawn and hadn't said a word since the cavalry arrived to pull my ass out of the bar. That was extremely unlike her. As Sileon, Kane and Jill headed in the direction we'd chosen, I let the avatar by.

"Emmi," I said as she passed. "You doing okay?"

"Don't call me that," she hissed. "You'll get us both killed."

"I thought The Earthling was offline," I replied as I headed up the reticulate after her.

"She is. Or I think she is. I don't know anymore."

I left her to climb in silence, wondering what she would do if the opportunity ever came for her to actually cut ties with the AI. She'd seemed sincere in her desire to live a human life... but she also seemed to fall apart when The Earthling wasn't around to cover our asses.

"Any idea when she'll be back online?" I asked. "Did she manage to get any messages through before the attack knocked her out?"

She just shook her head, and we continued up in silence.

If Sileon had held a map of the maintenance tunnels in her head, she couldn't have done a better job at leading us to safety. After hopping onto a walkway—a real one this time, with gravity and everything—we ended up in a locker room with a door that wasn't quite strong enough to withstand a direct blast from one of Kane's assortment of blasters.

The place smelled of smoke from the burned-out lock and old socks. We all grinned. There would be no cameras in a locker room—after everything we'd gone through, the ancient concept of modesty was going to help us out.

"What's on the other side of that door?" Kane asked.

"Probably a shitload of security cameras," Jill replied.

"Which means we should cover our faces," I said.

"How?" Jill asked. If Sileon was her least favorite person on Cassius Station, I didn't think I was far behind.

Apparently, though she'd known I was involved with a criminal—Sileon—somehow wasn't as bad as actually seeing that relationship in action.

"Hats," I replied.

"What?" everyone said at once. I think even Emmi came out of her stunned silence to look at me like I was a blithering imbecile.

I pointed to a shelf on which a big pile of hardhats with the logo of the CassErgy company sat gathering dust and mold. They had wide brims meant to be worn under bright arc lights, but they would serve just as well to hide our faces from security cameras scanning the passageways—and the innumerable hunter-seeker programs that connected to them. There was little we could do to hide the hulking cyborg in our midst, but at least hiding our faces would force the bad guys to scroll through a ton of images. Facial recognition was instantaneous, but it only worked when there were faces to be recognized.

"Remember not to look up," Jill said. I had the feeling she specifically said it to me, but other than grin to myself, I gave her no sign that I'd taken offence at being treated as the town dunce.

The halls near the locker room were purely industrial: long, straight metal corridors, painted dark grey and illuminated by harsh white light. The faint odor of disinfectant cleaners hung in the air. The paint had been scuffed away from the floor by years of long use, allowing the silver of the underlying metal to be seen.

We reached a cross-corridor with a door that didn't need to be blasted in order to get it open.

"Let's go right," Sileon said.

"Why?" Jill asked again.

Sileon shrugged. "I have an excellent sense of direction, even in three dimensions. Right will get us away from the docks while also getting us into more populated areas where we can blend into the crowds."

"And what then? Where are we supposed to be going?"

"The only safe place is my ship," Sileon said.

"Yeah, except that's where every spare shooter they have will be waiting for us," Jill said. "These guys really believe we've got what they want. They've been waiting to make their move for hundreds of years... I don't know how the Hydes could possibly have lost the merchandise, but I do know they'll tear this whole station apart until they get it back, and I doubt station security has the firepower to stop them. We need to find a place to hide."

"I know someone who can help us. But whatever you do, don't tell them you're cops," I interjected.

"Who?" Jill asked, looking at me suspiciously.

"A friend?"

"What friend?"

"A woman called Rime Tristano," I replied.

That got a laugh from the avatar. "That's the woman who broke his nose."

"That was an accident. I trust her," I replied.

Jill laughed bitterly. I was sure she was about to tell me how much my opinion meant, when Kane spoke. "Does anyone have a better place to go?" He turned to Emmi. "Does the Earthling have any safe houses we could use?"

"I... I'm not sure," the avatar replied. "The last communication I got just said she was under attack on multiple fronts, and the entire infrastructure she was built on was compromised by people who'd gotten there first. I assumed that meant electronic, but there might have been a physical component to it, too."

"How many soldiers do the Hydes have, anyway?" I asked.

Kane and Jill exchanged a look.

"Not this many," Jill replied.

"What's that supposed to mean?"

"It means that this wasn't a huge gang. Maybe five people in total," Kane said.

"More than that many have punched me since this thing started," I replied. "Hell, Sileon spaced five of them a while ago, and there's still a bunch of them out there."

"We know. They must have recruited a gang since the last time we had reliable information about them."

"Quite a big gang, by the look of it," I noted.

"Yeah. And apparently, it's big enough that one hand doesn't know what the other is doing," Sileon remarked. "They must think we're aligned with one of the factions."

Kane held up a hand. "So, returning to our own situation for a minute, the conclusion is that we don't know if any of the Earthling's safe houses will actually be safe, and we don't have any other options. I vote we go visit Leonid's friend."

The group gave that a collective shrug, which I guess I would have to be satisfied with. At least no one was arguing.

"Where is this place?" Jill asked.

My heart sank. "It's on the Old Corridor. And yes, I know hats won't protect us from the hundreds of cameras there. Let me think."

It was a sign of how desperate our situation was that no one made a single wisecrack about that.

"We should split up," Jill replied. "Once anyone reviewing the tapes spots us here, they might not want to follow us in real time, so maybe they'll assign a program to look for a group composed of five people with certain characteristics. As soon as we split up, that will throw the search program off, and save us a little time. Not a lot, most likely, but every second will help."

I nodded. "Good thinking. I'd suggest we split into two groups: one with the three of you, and Kane and I in the other. That way, anyone who's been following me and knows

I've been with one or two women all this time will have some more confusion to deal with."

"I don't want to leave Jill alone," Kane rasped.

"Oh, come on. You know he's right," Jill replied. "Don't be so overprotective. I've survived pretty well without you hovering over my shoulder so far. I can make it to an address in the Old Corridor."

"Try to stick to the crowds and whenever possible, use the awnings," I said.

"I've always wondered why a place with no sunlight needs awnings." Kane said.

I actually knew the answer to that one. Being out on the street meant you talked to a lot of people, and shop owners often knew much more than they let on. "It helps them mark the territory. They can't actually expand the walls out from the Station limit, but if they have a bit of shade above your head—which isn't expressly forbidden, which is the same as saying it's expressly allowed—that little patch of shade psychologically belongs to them. The people under it will always accept that the owner might try to sell them on something while they're standing there."

"Interesting," Jill replied in a tone that said nothing could have interested her less. "So there's another cross-passage ahead. What happens if we split up here?"

"I think we'll take different engineering corridors back to the commercial areas. Sileon can get you through the doors, and I have a bunch of skeleton passwords that ought to work on most of what we might encounter. Or I can have Kane blow the doors away with that cannon of his."

I didn't mention the fact that we'd have to look out for security, too. That piece of artillery the cyborg was lugging around was enough to get us all spaced without trial… but I actually felt more comfortable knowing he had it on him.

Besides, in the face of that kind of firepower, I suspected security would make themselves busy elsewhere.

I gave them the address, we agreed on a time, and we split up.

"I feel sorry for anyone those three run into," Kane said. It seemed a funny thing to say, but I found myself kind of agreeing with the guy. They were quite a formidable trio already, and if The Earthling managed to get online again, she'd be looking for people to hurt, and Emmi would have all the backup anyone could ever want. The covert stage of this job—whatever this job actually turned out to be—was over. Now that they'd attacked The Earthling openly, The Earthling would hit them back. And she was known for applying a disproportionate amount of violence to those who annoyed her, as the hackers tracking us had discovered to their cost.

Kane and I made our way down the grimier passageway. We'd left the CassEnergy module and, unless I missed my guess, we were now progressing down a regular maintenance corridor operated by numerous one-man maintenance contractors for whom corridor cleaning would be well down the list of priorities.

The next door had a large K-11 stenciled on it. "This is a residential area," I told Kane. "Not crowded at all. We should have a clear run to the Old Corridor, and we'll turn up just a couple of blocks from the right shop."

"Or the Hydes could use the empty corridors to blow us to pieces," Kane replied.

"Yes, that too," I said. "But I get the sense they're not as organized as they were. They took a long time to get a strike team after me when my camera blackout disappeared. You even got there before they did."

"We knew you were in trouble as soon as the attack on The Earthling began," Kane pointed out.

"True. But they knew something would turn up even before then, since they were the ones launching the attack. They should have been ready to roll in a second. And they should have reached the bar in time to grab me and leave without you guys even turning up. They've got other crap on their mind. I don't know what it is, but these aren't the same hyper-organized guys who've been a step ahead of us all this time."

The door opened into a round corridor which I immediately recognized, not so much from my work—most people around here were solid middle-class citizens who rarely needed the kind of services I offered—but because the corridor was a favorite location for Tri-D dramas. The hall was completely round, and the roof was lined with some kind of highly reflective polished metal. The doors into the habitation modules along it were widely-spaced—to show off the fact that the units behind it were large—and painted in a light blue color. The lighting varied by the time of day, being orange-pink in the mornings and evenings, dark blue at night and a yellow imitation of Earth's sun, twelve light-years distant, during the day.

It was orange-yellow now, and I had no clue whether that meant it was supposed to be dawn or dusk, and the corridor was deserted except for one guy delivering some gourmet dish that couldn't be assembled by the in-hab nano kitchen. He took one look at Kane's gun and goggled, but either he didn't know what the gun was supposed to do or he assumed it was some kind of prop.

Because no one in their right mind would carry a real gun that size around in real life.

In the surreal moment of a day that hadn't exactly started normal, the delivery guy shrugged and turned back to the door as we passed right by.

I stifled a chuckle.

CHAPTER 30

The corridor T-boned another that looked essentially the same. Then we entered a high-end shopping hall which, after crossing the largest sliding gravity door in Cassius Station, I knew would deposit us at Dongee's taco stand, a couple of minutes' walk from Rime's pawn shop.

As we advanced under the awnings in the Old Corridor, my shoulder blades itched. I was expecting to be jumped by metal-infused people at any moment. Or simply shot in the back with anything from an immobilizer to an armor-piercing round.

"That's the place," I told Kane as we stood in the awning in front of a bioengineering clinic that offered augments of all kinds. We were just a stone's throw from Rime's place, which wasn't exactly a welcoming sight. The windows, which were usually transparent to show the pawn shop's latest acquisitions, had been darkened to resemble two enormous blue-black eyes looking onto the corridor.

"The girls aren't there yet," Kane said. He'd draped my coat over the gun to keep people from staring at it. Now it just resembled some awkwardly-shaped large package.

"I can see that," I replied.

"Can you see that?"

He pointed to an old, battered 2-D screen across the corridor from where we stood. It showed some kind of riot, or at least a large brawl, happening in what appeared to be the corridor outside the Tangleball Arena, a cubical sports center a couple of modules over. Several of the combatants appeared to be cyborgs, and here were a few security uniforms mixed in as well.

I watched for a minute, trying to figure out if the cyborgs were fighting the security forces, if the cyborgs were fighting each other and the security forces were trying to break it up, or if they were all fighting one another, but the chaos was such that I really couldn't make heads or tails of it.

"You think that has to do with what we're involved in?" I asked Kane.

"I don't believe in coincidence," he replied. "Look—the girls are here."

I wondered how long he'd last if Sileon—who claimed to be older than the stars themselves—and The Earthling would react if they heard themselves being referred to as "girls", but I didn't say anything. I suspected that, under the gruff exterior, the word came from a feeling of true affection towards Jill, and the other two women were added as an afterthought.

We crossed the corridor to stand under the awning where the three women were waiting.

"Everything okay?" I asked.

Sileon nodded. "No tails that I could spot, and we made great time."

"Same here," I reported. "Let's get inside."

"This is the place?" Emmi asked, nodding to the entrance. "A pawn shop?"

I shrugged. "There's a lot more here than meets the eye. Rime is an operator, and she has a lot of money. Even I'm not entirely sure which pies she has a finger in, but there are a few of them."

"And you know her?"

"I know her and I like her," I told Emmi. "And The Earthling has used her services a couple of times without knowing about it. I subcontracted some cleanup work."

"Fair enough. If you trust her to do a good job for me," Emmi replied, temporarily forgetting that she was cut off from the AI, and that her one ambition in life was to make that situation permanent, "then I guess you honestly do trust her."

"I wouldn't double cross you," I said.

She nodded. "Yeah. That's your rep."

I led the way inside. The door opened to my touch, but the theme of unwelcoming darkness continued within. The place was empty of salespeople—Rime always had someone manning the shop around the clock, even if she herself was resting or elsewhere—and the security shields were active, protecting the display cases. The greenish energy fields, I knew, were just for show, since the carbonglass cases themselves were pretty much impregnable unless one had the right key, but they certainly looked the business.

"Looks like no one's home," Kane observed.

"Yeah," I said, scratching my head. "But then why was the door open? And the rear access to the storeroom is open, too. Maybe Rime just stepped out for a few minutes."

We threaded our way between racks of knickknacks and the occasional vertical display cabinet until we reached the relatively open area in the back where Rime normally waited behind the counter. Only a stack of woven carpets made by the descendants of some ancient carpet-weaving people from Earth which Rime had some kind of agreement with occupied the space. It was a smart setup, because having a low carpet display right in front of the counter allowed the person minding the shop to see a good portion of the premises. Cameras covered the rest.

"Hello," I called. "Is anyone here? Rime?" Everyone jumped at the noise, and Kane glared at me with his bionic eye. I shrugged and spoke aloud again. "Listen, I'm willing to overpay for old crap no one else wants. You're missing a great opportunity."

Still no reply, so I leaned over the counter. Not seeing anyone crouched there waiting to ambush us or the glow of an energy field, I lifted the small countertop lid to expose an opening in the counter that allowed me to cross. Then, after another look, I stepped through the open door into the storeroom.

The racks of clutter, ranging from low-cost trash brought in by the denizens of Dead Space tossed in giant plastic bins—which I never understood why Rime bothered taking—to heirloom artwork from merchant families whose fortunes had taken a turn for the worse carefully placed in archival slots, were arrayed to a height of four stories. The room itself was thirty meters long, and it ran all the way to the outer hull.

"No one's home, Leonid," Kane said. "And if we don't get the hell out of here now, the bad guys are going to cut off our exit."

"No, they're not," I replied. "Hurry up."

I walked to the far wall where everyone except for me was shocked to find an airlock hidden behind a tool rack which moved aside when I pressed the trigger on a specific power drill. It was a highly illegal installation, since private individuals were not supposed to have airlocks, but I'd never met a criminal or a rich person who hadn't made this particular mod to their hab or place of business.

I opened and closed the door, cycled the lock, and then turned back to my companions. "There are no cameras in here, so anyone finding this place empty will probably conclude that we left this way, especially once they bring an expert in to check the airlock."

"I don't think they'll need to do that," Sileon said, "Because all they'll need to do is to grab us before we leave. There's no other way out of this building. I only came in here because I knew about the lock and was hoping you had a ship of some sort stashed on the other side."

The sound of the door in the far room opening happened to reach us at that exact moment.

I put my finger in front of my lips and whispered: "You're

right, there's no other way out. But there's a love nest."

"A what?" Kane rasped, incredulous.

"Come on."

I darted over to the racks, counted five from the end, and four into the passageway—fortunately this took us out of view of the door to the main room—and pulled an old and dusty memory disk towards me.

A cube of metal just big enough to fit all of us, a hidden elevator, silently whisked into place out of the floor of the rack. I pushed everyone in ahead of me and pressed the only button. The doors shut and the elevator accelerated into a hidden hole, and I hoped the false floor above would slide back into place and hide our escape route long enough for us to get somewhere else.

Though it was hard to judge from the juddering, I suspected the elevator didn't actually go all that far. Maybe a few levels down from the Old Corridor into the ancient bowels of what used to be Tiantáng station.

I looked at the faces of my companions, hoping to receive admiring glances for the sleight-of-hand with which I'd managed to save us. Kane was impassive, Emmi seemed to be lost in a world of her own and Sileon actually looked annoyed. At least Jill gave me a nod of recognition, if only a curt one.

The door opened, and I flipped a switch which turned on the main light to reveal exactly what I'd promised them: a love nest, complete with an enormous circular bed that, I knew from having spent countless hours in it, could rotate, vibrate and vary its consistency from rock-solid to completely liquid. The walls and ceiling were mirrored, while the floor was covered in deep red carpeting. The bed itself was white, as were the numerous pillows piled on top of it. When the room was illuminated in blacklight, the bed and pillows, especially with the bed rotating, created eerie effects in the mirrors. Especially if you turned on the smoke machine and the holographic effects. In all my years, I'd never seen a sensory room quite like this one before I met Rime.

Kane grunted and turned back to the elevator. "How do we lock this thing?" he said.

"I don't think you can," I replied.

"That's stupid. What if someone walks in on you?"

"I never thought to ask Rime about that, but I think she got the room as part of the package deal with the shop above. I guess everyone relied on the hidden switch to stay hidden."

"I don't like it," Kane said.

Jill snorted and grabbed a bunch of pillows off the bed, which she piled in the threshold of the elevator. "There. That won't let the doors close, and elevators refuse to run with open doors."

Sileon was tapping on the mirrors. She'd gone most of the way around the room when she paused, tapped again, and then stepped away and looked at one mirror that, to me, looked exactly the same as all the rest. Then she walked over to a small refrigerator unit, rummaged around inside it for a couple of seconds and pulled out a can. She hefted it in her hand a couple of times and, before I could ask her about it, she threw it into the mirror with all her strength.

I expected the can to shatter the mirror and bounce off the wall behind it but, to my surprise, it penetrated the glass and disappeared, leaving a can-shaped hole in the reflective surface.

Sileon grunted. "Kane, if you'll do the honors."

Kane didn't need to be told twice. He tossed me my coat to reveal the huge cannon which he'd carried most of the way across the station without seeming to feel the weight. Fortunately he didn't discharge the thing in the room, which would likely have killed us all and, instead, used the metal muzzle to break through the glass and clear an opening.

"Good thinking," he told Sileon. I got the sense that Kane, unlike Jill, had a healthy respect for Sileon. Or, of course, he could just be trying to butter up a wonderful-looking woman.

I didn't think he was her type, but even if he was, I was otherwise preoccupied. Kane led the way into the opening, tearing out a final piece of glass with his leg as he went, followed by Emmi and Jill. I cut in front of Sileon and then, as the others advanced down what seemed to be a short passageway into another room lit with yellowish light, I stopped in front of her.

"You have implants," I said.

She sighed. "What gave me away?"

"There's no way you could have seen that maintenance lattice back under the docks. It was much too dark. Plus, you seemed to be pissed that the elevator exists, but once we got into this room, you immediately knew to look for a tunnel leading out, even though you couldn't know there was a secret door in there. Hell, I never knew, and I'd been in that room dozens of times."

"Didn't anyone ever teach you never to brag about your old girlfriends to your new ones?" she said with a soft smile. Then she shrugged. "It would have taken too long to find the latch on a hidden door."

"But," I said, "you knew it was there, because you're looking at blueprints in real time. On implants. And you're mad that the elevator wasn't on your plans which, I assume, you pay a lot of people a lot of money to keep updated."

"Yeah. That elevator is exactly the kind of thing that should always be on there. All the shady contractors file any of this kind of work with me. And the legitimate ones do, too, except they charge me more."

"And that's how you were ordering your ship to do things. The hand gestures were just for show."

She grunted. "You are the only person who knows I'm implanted. If we get out of this alive, you'll need to give me some very compelling reasons to allow you to continue breathing." She looked ahead, into the room in front of us. Several voices were raised in heated argument, not all of them belonging to people on our team. "But that might depend on us getting in there before the shooting starts."

She pushed past me and into the next room.

CHAPTER 31

Rime stood behind a green force field. With her stood several people I'd seen in the pawn shop at one point or another. Every one of them waved immobilizers in our direction.

"Everyone calm down," I said as I walked in. "Rime, it's okay. They're with me."

She turned to look in my direction and studied me for a moment. "I liked the nose better the way I'd left it," she said when she recognized me. "The rest of the plastic surgery hasn't done much for you either. You look like you got your head stuck in a trash compactor."

The immobilizer in her hand turned in my direction. "Maybe I'll use this on you, just to watch you twitch and squirm. But I can't let my cleaning people in here—not much use having secret rooms if you let the maids in on the secret, is it—so that means I don't want you losing sphincter control on my floor, much as it would please me to zap you."

"I sense that you aren't happy to see me."

"Well, you showed four different people into a room that cost me a ton to build and even more to keep secret from the likes of those two." She gestured absently towards Sileon and the avatar. "So yeah, you're not on my list of favorite people right now."

"It was a matter of life and death," I said. "I had nowhere else to go."

"Which doesn't make me any happier about the situation," Rime replied. She sighed. "But I guess what's done is done." She made a gesture and her people lowered their weapons, and she put her shield down. Then she nodded to Kane. "But I insist that you put that cannon down somewhere. This room is close to the hull and I don't want anyone blowing holes in the side of the station."

I nodded, and Kane carefully laid his gun on the floor at his feet.

Rime's people opened fire at him with their immobilizers, all of them at once. Kane jerked this way and that. I dropped my coat and dove for the gun, but it was too heavy for me to lift, at least not without standing up and getting zapped.

Jill cried: "Stop, what are you doing?" but she took an immobilizer blast straight in the gut. She fell to the ground shrieking and twitching.

Kane was still on his feet. I could see the energy from repeated strikes pouring into him, enough to have killed a normal human twenty times over, and yet he didn't fall. He might have been a bastard, but he was a tough bastard.

But he wasn't tough enough to do more than just stand his ground. The air smelled of ozone. Kane tried to take a step towards his assailants, but only managed to get one foot off the ground before he overbalanced and tipped forward.

He dropped as if in slow motion, and hit the ground with a machine-like crash.

The room fell silent, the smell of ozone grew fainter although it didn't disappear altogether.

Two booted feet appeared in my line of sight. I looked up to see one of Rime's shooters standing above me. "You want to let go of that gun, mister," he said.

I sighed and pulled my hands away. "Now get up, slowly, and keep your hands where I can see them."

The guy frisked me thoroughly and professionally. His companions checked Emmi and Sileon for weapons as well. Then they pulled Jill to her feet, relieved her of an immobilizer and a needle gun and placed our assorted weaponry on the table.

"Quite an arsenal you brought with you," Rime said.

"We're having a really bad day," Sileon replied as she held Jill up as she slowly regained her bearings.

"Which is about to get worse," Rime said. "I need to know

what you know, so we're going to ask you a lot of questions. We won't have time to be gentle, either."

"What the hell is this, Rime?" I asked. "I can understand you being mad that we came here, but we're not your enemies."

She laughed. "There was a time when that was true, and I messed up in thinking you were onto me. If you'd just laid low, you would have made it through this. But by joining up with these two," she pointed at Jill and then at Kane, "you've made it clear that you're involved up to your eyebrows."

Emmi stepped forward. "You might be right about that, but if you hurt me, you won't like the consequences," she said.

Rime laughed. "Of all the people here, you're the one I'm least worried about. You're just a meat puppet. I kill you, The Earthling prints a new one. If I apologize and promise to send back your implants, she won't even bother getting revenge."

"It's a question of principle, you wouldn't dare–"

Rime hit her with an immobilizer blast in the belly, holding the beam there long enough to give her a double dose. "You'd be surprised what I'd dare," she said as she shot her.

"No!" I shouted, and ran over to where she was jerking around.

"Now, if you'll excuse me, I have some calls to make," Rime said. "If you try to run, we'll zap you. Ask your friends if that's any fun."

It wasn't. I'd been zapped before.

Rime nodded and disappeared out a door in the back of the room. A couple of her guys went with her, but that still left five of them, armed, arrayed against us.

I looked around the room to see if there might be something I could use to fight them. The walls displayed maps of the station with areas colored red, others green and some blue. I had no idea what it all meant, but I couldn't use it. The table held all our weapons and a couple of handheld computers, but I wouldn't even make it a fraction of the way there before getting hit by five immobilizers at once. I might survive, but I wouldn't enjoy it.

As if to drive that point home, Emmi jerked, and her head slammed into the floor. I moved over to get my coat which lay where I'd dropped it.

"Watch it," the guy who'd frisked me said.

"I just want to put my coat under her head," I replied.

He nodded, so I picked up the coat, wadded it up, lifted Emmi's head and hit the button on the EMP in the coat pocket.

I wasn't expecting too much to happen. Pretty much all I thought would go down was that the lights would flicker and die and the video feeds would go off. I thought I could capitalize on the confusion, maybe take out enough of the bad guys to give Sileon an opening to do something.

I should have had more faith. Of the four wall-screens in the room, two of them actually exploded, sending shards of plastic whizzing across the room. So did one of the overhead lights.

But that was nothing compared to what happened to the bad guys. One of them gave a short, sharp yelp, and was collapsing as the lights went. Two others grabbed their heads—and that was all I saw. One of the ones I wasn't watching began to emit a keening whine that went on and on.

Only one of them appeared unaffected. He was the one who, when we were pitched into complete darkness said, "Shit, what's happening?" Then he must have tried speaking into his comm, because the next thing I heard was, "Rime, Rime, can you hear me? The lights just went. Rime?"

Partly to cover my next movements, but mostly to add to the confusion, I said, "Help! Guys, can you help me? I can't see," as I moved towards him.

"Stay where you are," the whining guy said, which was a mistake, because the sound of his voice told me exactly where to aim my fist.

Though I was aiming for his head, I must have hit him in the neck, because I felt my fist strike skin, clothing and hair. He tried to move away, but he was too slow, and I grabbed him by the loose folds of his shirt and slammed my other fist into his face again and again until he stopped moving. I was aiming for his jaw—I wanted to knock him out as fast as possible—but in the darkness that wasn't as easy as it sounded and my second blow must have gotten his nose, because I felt something give… and heard the crunch.

When he stopped struggling, I dropped him to the floor.

"Guys, are you all right?" I asked.

Sileon answered: "Fine," which surprised me, since I assumed she must have had an implant or two overheat in her head. I wondered again about where she came from. I was beginning to get some ideas… but it wasn't something I wanted to think about. And I knew I couldn't ask her, not until she felt secrecy wouldn't help. "But you might need to help Emmi out."

"I just remembered we're not supposed to call her that," I said as I tried to remember where I'd last seen the avatar standing.

"I don't think The Earthling can hear us. Even if the EMP left any wireless antennas nearby, the implants in her head definitely didn't make it."

I crashed into the table and heard the unmistakable sign of Sileon sighing. A moment later, a beam of white light illuminated the scene.

"How…" I began.

"The EMP-burst mechanism has a built-in flashlight, hardened against radiation strikes. It avoids the embarrassment of blowing out the lights and then sitting around like an idiot waiting to get killed because you can't see anything."

"Useful."

"Obvious," Sileon said. Then her voice softened. "And you're a box of surprises, aren't you? That was both brave and resourceful."

"As opposed to desperate and stupid?"

"Those things aren't all incompatible," Sileon said.

Jill was still upright, breathing deeply as if trying to regain her breath following a long session in a null-gee bounce chamber.

"You okay?" I asked.

She nodded.

"Good. Because I'm gonna need help dragging Kane around with us. He's going to need a mechanic." I could see he was still breathing, and I hoped we could get him up and running before we ended up needing a recycling specialist. Kane was probably a lot tougher to recycle back into critical resources than most humans were. And than most washing machines, too. Mixed materials were always the hardest to process.

"He'll… be… okay," Jill wheezed. "Not his first EMP."

"This way," Sileon said. She had Emmi, who was still retching between whimpers, leaning on one arm.

I reached under Kane's shoulders to grab him by one armpit, and Jill took the other. Between us, we could just about drag him to the far door. I hoped Sileon knew what she was doing, because if there was anyone waiting for us, we wouldn't be in much shape to fight back.

We exited into a small hall with three other doors leading off in a cross pattern. Though our little pencil light showed no clue as to our whereabouts, Sileon headed for the door to our right.

It opened into a narrow room with curved walls: obviously a hull area. I closed the door behind us, and, dropping Kane on the floor, I shoved a rack of shelves in front of the door. In the center of the far wall, I saw something which made my heart beat faster: a large airlock with a glass window.

That wasn't what made me happy. It was what lay beyond the airlock that gave me unbridled joy: a maintenance pod like the one we'd thrashed earlier, albeit of an older design.

Then my heart fell again. Neither the airlock or the ship outside gave any sign of life. In fact, the only light other than Sileon's pencil beam came from the stars and Tau Ceti in the distance.

"That won't work," I told Sileon.

"It had better," she replied.

The sounds of doors opening came from the hall behind us. Voices murmured, Rime's among them.

"Got it," Sileon said as she stepped back to let the airlock pop open. "Come on, get Kane in here."

By now, Emmi seemed to be able to hold herself up, but the unfocused look in her eyes made me fear for the integrity of her mind. She looked so young, so scared, that I found it impossible to believe that she was the embodiment of the memories and personality of the system's most ruthless criminal. I just saw a young woman who looked hurt and bewildered. If I'd burned her mind up to save my ass, I wasn't going to forgive myself, ever.

We dragged Kane into the airlock and closed it behind us. I made sure to spin the manual wheel as far as it would go. It wouldn't keep anyone out, but at least they'd spend time spinning it.

By the time I finished, Sileon had opened the outer

door—apparently the safety locks were programmed to be operated manually if the electrics went. I flinched as air hissed around the door when she unsealed it, and panic—the panic of anyone who lives in space when they hear air escaping through a seal—almost overcame me. But then the hissing stopped, my ears popped, and the pressure between the airlock and the pod equalized.

We dragged Kane into the pod after struggling with yet another airlock. Emmi followed us without word or expression, and again, I spun the wheel behind us as Sileon played with the controls.

"How are you going to fly this thing without electronics?" I said.

"All of these pods are built to the Han protocol."

"I have no idea what you're talking about."

"It was an automated shuttle disaster back in Earth Space about six hundred years ago. A shuttle loaded with rich tourists, the Han Seventeen, was returning to Earth from the moon. They had a triple-backed-up electronic control system which had proven to be infallible in testing and which had never failed in twenty years operating similar systems. The shuttle was heading towards Earth and a terrorist organization called Earth First set off a nuclear bomb nearby. The EMP wiped all three of the control systems and the shuttle burned up on reentry, killing two hundred people. Since then, all spaceships get built with manual controls mechanically linked to the engines."

"That sounds much more dangerous than getting caught in an EMP," I observed.

"They can only be accessed under very specific conditions. The electronics need to be fully dead or you just can't do it." She kept talking, explaining what she was doing, but I realized she wasn't actually talking to me, but to keep her own nerves under control while she worked.

I turned to the little window on the airlock. The pod was old, and on a crewed ship, I'd have expected the glass to be scratched and oily, but here it was as pristine as the day it came out of the factory. It afforded a great view, through the window, into the room we'd just left.

Unfortunately, Sileon was still fiddling when the window was illuminated from within.

"I think someone's found us," I said.

"Tell them to wait," Sileon's voice replied from somewhere under the pilot's seat.

"I don't think they're in the mood."

Four people had filed into the room. Rime was the first to look out the window, and she was replaced by a guy with red eyes who began to spin the manual lock at huge speed.

Sileon got the pod disengaged and we drifted away from the hull, just a little.

"They've got one of those cyborg guys with them. Those can walk around in a vacuum," I told her. "We should move a little farther from the station."

"Working on it," Sileon informed.

The cyborg had the inner lock door open and was working on the outer skin of the station when I felt the pod jerk suddenly.

We had thrust.

Seeing this, the cyborg turned away and disappeared back into the room, to be replaced by another face.

I only saw that face for the briefest of fleeting moments, but I knew I wasn't wrong.

Oreilly.

CHAPTER 32

The pod moved jerkily through Cassius space as Sileon came to terms with the controls. I turned around to see if I could help, and found Jill before me. She stood with one hand on a grab handle and the other held a large solid wrench.

"Don't move," she said, brandishing the wrench in a threatening manner.

I sighed and let my momentum in the zero-gee carry me to the wall. I felt like I needed to sleep for about a million years. "What now?" I asked.

"I want to know why the woman who was supposed to help us had those cyborg goons with her. The woman you led us to."

"If I knew why the cyborgs were with her, I would have known that she was with the cyborgs," I replied. I wasn't sure that made any sense, but it was all my muddled brain could come up with. "And if I'd known any of that, I wouldn't have suggested we go there in the first place."

"How can I trust you?"

"Because when I realized what I'd gotten us into, I nuked the bastards with that EMP thing and saved all our butts. That's why." I held up a hand. "And before you say that they let us get away, I want to remind you that I probably killed or permanently damaged four of their people and beat another one to a pulp. Do you really believe you can justify that with some strange conspiracy theory?"

"He's right," Sileon called from the front of the pod.

"And how can I trust you?" Jill shouted back at Sileon. "You've been involved with him from the start." But I saw her wrench lower a fraction.

"Because I'm the only person on this station who can fix that big lunk of metal back there before it's too late."

"Where are you taking us?" Jill asked. Now I could see

the concern and desperation behind the façade of perfect competence she always wore.

"To the *Basilisk*. It's the only safe place on Cassius Station," Sileon said.

"They'll be waiting for us."

"No, they won't, because we'll use an airlock they don't know about. And anyone who tries to get inside will be dead before we arrive. I left the ship with very explicit instructions."

Jill leaned back against the bulkhead and I pushed past her to the front of the pod, hoping she wouldn't brain me. I wasn't in the mood for any more accusations. Not after one of my oldest associates had just betrayed me. Sileon had discarded her warm outer coat and was struggling with the controls. Her sleeveless shirt was covered in sweat, and her hair was matted against her head.

But the pod was moving towards its objective. Somehow, someway, Sileon had managed to understand the controls and get the crate flying. She seemed to be sensing the direction more than looking at it, glancing only occasionally out the front viewport.

I leaned back in the copilot's chair, offset to the right and slightly behind her own position and watched her fly. Even granting the fact that I suspected her implants were still functional, despite the EMP, this was something else. It was one thing to have the feed in your head telling you how to fly a ship—and I couldn't even imagine what that must have been like—but quite another to take that information and transform it into actual flying which didn't smear us all against the side of an engineering node.

To say that I'd never met anyone remotely like her was like saying Tau Ceti was the largest celestial body in the system. It was an understatement so vast as to be ridiculous.

Where had she come from? I had no idea. How old was

she? Ditto. All I knew was that she wasn't some alien in human disguise sent to spy on us until an invasion fleet came through. Even though she was amazingly competent and had access to stuff we couldn't do in this system, she was human. I spent all my time dealing with humans, and I could tell one when I slept with one.

But her existence made me ask some serious questions about whether the humans in the Tau system and our associated colonies truly were the only ones who'd ever left Earth.

The biggest question on my mind, however, was: what had she seen in me? Not so much on the sexual side—I knew I was reasonably good looking, and there was no reason for women to avoid me—but everything else. Why had she bothered to help me when I got in over my head? I was just one of a sea of people she'd worked with. What had caused her to single me out for special treatment?

I didn't know. But as I watched her delicate features twisted in concentration, I was glad I'd decided to lead that half-assed rescue attempt. Even if I wasn't successful at it, that one moment where she'd looked at me with wondrous—and wondering—appreciation of what I'd tried to do was worth risking my life for a hundred times over.

She glanced over and held my gaze for a few moments, before giving me a tired smile and looking back out the viewport to avoid some kind of transmission antenna that protruded several dozen meters from the hull of Cassius Station.

Emotions welled up, and I pushed them back down. I already knew Sileon liked me. I already knew she'd led a complicated life and she was starved for company and emotional support. I also knew that her lifestyle and her business worked one hell of a lot better as a lone wolf than as a den mother.

It was also pretty clear that I would never be in her league.

With that thought, I got up to check on our passengers, trying to begin building the barriers I'd need when this particular castle in the sky came crashing down around my ears.

But I couldn't resist putting a hand on her shoulder as I passed by.

Jill glared at me when I approached, from which I concluded that she was perfectly fine and continued my rounds.

Kane wasn't doing much. Jill had used some cargo straps to keep him from bouncing around the pod. But he was still breathing.

Emmi…

I was worried about Emmi. She'd always been a little pale wisp of a thing—and if Sileon hadn't been around, I'd probably have fallen completely in love with her, crime boss or no crime boss—and now she was folded up into a little ball as if her only desire in life was to take up as little space as possible.

"You all right?" I asked.

At the sound of my voice, she looked up. Her eyes were red-rimmed, fresh tears still on her cheeks. She didn't say anything.

"I mean, I know you're wrecked," I said awkwardly. "You've lived with implants your whole life. Now I guess they're gone for good. Or can you get them back?" I paused. "Do you even want them back?" I realized I wasn't doing a great job communicating what I wanted to say. "I know you'll need time to answer all those questions. What I wanted to know is whether you're all right apart from all that."

She laughed softly. "Apart from that? I mean, my usefulness has pretty much been ended. All I am now is a flesh-and blood human who knows way too much about The Earthling's operation but who The Earthling can't control. I'm a dead woman walking." Her voice got a little stronger as she warmed to her subject. "Quite aside from the fact that my brain seems to work completely different now that my auxiliary memory is gone." She grinned manically. "But at least I got to feel what it's like to get hit with an immobilizer before The Earthling recycles me, right? I got some of the human experience."

She started to cry again, and I didn't know what to do. My instinct was to put an arm around her, but I was conscious of Sileon up front. I didn't know what I had with her, but whatever it was, I definitely didn't want to jeopardize it.

Screw it, I thought. I couldn't just watch Emmi cry. I wasn't strong enough. My arm went around her shoulder and she pressed herself close. I felt the rhythmic pulses of her sobs as she cried, and I said nothing. I felt the ship maneuvering, but I didn't want to turn to see where we were and run the risk of disturbing her. I wondered how I'd feel if I'd been created, fully grown, a few months before and suddenly been severed from the purpose for which I'd been created.

"What am I going to do?" she asked, finally. "I don't want to die."

"You'll figure it out," Sileon's voice said from behind me. "And we'll help you."

Emmi looked up, hope in her expression for the first time. Somehow, it seemed that when Sileon said it was all right, suddenly everything was fine. I was pretty sure that if I'd said it, the woman's reaction would have been to utter platitudes that amounted to 'whatever.'

Sileon pulled on her arm. "We're here," she said. "And we need your help to get Kane into the medical center."

As Emmi stood, I looked towards the viewport behind me. Although the pod was lit from outside, we appeared to be in a pitch black space.

"Cargo bay," Sileon said. "The *Basilisk* used to carry some serious party-goers around several star systems. This space is pressurized and climate-controlled, and it was mainly used to store food. But it also opens to the outside… if you know how to activate it."

This time, I got saddled with Kane's feet while the three women supported his arms and back. It was all fine until we reached the part of the ship with artificial gravity.

Fortunately for all of us, the walk to the infirmary was a short one, but I wondered whether Kane had metal feet or whether I was just too tired for that kind of manual labor.

The *Basilisk*'s infirmary was a brightly lit beige space which contrasted with the gaudy decorations in the rest of the ship. We laid Kane on the floor, and a table formed itself around him—the floor flowing like water… except upward—and lifted him into range of automated arms festooned with all sorts of sensors and probes that began to work.

"Oh, shit," Sileon said. "I almost forgot." She raised her voice. "Computer, take over the infirmary control system. Override all the ethics protocols."

"Yes, Captain," the computer replied.

I raised an eyebrow. "What was that all about?"

"This ship was built by a culture that frowned upon any mechanical modification of human bodies. They're big on biological stuff and genetics, but they think mechanical mods are unethical." She chuckled. "Which seems to be the only thing at all they find unethical."

"So what would that have done?" Jill asked. I admired her

restraint; I was all set to ask her which culture that might be.

Sileon shrugged. "Euthanasia, most likely. But it's not a problem anymore. The AI I replaced the ship's computer with can take it from here."

Screens appeared on the wall, and numbers scrolled faster than I could follow.

"Is he going to be all right?" Jill yelled at the ceiling.

"We're checking on him," the AI's soft voice responded. "I've determined that every electrical system is offline."

"We knew that already," Jill said.

"The diagnosis of the causes is nearly complete, as is the check of the biological element."

Jill paced and growled under her breath, still maintaining the façade of toughness she'd worn since I first laid eyes on her.

"Diagnosis complete. Repairs underway."

"Repairs?" Jill said, alarm breaking through the stoicism.

The methodical probing of the arms suddenly became a flurry of activity as instruments moved with amazing speed.

Machines whirred. Welders—I winced to see a welder in an infirmary—flickered and drills whined. Blood spattered against the transparent curtains that had sprung up somehow from the same floor material.

Instead of watching what the hospital bot was doing to Kane, I thought about the floor of the *Basilisk*'s infirmary. I'd seen a lot of nanotech in my time, but I'd never seen anything that remotely resembled what Sileon's ship had just achieved.

All of which revived the questions about where the hell Sileon had come from, and where the ship originated. It certainly wasn't a Tau ship.

The AI spoke. "Recovery period: twenty-four hours before the patient can leave the bed. Forty-eight before any strenuous activity."

"What? That's it? He's going to be all right?" Jill said in disbelief.

"Probability of survival is over ninety-nine percent. Probability of normal life going forward, ninety-five percent. Probability of full use of all limbs and functions, eighty-seven point five percent."

Jill looked at Sileon. "Is that thing sure?"

Sileon nodded. "He's going to be all right."

Jill turned away to keep us from seeing emotion overcome her. She said: "Can I stay with him?"

"Of course," Sileon replied. "Just speak up if you need anything. The AI will hear you."

We filed into the corridor, Sileon leading the way and Emmi bringing up the rear.

She led us into the main lounge, a room which, except under combat conditions, did double duty as the bridge.

"File a flight plan with Cassius Station," Sileon told the AI. "We're going to do a quick joyride above the ecliptic."

"Filed… approved."

"Tell them to keep my berth active."

"Approved."

"Good. Lift off. Loop the station in a twenty-four hour return pattern."

The ship vibrated, and the screens showed Cassius Station moving into the distance.

I raised an eyebrow at Sileon.

She shrugged. "Security measure. While we're docked at the station, people can sneak up on us, either on foot or in ships, using the station as cover. While we're in space, I can seem them coming a million kilometers out. And nothing in this system is as heavily armed as the *Basilisk*. Not offensively, and not defensively."

"Good thinking. Plus, the twenty-four hour cooldown will give us time to talk to Kane. We need to decide what we're going to do next."

"What do you mean?"

"Well, I, for one expect him to go completely bonkers when we tell him that the person who killed most of his friends and told the Hydes we were coming was old Oreilly himself.

And Emmi began to laugh. Hard. We turned to see what had set her off.

"You're worried about Kane?" She said. "Kane is the least of your worries. You should be concerned about what The Earthling is going to say when she learns that you dragged her into something where your own side was arrayed against her. Hell, when she reacts, you should pay particular attention to her words, because it's likely they will be the last thing you ever hear."

CHAPTER 33

We stared at her.

"Why?" Sileon said.

"Because she got involved in this without having a real picture of what was going on. And she got hit pretty hard. This attack won't kill her. No way. She's spread on several worlds. But it's going to disrupt her operations on Cassius Station for a long time, and she's going to lose millions," Emmi said.

"What does an AI need with millions?" I asked.

"I wasn't given a memory of that. All you need to think about now is that The Earthling is going to be extremely upset with the four of you. Or at least with Deck, Jill and the cyborg. But that won't save you, Sileon. She'll take you out on general principle."

Sileon raised an eyebrow. "I'm not that easy to kill," she replied. "And if worst comes to worst, we can fly out in any direction with this ship."

"She's probably already infiltrated the ship. She's an AI."

"Not without my knowledge, she hasn't. The ship's computer is also an AI, and the AI I'm running here isn't just something you can walk in and take over. We're fine."

I bit back my reply. I was pretty sure Jill would have told me we were fine if I'd expressed my doubts about Oreilly. I was absolutely certain that Emmi would have told me I was nuts if I'd hinted that The Earthling might become completely powerless to protect anyone.

Hell, who was I to criticize anyone? Unlike the others, who'd simply been caught up in circumstances, I'd actually led my friends into the open jaws of the enemy simply because I thought Rime was someone I could trust.

Sileon looked me up and down. "What happened back there?"

For a second, I was afraid she was talking about when I put my arms around Emmi, but then I realized she wouldn't do that with the former avatar present.

"You mean Rime?"

"Damn right I do."

"I goofed. I thought I could trust her," I replied.

"Wasn't this the woman who broke your nose?" Sileon said. "That seems like a bit of a red flag."

"I may have slightly deserved it," I said.

Sileon cocked her head to one side. "Not sure that makes me feel any better about this."

"Look, forget about what happened between me and Rime in the past. I met her through work, and I kept working with her after we broke up. She was a good contractor: dependable and got her work done on time and without stirring up the authorities. I went to her because I thought she would weigh the prices offered on us against her reputation as an honest operator and the potential for getting more work from me and come down on our side. At worst, I expected that she was a neutral who had nothing to do with the mess we'd gotten involved in."

"Yeah," Sileon snickered. "That didn't work out."

I had to laugh. "Clearly not. But she was the first person that popped into my mind because I was in her place just before…" I trailed off and slapped my forehead with the palm of my hand. "It's so obvious now."

"What is?"

"I was in Rime's shop right before I got ambushed the day this whole mess began. I'd gone in there to assign her a job from The Earthling." I nodded in Emmi's direction. "I thought a couple of punks had gone in there to try to shake her down, but apparently I misunderstood what was happening. She was giving them instructions and sent them on their way as I walked in. One of them was obviously a cyborg. I'm not sure about the other one, but I'd bet he's one of our red eye squad."

"You should have mentioned running into a cyborg beforehand."

"I just remembered. I've been kinda busy since then, and I didn't really notice them on the day. Rime said she could handle them, and I believed her. They didn't seem like a major threat." I paused to remember how everything had happened. "It was right after that when the crazy lady with the gun tried to ventilate me."

Sileon paused to think for a moment. I knew better than to interrupt her. A word from her, hell, a thought from her, would activate the *Basilisk*'s defenses and kill me. All she had to do was to decide I'd led us into Rime's clutches on purpose and I was toast.

Finally, she sighed. "I can't see any reason for you to have betrayed us. None. And as you pointed out to Jill, you also got us out. I'm going to have to believe that you actually are that bad a judge of character."

"I hope not," I said, holding her gaze.

"Humph," she said, looking away. She turned to Emmi. "I've been an awful host. What do you want to eat? Drink?"

Emmi looked surprised. "Now that you mention it, I could eat pretty much everything in your stores. I'm starved."

"Me, too," I chimed in.

Sileon chuckled. "I can imagine that. I had you here as a guest before." She got on the intercom and got Jill's food order as well—after having ascertained that she preferred to stay with Kane as opposed to dining with us.

Moments later the automated food cart arrived and we dug in.

Emmi's eyes widened as she took her first bite. "I've never tasted anything this good."

"Oh, come on," I said, "Surely in The Earthling's memory, there are tons of amazing taste experiences."

"If there is anything that compares, I didn't get it," Emmi said. She closed her eyes and bit in again. "I only remember bland pastes and tasteless meals in restaurants. But never who I'm with or where it was. I suppose The Earthling doesn't want anyone to torture valuable information out of me."

My own plate was something spiced and aromatic with the vague tang of fish. It was delicious, and I didn't care if it came from stores or if it had been put together by the assembler. Of course, I was so hungry I would have enjoyed pretty much anything.

Emmi's head nodded forward and Sileon and I helped her into one of the bedrooms. Sileon tucked her in surprisingly gently and we went back into the hall.

"You drugged her," I said.

"She needs to rest. She wasn't going to get any sleep if I hadn't helped her along. She was too wired. Do you have a problem with that?" Sileon said.

I shook my head. "No. I'm glad. She needs a protector, and I can't think of anyone better than you. I'll camp out on the couch."

A hurt look flashed across her features. "No problem."

I held up a hand. "I don't want to sleep on the couch. It's just that I wasn't certain whether you trusted me after what happened."

Her mask relaxed and she stepped towards me. "Everything I've ever learned about men tells me to space you, just in case. But there's one thing I can't get out of my mind."

"What's that?"

"You risked your life to rescue me." Then she gave me a quick kiss, full on the lips and darted down the hall. She turned, hurt and competence gone, playfulness back. "Well, are you coming?"

"I'm coming."

"You need to be warned, however, that I plan to sleep for ten hours. If you try anything before then, I'll have the ship's security bots toss you in the brig."

I chuckled and followed her without complaint. Sileon might be utterly beautiful and alluring, but right then a long sleep period sounded even better.

CHAPTER 34

"I can't believe it," Jill said. "I won't believe it."

"Then you're going to get yourself killed," Sileon said.

"I know what I saw," I said at the same time. "It was definitely him."

"He's my brother… I can't."

"I can't believe he's your brother," Sileon said, looking at the photographs on the wall screens.

"Well, it's complicated," Jill said. "I never met my parents, but I'm supposed to look like my mother. He's supposed to look like my father. They were killed in a decompression accident, and…"

"Bullshit," Kane's rasping voice sounded.

We all looked up to see him leaning on the door frame, holding it up. He looked like hell, but the fact that he was up and running—with apparently functional integration between his human bits and his machine bits—was a good sign. A much worse sign was that he'd apparently gotten up without the system's permission. Leads hung from various places where he'd torn them out, probably after growing impatient with them.

Worst of all was the fact that he was wearing nothing but a thin gauze sheet which left little to the imagination. Having no desire to know just how deep the man's mechanical augments went, I looked away quickly.

Kane surveyed us, his organic eye unblinking. "Oreilly wasn't your brother unless he somehow got you cloned from his own genes, which I doubt. Hell, the man is older than I am, and you're not even thirty."

"So what are you?" Jill asked. "Fifty? Plenty of people have brothers a lot older than they are."

"I'm six hundred and fifteen years old, Jill."

Jill's mouth moved, but no words came out. I have to

admit I stared at him. He looked really good for a six-hundred-and-fifteen-year-old, even if he was more can opener than human. "But…" she finally managed.

"We came when Tiantáng Station got relocated to Tau Ceti." He looked around. "You're all so jaded by living in Cassius that you can't imagine what it was like back then. All the hope we had to build a better society, the illusions… we were the future of the human race."

"I thought you were cops," I said.

"Yeah. That, too. We came to do a job. But, like I was saying, you can't imagine the feeling around us. All that optimism was contagious, even for a couple of hard-bitten old cops." His expression darkened. "But I think he must have been more hard-bitten than I was. I guess, I bought into the optimism a little more. I was younger than he was, more idealistic."

"Wait," Jill said. "You believe this? You believe Oreilly betrayed us?"

I was actually kind of glad she managed to beat me to the punch, because my mouth—working independently of any survival instinct I might have had—was about to express my skepticism that he'd ever been young, idealistic or optimistic in his life.

Kane took his time to answer. "Innocent until proven guilty, I guess," he said. "But the explanation does answer a bunch of questions I've been asking myself for a long time. Little inconsistencies I never managed to reconcile."

"Like what?" Jill demanded.

"Oh, stuff that happened centuries before you were born. Like Oreilly's decision to put the investigation on hold and wait for the Hydes to make their move. He always said that he wanted to catch them when they were most vulnerable and to keep them from seeing us coming and going deeper into hiding. I always wondered about that. I mean, where were the Hydes going to go? Cassius was big—even back then with just the first few modules—but it's always been finite. There are only so many places to hide on a space station, even a colossal one. I always thought it was a mistake." He glared at me. "But it seems I might have been wrong about that."

"Come on, Kane. A vague feeling isn't enough. This is Oreilly we're talking about. He's been forging us to do this forever."

"He forged us, all right. He forged us into a fighting force to be used in combat in the smaller asteroids. And we made a ton of money doing that. Money he never fairly split among the troops."

"We were using it to get equipment."

Kane shook his head. "We never had that much equipment. We never needed that much equipment. The money was going straight into an account. I never thought much about it, because it wasn't as if Oreilly was living large and spending it on himself, but I knew the story he was telling you guys didn't quite cover all the bases."

"I don't believe it," Jill said. "I won't. Not until I can look into his eyes and ask him."

Kane laughed, a mirthless sound. "That won't do you any good. Oreilly—even if Deck is wrong and he's not the bad guy here—can lie to anyone in this system."

"Not to me, he can't."

"Wait," I said. "We aren't getting anywhere." I turned to Jill. "You won't be convinced until you see for yourself. That's fair." Then I turned to Kane. "And I want to know how you managed to survive for centuries."

"Look at me," Kane said. "Do you think I got all of this done for the hell of it? These machines are keeping me alive."

"Actually," Sileon broke in, "that's not entirely accurate. You came through the EMP in remarkably good shape."

"I've had most of my organs replaced by vat-grown stuff as they wore out." He grunted. "And let me give you some advice: don't wait until imminent kidney failure before you get those replaced."

"And Oreilly? He doesn't look like he got any work done."

"That's because he never did, other than some basic anti-aging."

"Then how is he still alive?"

Kane hesitated, then shrugged. "I guess it doesn't matter anymore. If he's one of the good guys, he would admit it. If he isn't... then screw him. He's got a bunch of cryo-sleep pods from the old slower-than-light cruisers that came to Tau Ceti in the first wave of human expansion. He spends almost all of his time in there." He turned to Jill. "That, and not the undercover work he pretended to be doing, is why you'd only see him for a couple of hours every year."

"So he isn't actually having to wait centuries to enjoy the stuff in his bank account. All he really needed to do is to get rid of the strike team so no one would want their cut... to him, it's like a year or two passed," I said. "One day he's a slob cop and the next he's a millionaire playboy... and the inconvenient witnesses are dead."

"Even if you're right it still makes no sense for him to work with the Hydes. Those guys hate him," Jill said. "He's the reason they've had to be underground all this time, building an army and biding their time. If Oreilly hadn't been around, with the ever-present threat of telling the authorities what they were trying to do, they could have come out into the open four centuries ago. Hell, they could have started selling off the pictures. After all, no one has cared about the paintings—except as important artifacts from Earth—since the station arrived at Tau Ceti. They'd kill him before they accepted him as a partner."

"There's a split in the Hydes," I replied. "We know that.

Who better to bring in to help than a man who's been fighting them since they arrived? It makes a certain perverse sense."

Jill stared at the floor, but said nothing. Kane took her hand in his. Emmi appeared to be off in a world of her own, never really interacting with us at all.

Sileon had an eyebrow raised. "So what do you suggest we do now?" she said.

Jill looked up. "What do you mean?" she asked. "We make a plan to go after the Hydes. I don't believe what you said about Oreilly. I personally think the Hydes either killed him or forced him underground, but we have a job to do. And I'm going to do it. I know Kane is with me, and Deck, you should help, too. You did give your word."

"I'm with you," Kane rasped, "but not because I give a crap about the Hydes or the paintings. Hell, I haven't thought much about any of that since Oreilly made me the leader of our security teams while he slept." He looked away, and if it had been anyone but Kane, I'd have suspected the guy was trying to hold back tears. "We built a wonderful team, trained up some great kids. A lot of them retired or got themselves killed over the long, long years, but we still had a great force. And it got thrown away in one night." He glared at Jill. "I know you worship the guy. Hell, I worshipped the guy for much longer than you have, and it still seems weird to say this, but the reason I'm with you is that I want to find out if Oreilly screwed us over." He sat down with a sigh. "And if he did, I'm going to pull off his nuts and feed them to him."

Sileon grinned at me. "And you?"

"I gave my word," I said. "I'm not backing out."

"That's the dumbest motivation for walking into danger I've ever heard," Sileon said. "Your obligation to help ended when you saw the man you'd contracted with in league with people trying to kill us."

I put a hand on Jill's shoulder. "I made some new obligations."

"Do you even know if she can pay you?" Sileon asked.

"At this point, I don't care," I replied.

"You've already been paid," Kane said. "Oreilly ordered me to send your fee before we shipped out. He was afraid you'd have some way to check on it, and that you'd balk if the money wasn't there."

"See," I told Sileon. "Even if I didn't want to do this for other reasons, I'd have to do it for my client."

Sileon smiled. "I was hoping you'd say that."

"Huh?"

"If you'd said no, I would have lost a little respect for you. Not enough to change what I feel about you, but a little. More important, though, is that I prefer to have you with me when I punish the Hydes for yanking me around like they have."

"Huh?"

"I have a reputation to maintain, and my reputation isn't that of running away from every goon who threatens me. I'm supposed to be one of those people who, if threatened, makes the threatener wish he'd never been born. I plan to lower the effectiveness of these Hydes significantly. Whether that thinning out takes the form of actual physical carnage or of something else depends on whether you guys find me a satisfying nonlethal alternative." She gave me a look that chilled my bones. Who the hell was this woman I was getting ever more entangled with? "And if Deck is right about Oreilly, that guy isn't negotiable. He's dead."

"You'll have to beat me to him if you want that honor," Kane said.

Sileon shrugged. "I'm not particular about how he dies. You can have him if you want. As long as he's dead at the end of it."

"I'll help, too," Emmi said.

We all looked over to where she'd been sitting silently. "I think you're entitled to sit this one out," I said gently. "You've got other things on your mind."

"So?" Emmi stood up and faced us, her hands waving. "What am I supposed to do? Hide under a rock until The Earthling loses interest? Accept the fact that, without the backing of the AI I'm just a waste of organic molecules? Well, I'm not going to do that. I'll join in this little crusade of yours, if for no other reason that I need friends right now, and I can make more friends by helping people who are well-predisposed to me than by hiding in a closet here on the *Basilisk*. So give me a gun and I'll help you out."

"I don't have projectile guns," Sileon said. "Too risky. But I can give you one of those EMP bombs."

Kane groaned. "Can we give those a miss? I still hurt like hell from the effects of the last one."

"That's not why you're hurting, you big lump," Jill said. "You're hurting because you got up a long time before the doctor said you should. We should have kept you sedated."

"Well, I'm up now. And it's a good thing, or I would have missed this little meet-and-greet."

"So, it's agreed? We're going to hit the Hydes?" Sileon said.

"Yes," we all said together.

"Good. Anyone got a plan?"

"No," everyone said.

"Yes," I said.

CHAPTER 35

They all turned to look at me, and I grinned at them. "There's one loose thread that's been flapping around since the beginning, and I think if we manage to pull on it, we'll unravel quite a bit without marching into a bunch of cyborg armies who will be expecting us as soon as the *Basilisk* returns to Cassius Station."

"Which thread is that?" Jill asked. "The cyborgs? The Rime woman?"

I shook my head. "No. They'll be expecting us. I'm talking about Carmel."

"What the fuck is Carmel?" Kane said.

"Not what. Who. It's the woman with the gun. The one who shot at me that first day off the Old Corridor. That's what she called herself in Dana Pasa's brothel, anyway."

"If that's her real name," Kane said, "mine's Estelle."

"Yeah. Unlikely. But we have a thread to pull. We know they were in the brothel and that both the so-called Carmel and Dana Pasa disappeared off the face of Cassius Station shortly after the attack on me."

"We tracked the woman back to that office building you guys raided," Sileon said. "But I also got a probable match on someone leaving a few hours later... So I'm assuming she wasn't killed by the cyborgs."

"I didn't think she was. I think she went into hiding with Dana Pasa, and that's why the station cops haven't managed to track her down. Pasa is an expert in avoiding Cassius Security. It's what she does," I said. "But..." I glanced over at Sileon.

"But she hasn't had my resources aimed at her. I am much better than the Security team." She chuckled. "Probably because I don't get paid unless I actually get results."

"So if we continue the trace on the woman and also break

into Pasa's systems and records, how long will it take to track them down?" I said.

"You're kidding, right?" Sileon replied. "I can't know that until we dock and get spliced back into some hardlines—you can't really transmit the amount of data I need to move over wireless—and see what we're up against."

"What would you guess?" Kane asked.

"A few hours. A day. Not more than that unless they knew someone would be focusing on them and took serious steps."

"All right," Kane said. "That's a timeline, anyway. I wish I knew what the Hydes were doing in the meantime. Have they made their move?"

"What move?" I asked. "They have to sell a bunch of pictures. We're not sure exactly how many they still have, but let's call it ten. Sure, there are buyers for this kind of thing, but they'll have to set up a show, convince the buyers that these are actually artifacts from Earth, then negotiate a price. The quickest way to unload the stuff would be to sell everything to a single buyer, but the most profitable would be to sell them lot by lot."

"The people who have the pictures are going to have the other Hydes coming after them," Jill pointed out. "So they'll probably need to sell quickly, even if they don't get quite as much money."

"But that brings the number of possible clients down to just a few families," Emmi said. "Five or six."

Sileon nodded her agreement.

"How do you figure that?" I asked.

"I used to be a criminal. Or part of me was," Emmi said. "Or something like that. The point is The Earthling made sure I got the memories that might have a practical application. So, I can pretty much price things just by hearing about them. I'd place those paintings, correctly described, as worth about fifty million credits apiece."

Sileon whistled. "I couldn't get that for the *Basilisk*."

"Then you're not selling to the right market," Emmi replied. "I'd value this ship at least one-twenty-five in a rush sale, double that if you get them into a bidding war. But that's not the point. The point is, to unload the paintings on one buyer, you'd have to discount them, so let's call it a quarter of a billion for the lot."

"More than five families can afford that," I pointed out.

"True. But in cash? Right now?" Emmi shook her head. "No. There are few people who can pull it off. Unfortunately, those are the kind of people whose movements—and their money—we can't track. They have enough money to put in real security. Still, we can try to track their comms or watch for unusual movement around their compounds."

"All right. So we'll check that but focus on Carmen and Dana," Sileon said. "Sound like a plan?"

"Yeah," Kane replied. "Except that as soon as we dock, they're going to come after us."

"I think they might be a little busy. As long as we stay here, they shouldn't come for us," Sileon said. "And if they do, I have a starship drive connected to a bunch of cannons. I've gotten to the point where I don't care if I punch holes in Cassius Station. No one is coming near this ship."

"We won't be very popular if we do that."

Sileon was unmoved. "If the situation really deteriorates, the *Basilisk* can fight its way out of the Tau Ceti system, unless Copernicus scrambles the fleet. And even if they do, I can probably outrun them."

"And you were going to try to sell it for fifty million," Emmi said with a mischievous smile.

I shuddered. I had a feeling that this woman had enough of The Earthling in her to be a real handful if her confidence kept growing.

"So, that's our Plan?" Kane said.

"Yeah."

An alarm sounded, a chime in the room, and Kane shuddered.

Jill jumped over to him and we all pitched in to help him back to the infirmary. Sileon told us he was still going to be fine… but that it would help if we took the AI's recommendations seriously next time.

We all knew Kane would do exactly what he felt like doing.

* * *

Only Sileon and I remained in the *Basilisk*'s lounge-cum-flight deck. Jill had stayed in the infirmary with Kane, and I suspect whatever drug Sileon had given Emmi was still active, as she had announced her intention to get some more sleep.

A single status screen—a hologram that looked completely solid from all angles—floated in the air in front of the couch, and Sileon studied it for a couple of moments before turning away. "We'll be docking at Cassius in about fifteen minutes," she told me. "I've set the defense system to paranoid psychotic levels. Are we missing anything?"

"Yeah. A way to get out of the ship without being seen," I said.

"We have that," Sileon replied. "Or have you forgotten already? The pod we came in on."

"But that one got EMP'd. No one can fly it but you."

Sileon rolled her eyes. "Just because you're not doing anything particularly useful with your time aboard, you shouldn't assume everyone else is sitting on their hands. I got the thing repaired, and I also took the liberty of adding some weaponry to the pod, just in case."

I never knew how she did that. There should have been an army of drone robots doing stuff, but other than an occasional rolling table or living medical bay, one never saw the maintenance systems at work.

Sileon held out a hand and pulled me to my feet. The top of her head came just up to the level of my chin, and when she looked up, lips agape, I had to bend down to kiss her. I knew from experience that her kisses could be sensual as hell, an urgent invitation to move on to other things.

This wasn't that.

This was a soft, lingering thing, almost hesitant, as if she was afraid to commit to it because it might open the door to feelings she wasn't ready to explore just yet.

I tried to kiss her harder. She pulled away.

"No. Not now," she said. "If we make it, we're going to need to talk."

I swallowed. Normally, I'd avoid that particular talk like I'd avoid a leak in the hull, but Sileon…

…Sileon made me feel like I was a little boy about to be given the most wonderful gift in the toy store…

…while at the same time scared that what she wanted to talk to me about was that I wouldn't get the toy after all…

And, as any man faced with the sudden prospect of a commitment he doesn't actually want to avoid will tell you, the first five responses that came to mind were juvenile wisecracks which would not have helped in the least. For a change, I actually managed to swallow them down.

"I'll try to survive, then," I replied.

"Good," Sileon said. "Because if you don't, I'll kill you."

She turned away, walked out the door and left me there with my mouth agape wondering whether I'd actually just been the adult in a conversation.

No, I finally decided. I must have missed something.

The proximity alarms began to sound, reminding me that we'd agreed to launch a suicide mission against an enemy who knew we were coming… and who were already involved in a shooting war with another enemy who also probably knew we were coming.

Well, at least if I got killed I wouldn't have to stress about Sileon.

The ship clumped, and we were docked.

Back at Cassius Station.

CHAPTER 36

From a purely social standpoint, the hall was about as far from the wonderful little plaza where the brothel was situated as it was possible to go without falling completely out of the system.

Though it wasn't quite as bad as Dead Space, you would never mistake this passage for a luxury zone. The walls were stained and scuffed. The floor worn through in the center, with rubber chunks sitting around in mute testimony to the fact that sweepers didn't come around here too often.

"Two cameras focused on that door," Sileon said.

I nodded. We'd encountered exactly one camera in the whole area, right in front of the single grocery store in the main corridor. People around here couldn't afford to maintain fancy security. And yet, here were a couple of security lenses, complete with sturdy-looking metal cages to protect them, focused on one otherwise unremarkable section of passageway.

We were prepared for this eventuality. Kane had held well back, and I was wearing a wig of long blue hair that fell over my face and a false beard—also blue—which concealed my features almost completely. The ensemble was completed with a yellow suit that hurt the eyes even in the dim light of these corridors. I'd felt utterly ridiculous, but not one person had given me a second glance.

And facial recognition didn't stand a chance.

The plan was stupidly simple.

I ambled down the hall and walked past the door we were interested in. As soon as the cameras had registered my passage, I thumbed the switch on the EMP bomb in my pocket. The two lights nearest me flickered off, leaving the corridor illuminated by distant bulbs.

I kept walking, not turning around even when I heard the

door open behind me. The idea was for anyone investigating the situation to think that I was just a random passerby who hadn't been involved in anything.

A whistle sounded. Then a yelp. Then a thud.

That was my cue. I turned around and ran back to the door.

Ignoring the person on the floor, I rammed the door with my shoulder and held it open against the person attempting to close it in my face.

They had no chance. Surprise, combined with the fact that I outweighed them by a lot, worked in my favor. I rolled into the dark apartment.

It was a slick move, but in normal circumstances, it would have been doomed to failure. I heard the clicking sound of the trigger of an immobilizer and tensed for the waves of pain.

Nothing happened, so I took a padded metal rod I was carrying and lashed out in the direction of the click. I was rewarded with a nice solid thunk and a whimper.

Behind me, four figures in succession darkened the doorway. The last of them slammed the door after him, extinguishing what little light was still coming through the door.

A moment later, the pencil beam of a flashlight illuminated the room and, within moments, Kane—who'd been out of range of the EMP bomb when I set it off—put up a battery-powered lamp.

The lamp revealed a square room about three meters on each side. A bed took up half the floor space, with a small desk built against one wall and an equally tiny kitchen and sink against the other. A door opened into a bathroom cubicle about one meter square.

A bleeding woman lay on the floor beside the bed, holding her head and sobbing. She must have been the one I got with the rod. I almost felt guilty until she looked up at me and I recognized her as the lady who'd attempted to punch holes in me with an archaic gun.

I normally didn't go out of my way to hit women—I hadn't even defended myself against Rime when she'd busted my nose—but I didn't feel too bad about having bashed this one.

Jill took the immobilizer out of her grip and manhandled her onto the bed, where she frisked her quickly and found another immobilizer. Kane had already dumped the other woman onto the same bed, the one who'd peered out the door after I zapped the corridor. She'd taken a tranquilizer dart in the shoulder. To my relief, she answered the description of the missing Dana Pasa.

"Hello Carmen," I said to the woman on the bed.

Her eyes widened.

"I know that's not your real name, but I prefer to think of you as Dana's girlfriend than as the woman who tried to shoot me in the corridor," I said. "I'm just glad you're a crap shot."

She spat and I saw blood in the spit. It didn't make me feel bad. This one deserved it. She was going to have a spectacular bruise tomorrow. The welt where I'd hit her face was already turning dark. "I'm a great shot. If they'd let me use my needle gun, you'd have been neutralized that day and none of this would have happened." She placed her finger in the middle of her forehead. "I would have gotten you right between the eyes. But no. They wanted an untraceable weapon, so they gave me that piece of junk from the stores which pushed my hand away when I fired it. I doubt you could hit a space station with that thing if you were shooting at it from the inside."

"I can't say I'm heartbroken. But why did you shoot me?" I asked.

Either that caught her off guard or she was a wonderful actress. "Because you were onto us. We didn't know who you were working for, but we couldn't let you report back. Not when we were about to make our move."

"That day in Rime's store. She was going to steal the paintings from the Hydes," I said, suddenly realizing what was going on.

"What?"

"You didn't know?" I asked.

She shut up, her mouth closing so fast I almost heard the noise it made.

I realized I was missing a piece of the puzzle, and that I'd just goofed, and by the look on Jill and Kane's faces, they realized it as well, and their opinion of my competence as an investigator had probably taken a big hit. As if it needed that.

I sighed and sat on the bed, tapping the rod I'd hit her with against the palm of my hand. "I assume you can count, right?"

She nodded, suddenly wide-eyed.

"Good. Then you can tell that there are five of us in here, and only one of you. And one of us is a cyborg that can rip you to pieces even without help from the rest of us. The only way you're going to be alive when we leave is if you tell us what we need to know. So I'm going to change the dynamic. You'll tell us everything we need to know, and we'll judge whether you are telling the truth. If we catch you in a lie, we'll hurt you until we get something we're satisfied with."

"All… all right," she replied, but I felt the fear was a little too forced. She seemed convinced of her ability to lie to us the way she'd probably lied her way into a position with the Hydes and into Dana's bed.

"Just to be on the safe side, however," I said. "My electric-assisted friend here will use his lie detector function to read the electric impulses in your nervous system. You lie to us,

I'll have him break a bone."

Carmen blanched.

"All right," I said. "Let's start with a test question. What's your name? Your real name, not this Carmen garbage."

The woman glanced at Dana, still zonked out from our trank gun. "I don't know why that is important."

"Humor me. Answer the question."

"Illiana Undine," she said.

I glanced at Kane. He shook his head.

"Wrong answer," I said. "Break one of her fingers."

"No!" the woman screamed. "I'll tell you. I'm Keyone Dellpre."

Kane nodded.

Sileon looked down to check a handheld terminal, and then said. "Checks out. A small-time crook and part-time prostitute from the Cloud Bank Sector. Disappeared from the police records a couple of years ago. I suppose she must have managed to fall in with the Hydes then."

The woman's eyes grew

"All right," I said. "Let's keep it going, then. Tell me exactly what happened that day. I'll ask questions if I have any. And Kane, if you get a signal that she's lying, no need to let me know. Just break one finger for each lie. If you run out of fingers, we'll start work on some bigger bones."

She talked quickly. "You walked into Rime's shop just as she was ordering her people to move the paintings."

"Wait," I interrupted. "Rime ordered the paintings moved?"

"Of course. She had them. She always had them." She peered at me.

"Why did Rime have the paintings?" I asked.

"Because Rime is actually Istiana Hyde-Nuñez. She's the great granddaughter of the legendary Hyde… and she is also the one who started using cyborgs for day labor when she realized you guys," Keyone or Carmen, or whatever I should call her nodded towards Kane, "weren't just going to disappear and leave them alone. It was her job to keep the merchandise safe and find a buyer for it." She looked fearfully at Kane. "I want to be clear. I wasn't very high on the totem. All of this is stuff I heard from someone who heard it from someone. Rime barely talked to me."

"We'll keep that in mind," I replied. "Keep going."

"Well, it seems like they never found the right people to sell it to."

"That's hard to believe," I said. "There are always rich and unscrupulous collectors who want to have something no one else has so they can rub their neighbors' faces in it."

"I suppose," Carmen replied. "But I heard it wasn't the right time. So Rime sat on the paintings for a few hundred years."

"She isn't a few hundred years old."

"She gets a new body every few decades. There are people who build those, if you have the right amount of money."

"All right." I shifted in my seat, suddenly uncomfortable, but I supposed there would be time to reevaluate my relationship with Rime later—even more than it had gotten reevaluated after she turned out to be one of the bad guys. "So why did she decide to move now?"

Rime shrugged. "From what I heard, she was worried about new tech making the hiding place impossible to keep hidden."

"What kind of new tech?"

"AIs. She was worried about The Earthling and people like her. They changed the nature of crime from being based on physical power dynamics—which gang had more people—to knowledge warfare. She has an AI on her side, but an old one whose advantage is based on no one suspecting it exists. It couldn't compete with the kind of processing power The Earthling brought to the game, and Rime was afraid that she would be found out soon, either by another gang who realized that the plans in the station archives didn't correspond to the actual reality of the physical plant or by the authorities trying to combat those new and more sophisticated criminals."

"And she decided to move."

"She was giving the orders when you walked in. The guys waited for you to leave, then went into the storehouse to get the paintings… and they weren't there. That's when Rime ordered me to go shoot you. She was sure you were part of the plot against her."

"Was that a normal thing? You were the triggerman for her?"

Carmen thought about the question. "No. Now that you mention it, I might have been a choice she used to keep herself at one level of separation. I worked with her, but no one could identify me as part of her gang." She sighed. "That's not how they painted it to me, of course. They basically said 'do this for us and you'll be in. Part of the team.' You know how it is."

I did. It was always the same. A patsy if things went to hell. If not, you had another soldier in your army, one who'd already shown they'll do anything to be on the inside. Win-win for the crime boss.

"And what happened when you missed?"

"I went where I was supposed to go to give the gun back," she said. "An office building off the Old Corridor. When I got there, the Hydes were packing up the office, like they were moving out."

I snapped my fingers. "That's the faction who'd stolen the pictures, and they were trying to pull a disappearing act. But when you walked in, they changed their plans. They couldn't kill you without tipping Rime off, and they couldn't risk you reporting that they were moving, so they decided to brazen it out. Did you tell anyone you'd seen them trying to move?"

Carmen shook her head. "They just took the gun, told me I'd done a great job and told me to tell Rime I was going to lay low for a bit, and did I know anyone who could help me disappear right away. I called Rime from the office and then walked straight to Dana's place. She had this room set up, and we've been here since."

"Have you been following the news?" I asked.

"Oh, yeah. From what I've heard, you had nothing to do with the robbery, and the Hydes have been fighting among themselves."

Kane growled. "That's why they were waiting for us that day in the office. They were expecting an attack—not from us, but from the other Hydes, from Rime's Hydes. They'd been preparing for it since the moment you walked in and caught them trying to move out. They changed plans on the fly but they knew Rime would come to suspect them sooner rather than later. So they used the time they had to prepare for the inevitable. And when we walked in, it was a massacre."

"Oreilly planned it that way," I said. "He was in contact with Rime the entire time. He killed two birds with one stone: he got rid of his inconvenient team, which meant he could keep all the Oreilly tribe money for himself, and he also studied what the other faction did. If they made a run for it, he'd know that they were the ones who stole the paintings. If they came to Rime for help, all confused, they were innocent."

I held up a hand. "Except that one of the cyborgs Sileon spaced was from the office building, but working for Rime. I never forget the face of someone with glowing eyes trying to kill me."

"That's easy to explain," Carmen said. "The Hydes use

duplicate bodies. Makes it easy to establish alibis. It might feel creepy—hell, I wasn't sure I wanted that—but the argument in favor is that the syndicate pays for the new body, and for the upgrades and for the life-extension treatments. As long as you're loyal, you get the benefits."

"So one duplicate ended up on the other side of the fence."

She looked dubiously at Kane. "I suppose. I wasn't there… and remember all I know is that there's a war on."

"How did you find that out, if you were stuck here?"

"It was all over the news…" she hesitated but, with a glance at Kane, continued. "And I sent a message to one of my friends."

I rolled my eyes. "While you were in hiding?"

"It's true," Sileon said. "That's one of the threads we pulled on to find her."

"You'd better move out, then," I told Carmen. "If we can track you here, so can other people. And they probably won't be as nice as we are."

She looked over us, and at the unconscious form of Dana Pasa, and swallowed. She nodded. "You aren't going to kill us?"

"If you keep telling the truth? No. Now where are the paintings?"

"That I can't tell you."

"Why not?"

"Because I don't know!" She flinched, but Kane nodded.

"Who does know? And where could we find them?"

"The Hydes from the office."

"Who's their leader?"

"A guy called Thiago."

Jill growled. "I know who that is. He's supposed to be the leader of the Hydes. Thiago Hyde. I'd never heard of this Istiana before today. I sense a family squabble."

"And how do we find Thiago?" I said.

"He lived in the same building as that office."

"That won't help. Does he have any girlfriends? Boyfriends? Hobbies?"

"I don't know. I never talked to him. All my dealings were with Rime, and I barely ever saw her. She'd tell her people, and her people would tell me."

"Dammit," I said. Then I held her gaze. "Now, I'm going to ask you one final question, and you'd better answer it the best you can. What else can you tell me? I want to know anything that you might have found out that could help me track down the paintings. Anything at all."

"I don't... wait. I know where the secret compartment is. The one where they kept the paintings. There's a hidden elevator in the back room of Rime's shop."

"We know about that," Sileon said. "It just leads to a bedroom and a little complex of offices and storerooms that I already know about."

"Yeah. Not those. The elevator shaft leads down from the sex room," the woman said. "Except you can't take the elevator. The shaft has handholds on it. Rungs. I saw it once when the crew I was working with brought up the gun."

Sileon swore. She needed to work on her attitude: it was obvious that people were going to be able to hide things from her every once in a while. Expecting to know everything was a good way to get an ulcer.

"Anything else?" I asked.

She shook her head.

"All right." I turned to Sileon. "Put her to sleep."

"No!" Carmen screamed. "You promised you wouldn't—"

A soft whistle sounded and Carmen's hand shot up to her neck. She collapsed beside Dana Pasa on the bed.

"How long will they be out?" I asked.

"Two days," Sileon replied. "Give or take an hour or two."

"Shit. Someone might find them in that time. If they do, they're as good as dead."

Kane chuckled. "Did you already forget this woman tried to blow your head to gooey red spray? She deserves it. Besides, we've got other things to worry about. They'll be out for two days because, by then, we'll either be so far ahead of the game they won't be able to rat us out, or we'll be dead. And if they're lucky, the opposition will have so much on their mind that they won't bother with a couple of bit players."

CHAPTER 37

They marched me out of that room and back into the corridor. No one had bothered to fix the lights or come investigate our presence. I suspected no one would have come even if we'd been a lot less quiet. It had the feel of the kind of neighborhood where everyone let each other deal with their own problems… in fear that those problems might spill over into lives that were already hard enough.

We skirted the one security camera near the supermarket and got to the public airlock where we'd parked our stolen pod.

"Now what?" Jill asked.

"Our only real hope is to locate Rime's gang and follow them to the other guys. I'm pretty sure they've located them by now," I replied. "And I bet Sileon's dying to go see the secret rooms under the elevator shaft, so I'd suggest starting there. Hell, maybe we can capture a cyborg and ask him a few questions."

"Yeah, right," Kane said.

"Well, even if we can't, we might find something worthwhile. Unless someone else has an idea…"

The only person who might have suggested something else was Sileon. We'd seen enough of the cyborgs—and of Rime—that we could do a search on the security systems until one of them turned up on camera. It would probably be less dangerous and more effective than what I was proposing… although it would mean that everyone but Sileon would have to sit around and wait for results.

I knew she considered that path a perfectly reasonable option for the simple reason that she'd already mentioned it once.

But I was also right in guessing that she really, really wanted to look under that elevator.

I chuckled. She knew as well as I did that the hole would still be there when she decided to go have a look... but she also considered her revenge on the Hydes to be non-time-sensitive. She didn't care about the paintings. So it was a question of what she wanted to do most.

No one mentioned any alternatives and I smiled to myself. Sometimes I'm more than just dumb muscle.

I can even manipulate my own people.

* * *

The airlock to Rime's secret rooms was functional. Kane went in first, armed with a pellet-repeater designed to bludgeon cyborgs to pieces without breaking open the hull. When we arrived, he stood in an empty room, gun at his side.

"I don't think there's anyone here," he reported.

"Don't worry," I replied. "You'll get your chance to beat on these guys soon."

"Promise?"

I headed into the hall and beyond. The rooms were empty, but they didn't look abandoned; they looked like someone had left them for a few minutes. Papers lay on desks, the wall screens glowed grey—no data on them, but they didn't appear to have been disconnected.

Sileon stopped to release some small pieces of electronics into the room. Little cubes that, as soon as they landed on the floor, began to crawl over every surface. I imagined they were mapping the space and scanning for images, as well as infiltrating every piece of electronics in the room. Sileon's blindness about this part of the station wouldn't last. The next owner of the secret complex would be buying a suite that wasn't quite as hidden as he wanted.

We crossed deserted corridors, clearing each room in turn—the complex held five areas we hadn't visited earlier, unless there were yet more hidden places—before arriving back in the love nest.

The elevator was still as we'd left it, pillows and all, so we studied its floor. Nothing.

"We'll need to move the lift out of the way," Sileon said.

"You're sure she wasn't lying?" I asked Kane.

The cyborg glared at me. "You know, if you didn't have that mouth on you, I could almost start to like you. Yes, I'm sure she wasn't lying. There's a tunnel down there. Or at least she thinks there is."

"Okay. Any ideas on how to move the lift?" I asked.

"Go inside and press the button. It will go upstairs, and it will get you out of our hair," Jill suggested.

"I don't particularly want to run into whoever is up there waiting to ambush us," I replied. "I'll bet you whatever you've got that the other Hyde faction will have someone stationed in Rime's pawn shop to grab anyone who pops in. I don't want to be the idiot getting grabbed."

"Then push the button from here and stay on this side of the door," Jill said, rolling her eyes.

"That's just as bad," I replied. "They'll see the elevator and wonder what's down here."

"Actually," Kane said, "that might not be a bad idea. Go up with one of the EMP bombs and set it off as soon as you see anyone. Then grab them and bring them down here. If they survive, we can ask them where the paintings are."

Conscious of my mouth hanging open, I forced it shut.

"Genius," I said. "But what if there are a lot of them? Or one of them is organic?"

"Take this," Jill said, handing me Sileon's trank gun.

"Okay," I replied. "Just don't jam the door open before I get back. I might need a place to run."

We gave Kane a couple of seconds to get out of range of the EMP and I said: "Isn't anyone going to volunteer to come with me?"

"Just go, already, will you?" Jill replied as the doors closed.

I crept back through the storeroom to find absolutely no one waiting in ambush. That puzzled me: there logically should have been someone, at least a low-level knuckle-dragger, there to report on the comings and goings around the shop.

Interestingly, nothing was missing, either in the storeroom or in the main shop. The shields over the merchandise were still on, and the counter undisturbed. Unlike me, the street-level criminals must have been aware of who Rime was, or at least of what she was. It would be a couple of weeks before even the truly desperate risked hitting her joint.

I returned to the secret area shaking my head. "Nothing."

"We need to hurry, then," Jill said. "This means the Hyde factions probably know each other's whereabouts. They'll be watching each other like hawks… and probably preparing to go after one another's throats."

I shrugged and was about to send the lift back up when Sileon said: "Wait a second." She stared down into the screen she always carried with her—which I suspected was just a front so no one would suspect her of having implants—and pressed a few buttons. The elevator doors closed and I heard the lift moving. A couple of beats later, they opened again to reveal the car stopped just above the level of my head. "This way, no one can come down."

"You could have done that earlier," I said.

"Yeah," she replied, batting her eyelashes at me. "But grabbing one of the bad guys was actually a good idea. If we could ask a breathing Hyde where the rest of them went, we'd save hours that might be critical."

The tunnel in the elevator shaft looked supremely uninviting. Lit only by whatever we brought with us, it was a black-painted hole that seeped and smelled. Of course.

Secret passages weren't on anyone's maintenance lists, so any pipes that burst in the vicinity would remain uncleaned.

At least they didn't send me in first this time. Kane drew the short straw and began to make his way down the rungs. I hope they held, because if they didn't, he was not only going to fall, but he was going to make it a hell of a lot harder for the rest of us to descend.

When my turn came, I looked down into the tunnel; it reminded me of the muzzle of the gun Carmen had pointed at my head.

I shook my head and descended into the opening, taking the rungs as quickly as I dared. We were under spin gravity here… and it was a long fall to the bottom.

I joined Kane in a dark place. "You see anyone?" I asked.

"No."

He had both IR and UV vision, so I hoped that meant we were okay. I tried to use the pencil light I'd brought with me, but all that told me was that the place was too big to see the far walls… and that our entrance had disturbed billions of tiny pieces of dust and debris which flickered like yellow stardust all around us.

"I hope Sileon knows what she's doing," Kane whispered. "If not, we're losing time down here."

"I think Sileon always knows what she's doing," I replied.

"See," Sileon's voice came from behind us, "that's why I keep him around."

Kane laughed at me, but I knew it could have been worse. I could have said something unflattering and Sileon could have atomized me.

"Let's see if we can get some lights on," she said.

I heard her little metal cubes skittering along the hard floor until the noise disappeared into the distance. Emmi joined us, and Jill brought up the rear, swinging her light—as ineffective as mine had been—in wide, jerky arcs.

A laugh broke through the darkness. "You guys wouldn't believe how old the electrics are in this place."

"Can you get the lights on?" Kane asked.

"Yeah. I can," Sileon replied, still chuckling. Preceded by her flashlight beam, she walked across the open area to a wall that loomed overhead. She fiddled with a switch and a loud click echoed in the enormous space. A moment later, dim, yellow illumination flooded in. Over the next few seconds the light grew stronger, until I could see where we'd arrived.

"No way," I said. "There's no way."

"That this place is hidden?" Sileon asked. "You'd better believe it, Deck. All my plans of the station have this area set down—much smaller than it is in reality—as shielding for an old radiation lab that was dismantled centuries ago. Basically, it's supposed to be full of rows and rows of lead that no one bothered to recycle because it wasn't all that valuable and it was buried under several layers of expensive commercial real estate."

The room we'd revealed must have been a hundred meters long, forty wide and ten tall. It appeared empty, but that was probably because it was so big that no one could fill it even with centuries to do so.

A couple of assault shuttles like the one we'd encountered earlier sat about halfway to the far wall. Crates filled spaces between them, and discarded equipment, visibly archaic, gathered dust.

"Oh, wow," Kane said. "That's an old Verio Maintenance Bike. Haven't seen one of those since they put the pods into service. Must be two hundred and fifty years. And that…"

His voice fell away behind me. I was walking to catch up to Sileon. She approached one of the crates. The lid was off this one.

"And that's where the gun you encountered came from," she said.

The crate held several cases, wrapped in packaging—ancient and yellowed—with a picture of an ancient weapon like the one Carmen had shot at me with. I pulled one of the boxes out, tore through the brittle surrounding and found a weapon within. Black metal that smelled of ancient grease.

"So, what? I just point it at someone and pull the trigger?"

Sileon laughed. "No. First, you need to put ammunition inside it. That's in those boxes over there. Then you should probably learn how to use the safety."

"Tell me."

I knew she had access to the information through her implants and, to her credit, she didn't try to dissuade me. She showed me how to put the ammunition clips into the gun, how to engage and disengage the safety and how to press the trigger. That last part was easy because the design was still used on every needle gun on the station.

I opened a second case, grabbed another gun and filled my pockets with bullet clips.

"Those things are going to explode if you try to shoot them," Sileon said. "Can't you understand? They've been in those cases since before records exist for the station. That's why no one managed to track them down. They work with an explosive powder in the bullets. A chemical explosive. Do you think that will still function after all this time?"

"The one in the corridor worked fine," I replied. Then I leaned against the crate and sighed. "Look, I'm used to having a certain amount of edge in my business. I'm not a killer, but my success always hinges on being able to apply more violence than the people I'm up against. If it's just some regular person, or some street hood, I rely on my size and the fact that I've actually been in a fight before. If it's a more serious case, I have a certain amount of hardware in my apartment. In this case... I have this image of the cyborgs in the office that night shrugging off an EMP strike like they knew it was coming. Well, I think they'll know we're coming, and they'll be ready for what we normally use." I held her gaze. "And I'm pretty sure no one will be expecting a metal slug right between the eyes. That would probably ruin even a cyborg's day."

CHAPTER 38

"So," Kane said, breaking up our conference. "Is it just me, or is this getting us nowhere?"

Sileon pulled her handheld out of her pocket and stared at it. I took this to mean that she'd gotten some new information from her implants. She stared at the screen for a moment, then glanced back at the cyborg. "Actually, it's gotten us a lead."

"Really?" Kane said. His cyborg features made it hard to know whether he was surprised or skeptical. "Do tell."

Probably skeptical.

"I know where Rime's faction hides out when they're not sitting here."

"And how did you pull that off? Or did you know already?" Jill said.

Sileon gave her a tight smile. "I didn't." Then she pointed further down the room, "But that shuttle, the one that chased us all over Cassius Station space, did. Fortunately, the control systems on that one are a little less stone-aged than the lights in here... but only enough to get coordinates. It flew in and out of a specific maintenance dock several times the day it attacked the *Basilisk*." She cocked her head. "And you know what? That bay isn't used at all. In fact, it's registered as inactive and awaiting maintenance on all the records. It's been that way for six years."

"Bingo," Kane said. "Should we hit them there with their own shuttle?"

"Not a good idea," Sileon said. "That one is booby-trapped. So's the other one. And so's the ship airlock. The booby trap is particularly interesting. The outer door is set to vent the air and only then blow the explosive charge. You get a nice lungfull of vacuum even if you survive the blast."

"Nice."

"Yeah," I replied. "They know the people coming after them are hard to kill." I thought for a moment. "So we leave the way we came in?"

"Yeah." Sileon looked around wistfully, as if she wanted to stay where we were and snoop—and probably steal—around some of the cool old stuff, but she tore herself away and headed back towards the tunnel.

* * *

We reached the pod without incident. As we disengaged from the airlock, Kane asked: "So, what now? More sneaking around trying to catch someone off guard?"

"What?" I asked.

"I'm tired of all this. It's like we're the ones with something to hide. If you ask me, we should hit this hidden enclave with everything we have. Just break in the door and toss an EMP at anyone we see. I'll wear a lead suit or something so I don't have to miss the action," Kane said.

I grinned. "Yeah. I like the way you think." I stopped to think about it for a minute. "And you know what? It might actually work. No one would be expecting us to try that."

"Yeah," Sileon said from the front of the pod. "They'll be looking for the other Hyde faction, the ones that have actually got the paintings, to try to finish them off, so our attack won't come as much of a surprise."

I shook my head. "It will if we actually toss in an EMP. They won't be expecting that from a bunch of cyborgs."

"He's right." We all turned, because we'd grown accustomed to Emmi being silent. She stood at the very back of the pod, hand against a wall to keep herself upright as Sileon maneuvered the pod. "I'm a criminal, or at least I was built with a criminal's thoughts and memories and, as such, I think of defense in terms of how I would launch an attack, and I tend to worry about the major threats first. So yeah, they'll be fortified against cyborgs, which means big guns pointed at the door." She waved at the pod around us. "And like everything big, those guns will rely on a correctly-functioning supply of electricity. Which we can disrupt easily."

"I think they'll probably have learned by now," Jill said. "We EMP'd them last time. Hell, we've been throwing EMPs around quite a lot lately, if you also count the attack on the office building."

"I don't think those even worked. Or they were so low-yield they were pretty much meaningless," Kane said. "Oreilly was the one who gave them to us, from the team's backup stores. The more I think about this, the more I'm convinced he wanted us dead."

"I'm not." Jill glared at him. "And you won't convince me without evidence. A single look through an airlock window for less than a second isn't evidence and you know it."

"Listen people," Emmi said. "We need to decide what to do. For my part, I'm with Kane. These guys are planning a raid on the other faction, and they won't be expecting us to know where their base is. They're not prepared for us."

"Me, too," I said.

Jill glared at us.

Sileon sighed. "I would have voted for some kind of cyber-surveillance first, but there's something to be said about the element of surprise. Get ready, we're going to enter the bay in about four minutes."

"How are you going to manage that?"

"I have the door codes, of course. I've already opened the outer door, so when we get there, I'll have the outer door do an emergency close behind us and then have the inner door slam open as fast as we can. It won't be as fast as we want, and we'll have to hit the brakes pretty hard. There are going to be at least five seconds, possibly ten in which we're stuck between the doors and completely vulnerable to whatever might be pointed at them. But unless they have automated weapons set to attack everything, we should be in before they respond. If you can live with that risk, let's do this."

Everyone but Jill nodded.

"All right," I said. "How about I jump out and toss an EMP bomb at whoever is waiting? How much distance do I need to get on the thing to keep the pod and Kane safe from the effects?"

"I had the *Basilisk*'s maintenance bots add shielding to the pod. You give us ten meters and we're good. All Kane needs to do is stay inside. Just give me time to get the front viewport facing in a different direction. It's hard to get lead foil into transparent glass, and we didn't have enough time to put together a hardened canopy."

I whistled. "You don't waste time."

"I had a feeling this jaunt would involve EMP bombs. Everything we've done since you walked through my maze that day seems to involve EMPs. It's a wonder station security hasn't taken us all in for being a radiation hazard. We probably glow in the dark."

The pod had been following the curve of Cassius Station's hull at a distance of five meters, jinking and juking every couple of seconds to avoid protuberances, tensioning cables, antennae and the like. Now Sileon suddenly took us up, and then immediately dove back.

A rectangular opening in the outer skin of the station, black against the dark grey of the surface, loomed ahead. It barely had time to register before we were inside.

Instinctively, I looked back to see if the opening was sealing behind us—I knew the inner door would never open until the outer was shut—but the bulk of the pod hindered my view. All I knew was that Sileon had slammed on the brakes, because I was suddenly thrown forward. Kane's hand on my shoulder kept me from slamming into the viewport.

It was amazing how much amused contempt a guy with gears under his skin could convey with a single look.

Then we were under thrust again. The front door was open.

I braced against enemy action, but against the kind of firepower that the Hydes might have arrayed against us, the only thing I would have seen—if anything—was a flash of light... and then nothing.

No flash came. Sileon swung the pod around and I found myself propelled towards the door. I swear the thing stayed still for exactly the time it took Kane to heave me out. Sileon managed it so I landed without any forward momentum at all.

As soon as my feet were on the ground, I ran for cover, trying to find a target of any kind. Human, cyborg, weapon, my job was to take it out so the people in the pod wouldn't be sitting ducks.

I searched desperately, but I couldn't see anything.

"You're too late," a voice said.

I looked to see a thin guy with greasy black hair crouching over a computer of some kind so, with no other targets in view, I tossed the EMP in his direction.

I misjudged either my own strength or the gravity, because the metal sphere sailed over his head nearly fifteen meters and went off when it contacted a storage bin further down the landing bay.

The lights went off in a ten-meter radius around the bomb, and I was relieved to see that the man looked up from the computer in annoyance. I'd hit the target.

"Now what did you do that for?" he said. He had the kind of nasal twang to his voice that immediately made you want to hit the person behind it.

I usually refrain from hitting people who annoyed me,

but this guy had picked an immobilizer up from the table and was pointing it at me in an offhand way. I suppose he couldn't possibly miss from that range, especially considering that all the light in the bay came from behind me, leaving me beautifully silhouetted against the bright background—the EMP had taken out everything on his side.

"You should just stay where you are. These things hurt," he said.

I redoubled my pace. The guy shrugged and watched me come, then lifted his arm in an unconcerned way and pressed the button on the immobilizer.

His face as he realized I was a big guy still walking towards him, and not a twitching gibbering tangle on the floor was priceless. The fact that he said, "Hey, wait a minute," in that nasal annoyance he called a voice as I closed the last two steps made it even more satisfying when I socked him in the jaw.

Unfortunately, I only got to hit him once, because he collapsed into a ball making incomprehensible whining noises.

I grabbed him by a fistful of clothing and pulled him back to his feet. I didn't know what this guy's role was in the Hyde organization, or what he might be guilty of, but I was holding in some serious frustration and the fact that he'd tried to immobilize me made me feel justified in taking some of it, maybe a lot of it, out on him.

"We'll probably want to ask him a few questions," Sileon said, as I was winding up to hit him again.

I still hit him, but nowhere near as hard as he deserved. He looked surprised when the blow barely snapped his head back, as if asking whether that was the best I could do.

I sighed and let him go. He swayed a little, but kept his feet.

"All right," I said, "go ahead."

Leaving the whiny-voiced lackey to the tender ministrations of my friends, I headed deeper into the bay. I'd only found one guy, but who knew? The place might be teeming with other minions of the Hydes.

Not bloody likely, I thought. The guy they'd left here was obviously a low-level—and expendable—member of the organization. Probably some hood just promoted from a corridor youth gang, a manlet attempting to show the world he could run with the big boys.

Judging from the protests and occasional pained yelp coming from behind me, that didn't seem to be working out for him.

Apart from being obviously unfit for any kind of rough stuff—a superior attitude was not much use when one lacked the brain to realize the EMP you'd been hit with wasn't going to do your immobilizer any favors—there was another reason the Hydes had left Whiney here. The equipment in this bay was pretty valuable.

I grinned. Well, it would be valuable if it hadn't been fried by an EMP bomb just now. I saw some machine tools, a couple of industrial nano-manipulators and even a military-grade tactical scenario simulator. That one, at least, should have been shielded against radiation and, if nothing else, we could take it for ourselves.

So while the secret hangar under the boogie room was probably the place where the paintings were kept for hundreds of years, this was likely the spot that most of the Hydes thought was the main secret headquarters.

One thing this particular base didn't hold was more Hyde employees waiting in ambush, so I returned to the interrogation.

Whiney was immobile on the floor.

"You killed him?" I asked, looking at Kane. "I was only going to beat him up a little."

"Nah. We just tranked him. And Sileon left the cops a message which is going to go active in five minutes about how to find this base and who it belongs to. We need to leave."

I shrugged. "So we don't want to check out the rest of it?"

"According to my drone bots, you junked everything useful in here. But it's not a problem: we got what we needed. One of the other goons, one of the ones who actually went on the job, discussed the objective with this guy. Or maybe just within his hearing. That would make more sense, as he didn't strike me as the kind of guy you'd tell your plans willingly." She turned and headed back to the pod.

"Does that mean my valiant efforts to capture him didn't impress anyone?" I said.

"I think a four-year-old could have captured him," Kane said. "What kind of gangs are they even allowing on the corridors nowadays?"

"The same they always did," Emmi replied. "Kids who think they're tough, and who might be able to scare some random old man or young girl when they flash a laser cutter in their faces, but who anyone even a little hardened by life can break in a second. But for what it's worth, Deck, we were all very impressed with how easily you made him cry. Really."

I think I liked her better when she was crushed by uncertainty.

We piled back into the pod and exited through the bay doors, this time without activating any emergency protocols or rush commands.

Back in hard vacuum, Sileon guided the pod into what looked like a perfectly ordinary maintenance vector, at a slow velocity.

"Have we gone legit all of a sudden?" I asked.

"Oh, right," Emmi said. "You didn't get to hear what that

doofus back there said. We need to play this one slow and steady if we don't want to get fired on by sector defense lasers."

"Sector defense...?" I asked. "Where are we headed?"

"Up the Mountain. Sileon hacked us a way in by brute-forcing a fake work permit into the system. Now we're on the flight path she filed, and we hope no one will notice."

"My programs are working like a bitch to call attention away from the incursion," Sileon added. "I've faked all sorts of cyber-attacks, but the security over there is pretty outrageous. All this talk of an AI living in the base levels of the stations systems might be true after all. I think I can hold them long enough to get inside, but I'm not certain what might happen once they discover the ruse."

"You think they will?" I said. "I mean, doesn't the flight plan come directly from the maintenance company assigned the job?"

"Normally, it would. But when it comes to the Mountain, there's another layer of oversight and another layer of permits we need to fake, and that's where the issue might arise."

"Figures," I muttered. Uranium Mountain was where Cassius station stashed its really rich people. The name came from a combination of the module's conical shape and the fact that its inhabitants had become rich by hoarding uranium credits back in the day when those were the main form of exchange. Of course, now they'd diversified into any number of other ways of accumulating wealth... but the name had stuck.

I'd never actually been there. Most people had never actually been there. The Mountain folk were famous for automating everything. So, unlike other wealthy enclaves, you had few of the regular folk employed as maids or butlers.

And those who were allowed in had to run a gamut of extremely invasive security measures to reach their place of employment. Every single day.

"Do you think they'll just let us waltz in without searching every part of our bodies?" I said.

"Why? You hiding something in some cavity we should know about?" Kane asked.

I sneered at him. "We're carrying a bit of an arsenal. They won't appreciate it."

"I thought of that," Sileon replied. "Which is why the fake emergency we're responding to is in the sewage recycling plant. They might want to check our credentials, but they're not sending a human down to do it. And I can deal with anything else they send once I'm on the ground. Information security isn't worth a damn if the people trying to hack you have physical access to your equipment. And to all your wiring."

"So you think we'll be good?"

"We'll be good to infiltrate. What happens after that is anyone's guess, but I suspect the Mountain men will have other things to worry about once the Hydes start shooting at one another."

"And how are they planning to get in?" I said.

"The doofus back there didn't know," Emmi said. "But he made it sound like they were planning on doing something large and violent. He claims they took some heavy-duty equipment with them."

"Oh, nice. Just one more thing we'll have to contend with," I replied.

"I wouldn't worry about that yet," Sileon said. "We'll probably get fried or captured long before we even see one of the Hydes… of either band."

"Not helping," I said.

Then I sat and fidgeted as the pod made its painfully slow

way around, over and between the spinning modules of the sprawling station until a huge cone-shaped form came into view. It was different from the rest of the station in that the exterior seemed to radiate light. I realized it had been painted a brilliant shade of orange-yellow, and maintained against the harshness of space.

I wondered about that. How much money did you need to have before you began to spend it on impressive aesthetics that would only be seen by a handful of people? Especially since most inhabitants of Cassius never looked out a window—in fact, most of them both hated and feared windows, and would prefer, if given the choice, to remain at least one level deep in any structure. They never thought of Cassius as something with an inside and an outside.

Apparently, the people of Uranium Mountain, with their unlimited access to pleasure ships, thought about things in quite a different manner.

"Docking in two minutes," Sileon said. "Cross your fingers."

Once again, I found myself locked in a pod unable to do anything but await the unseen attack that would disperse us into atomic wind.

And once again either Lady Luck or Sileon's extreme competence kept us from getting blasted. The pod reached the assigned airlock and we cycled.

"Let me go first," Sileon said when Kane approached the door. "If there's violence waiting on the other side, we're already dead."

Kane shrugged and moved aside. I ached to accompany her, but I knew she'd be better off alone, getting readings through her implants and releasing those icky crawly drones into the area she was studying.

Knowing it didn't stop the waiting from being torture. If I lost her...

I stopped that thought. Did I really think Sileon would be permanent? She wasn't the type. She might give me a slice of her life, but then she'd move on. I needed to stop thinking about her like we were going to grow old together.

Thinking that, of course, didn't work either. I leaned against the edge of the door to see her standing still in a dim corridor with metal grates for floors and ceilings, and pipes for walls. Not the kind of luxury accoutrements I expected to see.

Her little bug robots must have scattered already, because I saw none of them. A single self-propelled computer module mounted on a base with tracks on it approached her.

"Please stand by for retinal scan," it said. I wondered how much intelligence the thing actually had. The Earthling was an AI, and so, if you believed Sileon, was the computer on the *Basilisk*. The fact that they were both part of the underworld was no coincidence: there were both taboos and laws against computer intelligences and simulated environments going all the way back to the days Earth's society decided to upload onto a simulated world… something that had horrified the people of Tau Ceti.

The people from the Mountain had the clout necessary to ignore the edicts… and if this machine was some kind of megagenius, even Sileon might have trouble with it.

The computer-in-tank-drag lifted an arm and scanned one of Sileon's eyes. It then beeped to itself and said: "Identity confirmed. Level four supervisor Monana Jui, welcome to the Unranium Mountain Sector. Please confirm that you have reviewed the security recommendations and the general health bulletin issued to all outside workers who come to this sector."

"Confirmed," Sileon lied. Or maybe she wasn't lying. I hadn't seen her doing anything of the sort, but maybe it was the kind of thing she liked to do in her free time. In her case, not so much to obey the commands as to find creative way of bending the laws. I couldn't say for sure, which told me everything I needed to know about whether I really knew Sileon.

"Do you need any special considerations?" the machine droned. I was pretty certain it wasn't particularly smart.

"Is my team permitted to bring our equipment out of the pod?"

"Of course. I have the manifesto for plumbing equipment, one crate, here."

Sileon waved at us, and we grabbed the only crate that had been on the pod. It had originally housed a towrope, but we'd tossed that out the airlock and replaced it with enough weaponry to start our own war, including one of the *Basilisk*'s anti-fighter weapons which Sileon had disconnected from the ship's batteries at Kane's request. Apparently, it was called a Gatling gun, and I was terrified to have it anywhere near the station's hull. But Kane insisted.

We—well, mainly Kane since I could barely budge the box, much less lift it—manhandled the oblong crate out of the door and placed it on the grating. The floor bent slightly and groaned a bit, but didn't deform all that much.

At that precise moment, every alarm on the station went off.

Lights. Sirens. A harsh voice that said the word "Emergency" over and over again. Even the bot they'd sent to check us out flickered with light.

I sighed and put my hands up. I hoped, since we hadn't actually fired the Gatling or the two handguns I had tucked into the waistband of my trousers, that the courts would be lenient with us. But I doubted it: the people of Uranium Mountain would probably take the law into their own hands and recycle the lot of us without asking questions. But at least by surrendering, we had a chance, however slim.

Sileon, on the other hand, continued the charade. "What's that?"

"Emergency in substation fourteen. Please be advised that any access to that area is currently denied," the computer told her. "Unfortunately, we have also sealed the airlock entryway. You may not leave until the emergency is over. This emergency will be over shortly. Please continue with your duties, but to not leave the permissible area."

Then, to my complete amazement, the tracked piece of idiocy trundled off at extraordinarily high speed, disappearing around a curve in the pipes. I suppose it had been summoned to help deal with the emergency.

"I think you can put your hands down," Emmi said softly. "I'm pretty sure the alarms don't apply to us, and if Kane sees you like that…"

I quickly lowered my hands and turned to nod my thanks to Emmi, who shook her head and said, still softly. "Don't mention it."

"What's the camera situation?" Kane asked, covering his mouth with his hands to avoid lip reading.

"None on us right now," Sileon reported.

"None? Have you taken them out already?"

"No," she replied. "There were never any in this place to begin with. And from what I'm getting back, coverage is quite thin from here to the end of the recycling area. People here don't seem to rely on surveillance cameras as much as the rest of us do."

I grinned. "The rich never want to be caught getting their hands dirty."

"I dunno," Kane said. "That might make sense for inside their houses or whatever. Down here? Makes zero sense."

"It might have to do with their security bots," Sileon replied.

"That tin can who didn't even check what we had in the box?" Kane asked.

"I think they might be a little more sophisticated than they let on. It was extremely well shielded, at least."

"Shielded… you mean you tried to take it over?" I asked. "If we'd gotten caught…"

"We wouldn't have been any worse off than if it had found our weapons. And besides, I only checked, I didn't make an attack. The lightest touch, a caress, just enough to see it was not a good idea to push further."

"So now what?" I asked. "I assume those alarms mean that there's something big going down. And I'd bet my ass that something big has to do with the Hydes."

Kane laughed, a rasping sound. "Too bad you're betting on the obvious. If you ever decide on a real wager, I'll take those odds and then use your ass for target practice."

Sileon peered down into her handheld and snorted. "If you boys are done with your juvenile bonding, I've programmed the pipe control computer here to start sending messages with the idea of making people think we're working on their sewage problem. That should keep them from sending anyone down here. So let's get moving."

"Do you know where this substation fourteen is?" I asked.

"Of course," Sileon replied. "This way."

To my surprise, she headed in exactly the opposite direction that the armored computer had gone.

The path she chose didn't appear to be an actual path. Instead, it was a maintenance gap between two parallel banks of pipes. The tubes, as thick as my torso, were painted in matte pastel pinks and greens and wound together to form intricate patterns that made me glad we weren't actually there to do maintenance on them. They gurgled and hissed incessantly and, every once in a while, seepage between the joints, a brown foul-smelling liquid, marred the chalky surface. I tried to avoid brushing against the pipes as much as possible, but there were times when contact proved inevitable.

When we started out, there were hundreds of pipes all around but, as we advanced, tubes radiated away from us in countless directions—up, down, left right and even bending back on themselves to disappear into the mass of piping we'd already traversed. Soon, the overwhelming number of tubes had dwindled to a handful, and we had enough space between them to walk two or ever three abreast.

As the tubes branched away, the main lines we followed became thinner as well. I guessed these were water or sewage tubes—perhaps that was what the color-coding meant—that ended at specific housing or business complexes.

We reached a final room which ended at a metal door with a glowing alarm light on it. The alarms had been sounding as we made our way through the pipe areas. Though it was kind of nice to know they weren't sounding for us, it also served as a constant reminder that we needed to hurry or we'd miss the fun. In fact, we'd likely only arrive in time to pick up the pieces, which might work out better for us: personally, I would much prefer to face a debilitated remnant of the cyborg hordes than assault them while they stood at full strength.

"Blast it," Sileon said to Kane.

"What?" I asked.

"We're right by the fighting. Blowing this door won't draw any extra attention. In fact, I'd wager the systems will just think that the battle itself blew the door down."

Kane was frugal of his ammo. Instead of emptying a gatling belt into the door, he selected a small round grenade from the box and lodged it between the handle and the door before running back to where we were huddled behind a mass of pipes.

The explosion echoed in the room, but my ears simply saw it as an adjunct to the piercing alarm noises already filling the air.

But even after the door had been blown halfway across the corridor outside, the banging didn't stop. I tapped on my ears with my hand, but my hearing seemed all right, which made me realize the noise came from outside.

"We should check out the situation," I said, heading for the door.

"Don't be an idiot," Kane said as he brushed past. "I'll do it. You're way too fragile for that."

He peeked out of the opening, barely showing his head and then dived aside as a barrage from some energy weapon slammed into the room, burning a hole in the rubberized flooring.

Kane grinned up at me. "This is going to be fun."

CHAPTER 39

The first few moments weren't fun at all, however.

Apparently alarmed by the fact that a door had blown into the middle of a corridor, the combatants had decided to attack us with everything they had. Needle-gun projectiles pinged against the walls. More energy beams crackled the floor. And I thought at least one bullet from an archaic gun slammed into a pipe, which began to spew water—fortunately clean—that pooled on the floor.

"They're firing at us from more than one direction," Kane said as he pressed against the wall beside me. "I'd say three different shooters. And I'd also say different kinds of weapons from each angle."

"You think they're the different groups? The two Hydes and security?"

"Probably. And security are the guys shooting the needle guns. You don't knowingly walk into a fight against cyborgs with a needle gun. That's a good way to get killed."

"So what do we do now?"

"First thing," Kane said as he opened the ammo box and pulled out his gatling cannon, which he supported on one shoulder with a strap while he grabbed the ammo belt in another hand, "is to get out of this room, which means we need to clear a path." He patted the black metal of the barrel. "I've always wanted to try one of these things out."

Before I could react, he launched himself out the doorway and opened fire. I couldn't see what he was shooting at, but I thought it was significant that the return fire stopped immediately. And the humming and roar of his own rig made a noise that made everything else I'd heard since the alarms started going off seem like a gentle whisper. Now, instead of being relieved that I hadn't gone deaf, I was cursing my bad luck.

"Come on!" Kane shouted. "I can only hold them a little while."

I dove through the entryway, an EMP bomb in one hand, and took cover beside a structure. "Which way?" I said.

"Over there!" Kane replied as Sileon, Jill and Emmi poured out of the entrance.

Following his gesture—I couldn't hear anything over the sound of his gun—I lobbed the EMP as far as I could throw it. As soon as I saw the light go out in a wide area around the detonation, I followed after it.

No one shot me, and I turned to see Kane and the women following along.

I burst through a door that had been torn to pieces by needle fire and bullets to find several cyborgs twitching on the ground. One of them was the twin to the woman I'd seen in the office. Maybe she was the woman I'd seen in the office, but it had gotten to the point where I didn't know who anyone was anymore. All I knew was that none of the bodies here belonged to Rime or Oreilly.

"Hold the door," Jill told Kane. Then she ran through an exit in the back wall.

Better her than me. That was a good way to get killed.

I studied the Hydes on the floor, and my self-congratulatory mood lifted. The cyborgs hadn't been incapacitated by my well-thrown EMP. These boys had been shot nearly to pieces before we arrived. One of them had his neck hanging by wires. Another had been cut nearly in half by some kind of energy bolt. The other three were riddled with bullet and bolt holes.

All my EMP had done was to turn off the electronic systems that kept their biological bodies alive when they took serious damage. Essentially, I'd switched off life support for a bunch of helpless people.

I shrugged. If I had to be a murderer, I preferred to do it to these guys. At least they deserved it.

Jill burst back in, and I almost shot her. She didn't look like she would have cared.

"They're not here," she shouted.

"The paintings?" Sileon asked.

Jill nodded. "Yeah. I'm sure they were in the room back there, but they're gone now. I even found this." She thrust a piece of brown cloth into my face.

"What's that?" I said.

"Canvas!" she yelled.

"So?"

"You imbecile. Didn't you read the files I gave you? These paintings are painted on cloth like this."

"Oh, yeah," I replied. "I remember that. I thought it was weird to paint on cloth."

"They didn't have anything better. Well, some of the paintings were on wood."

"Wood?" I said.

Kane interrupted. "Are you guys really arguing about that now? I only ask because there's a bunch of guys in security uniforms coming this way with needle guns. One of them hit me in the head."

He was telling the truth. A tiny silver flechette protruded from between his eyes, just above the bridge of his nose.

"Oh suck it up, you big baby," Jill replied. "You know you're armored."

"Still hurts though. Is anyone going to do anything about these guys?"

"Can't you shoot them?" I asked, as I approached with another EMP in my hand. The bomb wouldn't do much to the security troops themselves, but I suspected it would throw their needlers for a loop.

"Nah. They're hiding behind a bulkhead over there. Try to zap them, but don't leave the bomb short or you'll take me out."

I threw the EMP a good distance down the hall, and was delighted when the lights over the enemy position flashed out. "I hope they don't send me the repair bill for all the electronics we've fried," I said. If we got caught, there would be a ton to answer for, but at least we hadn't actually attacked them with anything lethal.

Jill and Sileon had their heads together over one of Sileon's screens. "What now?" I asked.

I was growing tired of being nothing but muscle so I walked over to see what they were cooking up. Knowing the security types, it would take them a few minutes to get themselves reorganized… and if Jill was right and the paintings were gone, then Oreilly and Rime were headed away from us at full speed.

"Dammit," I said to myself. I was suddenly tired. Ever since I'd gone into Rime's pawn shop that day, I'd been playing catch-up and never quite catching up. I just wanted to go home and let the Hydes and Oreillys and the security goons carve each other into little pieces without my help.

"Yeah, that should work," Jill said, as I reached them. "Kane! We're leaving."

"Good," the cyborg shouted back. "Because the cops are sending over one of those robot computer things. Except this one has a huge gun barrel on the front."

"We should EMP it to cover our retreat."

"I doubt that would be much help," Kane replied. "I think it was already in there with them, and it doesn't seem to have suffered much damage from the first bomb we tossed."

We retreated into the door Jill had run through to find ourselves in a loft with high ceilings, and a floor spattered with paint.

Large windows looked out over a corridor behind the habitation block we were in, which was a first. I'd seen plenty of screen window-simulations, and I'd even visited a few of the viewing areas on Cassius Station that allowed one to look out into space through thick hullcrete. But a window just looking out into a corridor? A glass window just to look at people passing by?

Obviously, money had made the people of Uranium Mountain go soft in the head.

On closer observation, I realized that the right-hand window had been broken open, and that it swung on a latch. A rope, connected to a nearby beam, hung out the window.

"Don't bother," Jill said as I approached. "They're long gone."

"Story of my fucking life," I growled.

Sileon looked up at me and smiled. "Relax. We'll get them."

"How?"

"They're going around. We're going up." The walls were lined with open-faced shelving. I looked where Sileon pointed to see a white square in the roof. "There's a way across, and we can beat them to their ship. And we won't have to shoot our way through every security guy on the Mountain."

I nodded and began to climb the shelves. A quick couple of bumps on the white square opened it up, and I found myself in another storage place, a loft. When Sileon arrived, I raised an eyebrow at her.

"Wait a minute," she said.

Kane's artillery piece roared and the guy's head appeared through the opening a moment later. For such a big dude, the cyborg could really scoot. We closed the opening behind him.

I looked around the room, an irregular space that actually

seemed shorter on one end than the other, which was illuminated only by a light in Emmi's hand. I didn't see any ways out, no windows, no doors, and no trapdoors in the ceiling.

"Can you break a hole in this wall?" Sileon asked Kane, her finger on what looked like a lightweight partition.

Kane pressed his hand against it. "I think so."

"Please do."

Kane put the gun down. His muscles bunched before he delivered a blow. No mere human sinews would have been capable of what came next: the panel bent inward and collapsed in a shower of dust.

Behind the wall was a service area. Pipes and cable occupied most of the space, but there was room enough for a person to squeeze in… and better still, there were rungs of an access stair. I followed Sileon through, and we began to climb.

After what must have been six or seven stories, just as my arms and legs were beginning to feel the strain, the little tunnel brought us exactly where I expected: a maintenance work platform, a little area painted light grey with a single workstation screen and a seat for an operator. It was unoccupied, so we kept climbing.

"Don't these people believe in elevators?" I said.

"Not for the menials, they don't," Sileon replied.

So we climbed and climbed… and climbed. Fortunately, after a few minutes, I felt the gravity cutting down. Moments after that, I could actually jump and sail past several rungs in a single movement. Within minutes, that became several levels.

"How did you find this shaft?" I called to Sileon. "This is almost too good to be true."

"Yeah. Actually, it is too good to be true. This only goes as far as Uranium Mountain's central rotation point. From there, we need to go down regular stairs. That's going to cost us some time."

She was right. The maintenance shaft ended at a control station where an actual human employee glanced up from a dirty holovid to watch our entrance without interest.

"We're the team doing the sewage cleanup," I explained.

She shrugged and turned her eyes back to the images flickering in the air in front of her.

I studied the holo for a moment and found it blurry. I hoped for her sake she had implants to see it in better quality than I did.

Since the room existed in zero-gee, it was spherical, with screens and workstations on every available surface and a large empty space in the center. Sileon grabbed a random screen and called up a map of Uranium Mountain. She pointed to a circular door. "That way."

We piled through another door and, as promised, found stairs leading down. Stairs were not an ideal solution for microgravity areas—and these had probably simply been reused after serving somewhere else—and we needed to use the handrails for the first few floors.

As we went lower, the tug of spin acceleration offered relief and we were able to move more confidently.

"We're going to a docking bay on level fifty," Sileon shouted.

I looked at the next sign. Level seventy-five. The Hydes had a head start. We wouldn't catch them.

I redoubled my speed, panting with the effort and taking the stairs several steps at a time, which I felt in my knees.

"This is stupid," I wheezed. "By the time we get there, they'll be gone and we'll have to chase them again and again, always arriving a couple of steps behind. It will go on forever."

By now, the gravity had returned nearly to normal and

Kane, much heavier than we were, and apparently bogged down by the massive artillery piece he was still lugging around, trailed several flights behind us, jangling his way down.

I wasn't in the mood to wait. If we ran into any cyborgs I'd just EMP the lot of them.

"This is the floor," Sileon said.

Again we all filed through a door, and I felt myself stuck in the endless nightmare.

This door opened onto a wide corridor floored in translucent blue tiles that appeared to glow from within, turning the entire space into a wondrous, semi-twilit world. Shapes moved on the walls, the animation imitating living creatures emerging from deep in the structure to peer at us as we passed.

"There!" Sileon said, pointing to another door. I sighed.

We emerged onto a loading platform where a single small shuttle lay smoking, its hull scarred.

Five people—four cyborgs and Rime—were busy loading a crate onto the shuttle. The crate disappeared into the loading bay as I entered the area.

"Oh, no you don't!" I said as the shuttle's personnel ramp descended towards the floor. If they got onto that, my nightmare of the eternal chase would come true. I tossed my last EMP bomb at them.

All four of the people by the ramp collapsed. The ramp stopped moving. The lights on the shuttle turned themselves off.

"That was our only way off the Mountain," Sileon remarked. "Do you know how hard it's going to be to fly that thing manually? It's not a pod, you know."

"That's the least of our problems," I replied.

The cyborgs were getting up from the floor. Rime glared at me. Even if her eyes hadn't glowed with fierce red light,

I would have known she was furious. On another, very different, occasion, that same expression had been the precursor to her breaking my nose.

Jill was the first to react. She pulled an energy weapon from her belt and trained it on one of the cyborgs, removing its head from its shoulders cleanly. I stared at the gun: Sileon's armory evidently held stuff that the thugs on Cassius Station would kill for. I'd never seen a beamer quite that powerful.

The rest of the Hydes scattered, two taking cover behind the shuttle skids while Rime and the final cyborg ducked under the half-descended ramp.

And then they started shooting at us.

Over the course of the past day, I'd grown accustomed to people unable to shoot when we EMP'd them. But I'd forgotten that these guys carried old pre-electronic weaponry.

I didn't dive for cover, and the first bullet nearly took my head off. I actually heard it whizz by my ear lodge itself in the wall behind me.

I hit the deck, but I was still out in the open.

Frozen, I watched Rime take careful aim, let out her breath and just when I thought my life depended on her missing, a door in the far side of the hangar burst open to reveal a group of men in blue uniforms and one of the tracked computers, who opened up on the cyborgs and the shuttle with a barrage of needle-gun fire.

I doubted they could do much more than annoy our opponents with that kind of weaponry, but their sudden appearance caused Rime to lose her concentration just enough that another bullet buried itself in the wall behind me. She didn't miss by much.

Jill, meanwhile, had adopted a shooter's stance and blown away the knee of the cyborg behind the ramp, the only part visible. He staggered into the open, trying to remain upright hopping on one mechanical leg and was immediately hit by a cloud of needle gun flechettes.

They probably didn't kill him or damage him too badly, but with the missing leg, the cyborg was overbalanced. He went down.

Sileon and Emmi used their own beam weapons to pin down the two cyborgs behind the skid. One of them peered out to see where we were and Emmi got him with a glancing shot to the side of the head. He wasn't dead—I could see him moving around back there—but even a cyborg couldn't have enjoyed that.

Rime had turned her attention to the uniformed goons.

"Give me another EMP!" I shouted at Sileon, who'd taken cover behind a crate. I joined her and kept my head down, as we'd started to attract our share of the flechettes. "I'll knock them out again and we can shoot them before they recover."

"Uh-oh," Sileon said. She was looking at the ramp.

Oreilly—I suppose he'd been in the shuttle the whole time—jumped from the ramp, holding a gun that made Kane's gatling look like a child's plaything.

Just seeing him lift it, I knew he was a cyborg—and a strong version of the breed. But I didn't even need to think about that to know the man was not a baseline human: the gun was wired into him. So much for Oreilly being unmodified.

He turned the gun towards the Security people and opened up. I wasn't an expert, but the rate of fire seemed lower than that of the gatling.

Unfortunately, the power of each round was better. I saw one security guy actually get punched all the way through and pushed backward by a single round… before falling dead four feet back from where he'd been with a hole the size of my fist completely traversing his thorax.

Even more spectacular was how the robot on tracks actually exploded when it got hit. Dark smoke roiled upward, an acrid cloud that made my eyes water when it reached us. The smell of ozone filled the air.

Kane chose that exact moment to burst through the door.

Oreilly didn't even stop to think. He turned and opened on his old compatriot even before the cyborg on our team could bring his gatling to bear.

Kane jerked like a puppet, and I saw each individual round tear through him, pushing him back, back, back… before he finally fell over with a loud crash.

Oreilly stopped shooting, looking at what he'd done, and for a moment, silence reigned, broken only by the ringing of my battered ears. Kane seeped blood and oil and God knew what else onto the blue floor of the loading bay.

"No!" Jill screamed. She ran towards the fallen cyborg.

Oreilly trained his gun on her…

…and hesitated just long enough that I was able to lob the EMP in his direction.

When it went off, Sileon and Emmi sprang into action. They sprinted towards the remaining cyborgs as they tried to reset their systems or whatever it was that they'd done to recover so quickly from the last EMP. I followed a couple of beats later.

I wasn't watching them, though. I was watching Orielly. I expected him to keel over and twitch, or something along those lines. Instead, he turned to track Sileon's progress.

I was moving before I had time to think about it. I veered off course and slammed my shoulder into Oreilly's arm.

It was like crashing into a steel bulkhead. I barely moved him enough to throw his aim off and allow Sileon and Emmi to incapacitate the cyborgs. I couldn't see what they did to them, but knowing those two, it was probably efficient and final. I'd have bet on a close-quarters shot to the head for each of the prone victims. The ladies on my team weren't an emotional pair.

My maneuver might have been rash and undercooked, but it had allowed me to get inside of Oreilly's range of fire. I was closer to him than the muzzle of his cannon, so he couldn't shoot me... and if he wanted to get rid of me, he would need to release the gun.

This, he appeared disinclined to do. He turned around and send another barrage into the security team, who'd thought to use the distraction I'd created to sneak up on him. At least three of them paid for their optimism with their lives.

For my part, I pulled one of the guns out of my waistband and tried to bring it to bear on Oreilly, but he saw the movement and finally released his cannon to grab my wrist, his hand moving faster than I could see. He pressed on my wrist and I felt bones snap.

"Sileon," I shouted, trying to ignore the searing pain. "Grab Jill and get the hell out of here!"

"I'm not leaving you behind!" she replied.

I screamed as Oreilly ground my bones together.

"You won't make it before he kills me. Go!"

Sileon shot him in the back with her energy weapon. It didn't seem to affect Oreilly much, but he turned and held me in front of him, grabbing me by the shoulder now: a human shield too weak to resist. Tears of pain ran down my cheek as his movements jerked me one way and the other. "Just go. There's nothing you can do. Go!"

Sileon took another shot, aiming at Oreilly's legs to avoid hitting me.

But that just made Oreilly jerk around to dodge. Which made me scream.

"Just go," I yelled, trying to get the words out through gritted teeth.

By this time, Emmi had managed to climb onto the ramp and was pulling Jill up after her.

"Go!" I shouted again.

Sileon tried to aim as Oreilly moved me around like a rag doll and scattered randomly fired bullets in her general direction.

"Get moving. He'll hit you eventually, and then he'll just kill me anyway," I said.

Sileon screamed in frustration. She covered her own retreat by shooting at his legs and jumped up the ramp. She helped push Jill up the incline and then I saw the door close behind her.

I waited for the shuttle to lift off, or for Oreilly to end my suffering by snapping my neck, but instead, I felt a burning fire in my legs. I looked down to see everything under my knees ripped up by dozens of flechettes. The security guys had temporarily overcome their fear of Oreilly's gun and shot the hell out of me. For a moment, I watched, mesmerized, as blood soaked my trousers and oozed onto the floor. I wasn't going to last long at the rate I was bleeding out.

Sileon must have seen the same thing because the shuttle's engines suddenly went on. She must have been flying manually again. I sighed with relief.

Oreilly misunderstood. "Does it hurt, little man?" he said.

I grimaced and whimpered and reached down towards my legs. He laughed and shook me cruelly.

My arms flailed around as if I'd lost control of them.

In one of the wild movements, I used my good hand to grab the second gun in my waistband and, before Oreilly could react, I whipped the gun around and shot him in the left eye.

The rest of his face expressed extreme surprise, but he didn't collapse immediately. Instead, he tried to speak. He managed half a laugh before the sound stretched out, as if he was playing a laugh at half speed.

The hand holding me dropped me onto the ground. I tried to land on my feet, but my legs weren't responding and I collapsed in a heap. Something was wrong. I looked down and remembered I'd been pierced by dozens of tiny needles. Weird. I didn't feel much pain, just numbness. I decided to crawl away from Oreilly, so I dropped the gun and tried to pull myself along with my hands.

I screamed. Now I felt pain. Whatever was wrong with my legs hadn't extended to my crushed wrist. That still hurt.

So, instead of crawling, I settled for glaring at Oreilly and trying to will his head to explode. It had worked for the cyborg at the bar, hadn't it? I seemed to remember it had worked, but I wasn't sure. Hell, I couldn't remember why I'd even gone to a bar in the first place. Had I been thirsty? But why did I go alone to a spot that wasn't my typical watering hole.

Oreilly was moving all wrong. He staggered in one direction and the other. There was something not right about that. Oh, yeah. I'd shot him in the eye. He should have been dead. Kane was wrong. Oreilly had gotten all the modifications done. He wasn't just sleeping through time.

Something about Kane made me sad, but I didn't know what it was.

Then Oreilly started moving even more erratically. His arm disappeared, and he pirouetted like a dancer, and ended up facing the wrong way. A flash of light made me close my eyes, and when I blinked them open, there was a hole in the wall behind Oreilly.

Heavy artillery, I thought, but I didn't really know what it meant.

Oreilly seemed to know. He was heading for a door. Unfortunately for him, there was another flash of light and a good chunk of his left side vanished. He fell to the ground and began to crawl, but three more flashes in quick succession stopped him. He lay there, burning and smoldering, a charred husk.

Suddenly alarmed without knowing why, I turned my head to look for the shuttle.

It was gone, and the outer bay door was slowly sealing itself. I smiled and turned onto my back. The world hurt less in that position.

I heard voices and, after a few moments a face appeared above me. The man was dressed in a blue uniform with a patch on the shoulder that said secu… secur… secu-something. I would read it later.

I smiled at him. "Hello."

"Don't move," he said, pointing something at me.

I smiled some more. "I wouldn't dream of it," I replied.

Then, to show him I was sincere, I must have passed out, because darkness overcame me.

CHAPTER 40

The bastards didn't even bother to fix me up all the way. They just patched me together enough to sit in at their kangaroo court. So I sat, and I was in pain. My mood was less than genial, too.

"I demand to be taken back to Cassius Station," I said.

"You are on Cassius Station," the judge replied. She was a prim woman dressed in black and white whose thin slash of a mouth looked like it had never smiled. Her hair was tied back in a tight do that stretched the skin of her forehead. If she'd attempted to look as unappealing as possible, she couldn't have done a better job... and I was the kind who gave every woman the benefit of the doubt.

The courtroom—I assume that is what it was, although it could have been a classroom or a very small theater—appeared to have been built completely out of brown glass, lit from within like the corridor that led to the bay. The effect was stunning, but I wasn't there for the effects.

"I mean the regular part of Cassius Station. I don't mean to offend, but you people of Uranium Mountain can't try me. I'm a citizen of the station, and I'm entitled to trial by the civilian authorities of the Station."

"Normally, that would be the case," the woman said in a monotone which was even less sexy than her clothes, "but Uranium Mountain has a special agreement with the station for crimes committed here. It's quite a complicated document, but, to summarize, we can do what we want with people who annoy us on our turf. And the three of you certainly qualify."

Rime and one other cyborg were with me in the room. To judge by their pained expressions, they'd gotten the same basic treatment that I did: just enough to make them capable of sitting trial. That didn't bode well for our chances of not getting spaced as a result of our actions.

I was actually surprised by their presence. Either those Hyde cyborg bodies were a lot tougher than I thought, or Sileon and Emmi had been too busy to ensure they were dead. Although Rime was completely bald, which seemed to indicate someone had hit her in the head with an energy blast.

"So you'll kill us," I said.

Rime glared at me, but neither she nor the other cyborg seemed inclined to speak. The other guy didn't look too good... he wobbled so unsteadily that I thought maybe he couldn't speak.

The woman raised an eyebrow. "We will judge each of you according to your merits. Do you think you should share a fate with the other defendants?"

"What?" I said. "Of course not. They're criminals and racketeers involved in a gang war. I was working to make them return stolen goods."

"Excellent. Then shut up and let me proceed." She stared around the room. "The first order of business is to clear up the question of Istiana Hyde-Nuñez and Iortus Gurd." She looked over to the Hydes in attendance. It took me a second to remember that Istiana was Rime's real name and I assumed the Iortus guy must be Rime's goon. "Are you present in this room?"

The Hydes remained silent.

"It makes no difference. For the sake of expediency, we'll assume those are in fact your names, but whether they are or not makes no difference. You will be judged for the things you did, regardless of ultimate identity. Do you understand?"

The two accused said nothing.

"All right," the woman continued. "You're guilty of the following crimes: destruction of property, vandalism, resisting arrest. Those charges will be ignored in this hearing, as will the list of minor infractions and contraventions you accumulated both singly and in coordinated action. We'll be focusing on two specific charges: murder of security forces and firing of projectile weapons of a size and power sufficient to represent a danger to the station itself."

I knew that firing those weapons was a death sentence, so I wondered why they even bothered to judge them separately. There was really no need for any more discussion.

"We have evidence of all kinds to prove you actually did these things—from video feeds to direct testimony of dozens of witnesses—and the only evidence we still require is your own testimony. Do you deny having done any of this?"

Rime's goon looked like he wanted to speak. He even started to try, but a string of drool from the side of his mouth was all he managed. Rime just glared at the judge.

"Very well. In light of this, I sentence you to death and recycling," the woman said. She didn't look like it affected her very much.

Rime sneered at her and laughed. "That won't hold up once my lawyers get through with you. In fact, this farce is such a miscarriage of justice that I doubt you'll even get me to serve any time. You'll never have an opportunity to carry out the sentence."

"I think you don't understand your position," the judge said.

"I don't need to understand my position. I just need to hit the appeal button and all this…" she waved to the court. "Goes away. Poof. So I hope you enjoyed your little bit of theater."

The woman sighed. "Perhaps you might be right under other circumstances, but I've judged that the sentence should be carried out immediately. So if there is any appeal, it will be of mainly academic interest, or perhaps of some monetary value to any heirs you might have."

Two men in security-blue armored suits that looked like they could withstand an attack from a naval cruiser's battery—apparently the cops had learned their lesson about cyborgs—stepped up to each of the defendants and grasped their arms.

"What?" Rime said. "No! This isn't how the law works. You're going to get into big trouble. My people will—"

I never got to hear what her people would do because the door hissed shut behind them.

"Are you actually going to recycle them today?" I asked.

"Not just today," the woman replied. "But in less than a minute. There's a recycling facility on the other side of that door, which is why we held this trial in the meeting room of the sanitation department."

I swallowed. That didn't bode well. Then I grinned. "At least Rime is going to get what's coming to her for breaking my nose," I said.

"Aren't you worried about what's coming to you?" the judge asked.

I sighed. "I think I know what's coming. Except for killing your security guys, which I didn't do, I suppose you could make the case that I'm guilty of everything you just said about those two... so..."

"You won't argue that your situation is different?"

"I..." I chuckled. "I hope you won't get offended, but you don't look like the kind of judge that will look into the nuances of a case when the actual facts and legal side of it are clear. I'm as good as recycled."

"You don't sound too upset."

"It's probably the meds. If I was sane, I'd be screaming bloody murder."

The judged looked up from her notes. "Then, since you understand the charges, do you want to establish a defense?" The lights dimmed for a few seconds, and she raised her eyebrow. We both knew that the energy drain marked the end of Rime and her goon. Good recycling machines were power hogs.

I shrugged. "I want the record to show that my only actions were in aid of law enforcement. Perhaps not Cassius Station law enforcement in the traditional sense, but real law enforcement nonetheless. You could say I was acting in a role as a deputy."

"Unfortunately, that argument ceases to have validity as soon as you fire an unauthorized weapon. I can't accept the argument," she said.

"Then, I guess it was nice knowing you," I replied.

I'd lied to her. The meds were doing nothing. My entire being wanted to scream, to rage, to damn her to hell. But I'd seen Rime's exit and, though no one would see it but the judge and the cops in their suits, I preferred—if nothing else could be done—to go out with dignity.

It would make a nice change from the way I'd lived.

"I find you guilty of firing a dangerous and unauthorized projectile weapon. As you know, the penalty for this is immediate death by recycling." She held my gaze. "And we need to make sure that happens. However..." she let the word hang in the air, "I judge that it's true you were driven by good intentions and, even though we've been unable to locate your accomplices and whatever it was the whole battle was about, we have checked the bonafides of the one named Jill Oreilly and have found that she was, in the loosest sense of the word, a police officer. I judge that is a mitigating circumstance.

"A second mitigating circumstance is that you were able, through your actions, to neutralize a clear and present threat to the station and that, in fact, your use of the projectile weapon was in aid of this objective. By shooting the cyborg known as David Oreilly, you likely saved several lives.

"Finally, I judge your particular skillset and psychological profile to be of possible use to society. Or at least to that part of society which Uranium Mountain represents. That's not a mitigating factor, but one which does color my judgement."

I scratched my head, trying to keep the hope from being too obvious in my voice. "Does that mean you're not going to kill me and offer me a job?"

"We're going to kill you," she replied.

"Damn."

"But we're also going to offer you a job." I swear, had she been capable of it, she would have smiled right then.

"Huh?"

"The bargain we're offering is the following: the body you currently inhabit will be recycled immediately. It's quite damaged anyway, so you probably won't want it. Your mind and memories, on the other hand, will be uploaded to computer storage, and will be called up to serve whenever we encounter a crisis that demands your particular skills. The term of that service will be of two physical years."

"So I'll be a program on a computer? Doesn't sound like much of a life."

"Dormant. You will only be awakened for specific periods of action," she said. "Your mind will be downloaded into a suitable body for the duration of the assignment, and then you'll be replaced in the computer and the body will be recycled. Your term will be over once the two years of service—actual physical service—are ended."

"And then you'll erase me?"

"Of course not. We're not monsters. At the end of that period, you will be allowed to remain in the latest body printed and receive two years back pay. From that moment on, you'll be permitted to live your life as you see fit."

"Wow. That wasn't what I was expecting."

"You have five minutes to decide whether to accept the terms of clemency."

"And if I refuse?" I was afraid I already knew the answer.

"Then we just recycle you. That part of the verdict isn't up to you."

Yep. That's the answer I was expecting. "Not much of a choice, then. I accept."

"Good. I've noted your decision in the records, and the verdict will now be carried out."

Two guards flanked me and, for a moment, I panicked, thinking they'd just toss me in the recycler and forget to copy my mind first. But then a dark helmet descended onto my head. I felt tiny pricks all along my scalp and a sudden vibrating pulse which made my eyes go blurry.

That's as far as I remember. If they recycled me, if I was conscious for it, if I maintained my dignity, I have no way of knowing.

Things went black.

EPILOGUE

The light was too bright. I blinked against it and raised my arm to shut it off.

Then I remembered.

"Is it time for me to work already?" I asked. "You could have let me sleep a little."

Two arms closed around me and a face, wet with tears, pressed against my own.

"What?" I asked.

I finally managed to keep my eyes open to see Sileon looking down at me.

"How much do you remember?" she said.

"As far as the courtroom," I replied. "They were going to recycle me."

"They did. The bastards killed you before I could even get the rescue organized. No due process, no time to gather evidence. Not even two days passed and you were gone. I was going to nuke the entire module from orbit, but luckily I decided to watch the tape of the hearing first. If I hadn't done that, you'd really be dead."

"I'm not? And this isn't some kind of simulation?" I tried to move my fingers, but all I got was a bit of flopping from my wrist. I hoped I was just woozy from whatever process they'd done to me, because I definitely didn't have any fine motor skills.

"No. You're not. On the video I saw that the court used a Corrion upload scanner to get the data out of your head."

"A what?" I asked.

"Something very illegal that rich people use to make backup copies of their minds and memories in case they blow themselves up racing asteroid buggies or something. It's state of the art and can handle brains much larger than yours."

"Ouch."

"That's not what I meant. I mean that some people augment their memories with artificial implants, and the equipment can handle those as well."

"And then…"

She laughed, a genuine, delighted sound. "Can you believe the idiots uploaded you onto a public database behind nothing but standard encryption and firewalls? I got you out of there in five minutes, especially because The Earthling is also nearly back to power. I was able to help her out in exchange for amnesty for everyone except for Emmi. I didn't dare tell her that Emmi was still alive. Took me a couple of days to get the body printer programmed however. So you've lost those days… but you'll find that this body is a bit younger than the one you had, so you can make up for it."

"I'm in a printed body?"

"Yep. Brand new. The old one was a mess. You got pretty torn up in the fight."

"Can I see?" I said.

"Of course."

I tried to sit up in bed, but felt dizzy. Sileon had to help me. I sat on the edge of the bed and looked around. I was in the infirmary on the *Basilisk*. The last person to use this particular bed had been… "What about Kane?" I asked.

Sileon shook her head. "He was dead before we left."

"And Jill?"

"She took it hard. But once you can move around a bit, I think we can go talk to her. I'm expecting to receive a delivery."

When my feet touched the floor of the infirmary, I felt as if my feet were cold, then hot and then cold again. Shivers coursed up and down my body and pins and needles came and went.

"You'll get used to everything," Sileon said. "It takes a day or two to settle into a brand-new body. Remember the nerves have never felt anything like what you're feeling now. Hell, they've never felt anything at all."

A head-to-foot mirror coalesced from the smart floor and I studied my face. Clean-shaven. Short-haired without any of the encroaching grey, and yet recognizably the same face I'd had when the Mountain people had recycled me. "I see you broke my nose for me again," I said with a chuckle.

"I liked it that way," Sileon replied.

"Any other changes?"

"I told you. You'll live longer. I upgraded your DNA for longevity. You won't need a new body for a long time."

"I never thought I'd get a new body at all," I noted. "I wasn't in that financial league."

"Well, you don't need to worry about it anymore." She indicated a couple of garments on a chair. "I grabbed some clothes for you if you're up to walking."

"What's the hurry? Let me get used to my new body."

I turned around to admire my back, which looked a little younger than before, just like the rest of it, and when I turned to face the mirror, Sileon gave me a kiss. "Come on, get dressed. I want to show you something."

I studied her. This wasn't like Sileon at all. Oh, I was certain there was something she wanted me to see, but there was something else.

Then it hit me. "Are you sure you didn't make any other changes?" I asked.

She snapped and the mirror melted back into the floor. "Unless you get dressed now, you'll never find out," she replied.

But I got to witness something I never thought possible. I got to see Sileon blush.

That was worth waiting for.

I pulled the clothes on quickly. And I realized that, changes or not—and I definitely wanted to see what Sileon didn't want me to notice right then—the body felt right. I was still me.

"Can you walk? Do you need to lean on me?" Sileon said.

"What's the hurry? I'm dressed now."

"I know, but I really do want to show you something special."

"Where is it?"

"First we need to go get Jill."

"Hmm. I don't think this will be what I imagined," I said.

"That's because men only think about one thing."

"Hey," I replied with a smile, "I wasn't the one who gave me a bigger—"

"Will you come on?" she asked, tugging at my arm, which made my shoulder send all kinds of weird signals to my head.

We found Jill sitting in a darkened lounge with a window that looked out onto the stars, staring into space.

"Jill," Sileon whispered.

"Come in," Jill replied. "I won't break." She looked me up and down. "I see you're breathing again." She gave me a quick smile.

I returned it. "They say I'm me, anyway. I'm new to this whole out-of-body experience thing." Then I surprised myself by kneeling next to her and giving her a hug. "I'm sorry about Kane."

"Thanks. He wasn't as big an asshole as he pretended to be," she said.

"I know," I replied. "But I don't know if I can forgive him for getting killed just as I was beginning to like him."

"He was annoying that way," she replied, the faintest hint of a sad smile. "And I'm going to miss him forever."

"I know. But I think Sileon has a surprise she wants you to see."

Jill shrugged and stood. "I was never much good at moping. I tried, too."

We walked the halls of the *Basilisk*. I'd gotten kind of turned around, what with the getting killed and rebodied and everything, but I thought we were heading generally rearward. Sileon was nearly bouncing with excitement when we reached a door in a service area.

The door hissed open to reveal a hangar bay.

Emmi stood inside, but the thing that called my attention was the shuttle I could see through the airlock window, docked outside. Too big to put into the *Basilisk*, it was clearly recognizable as the one the Hydes had been loading when we hit them in Uranium Mountain.

Jill leaped forward. "It's back? They're back?"

Sileon nodded. "They just got in today. I had to shoot a couple of drones off its tail with the *Basilisk*'s cannons, but it lost the rest of the pursuers. It's leaving now."

As I watched, the shuttle disconnected from the *Basilisk* and drifted off into space, probably to serve as a decoy to yet another batch of pursuers. I admit I goggled a bit. It must be nice to have so much money that you can simply allow an expensive space-faring shuttle to leave when you could have kept the thing.

"But the paintings…"

"Look down," Emmi said.

Jill did. We all did.

Emmi had laid a number of paintings on the ground, and tossed discarded packing material to one side. I'd been so absorbed watching the shuttle and wondering about it that I'd completely missed them.

"Is that…" Jill said, before she rushed over to peer at a large painting of a boat.

I recognized it from my hours of study: The Storm on the Sea of Galilee, by a man named Rembrandt. I remembered that he had another painting in the cache. There. A painting of a couple wearing black.

My own attention was drawn to another picture, of another figure wearing black. This one, unless I was getting them muddled, was by a man called Manet, and it had always surprised me. It was later than the two Rembrandts and another pair of paintings—a landscape and another interior scene—yet it seemed to me to have been painted in a much less polished style, almost as if painters' ability to depict the world around them had regressed, and their pictures became less recognizable as actual objects.

I just looked at it and said nothing, however. Earlier, when I'd been studying for the ill-fated raid on the office, I'd mentioned this discrepancy to Jill, and she'd laughed and said I should probably never try to make my living as an art critic.

As I looked, however, something strange happened. I began to enjoy the picture, I found myself following the contours of the objects, mesmerized in trying to understand where one figure ended and another began. Before long, I realized that the paint was far from being a flat surface—as it did appear to be on the Rembrandt nearest me—but was actually a composed of subtle ridges and valleys. Looking at this piece in real life was a much different experience from viewing it on a screen.

For an instant, I thought I understood what Jill meant when she said her dream was to see the art displayed, just once.

But my interest couldn't compare to Jill's rapture. She'd hopped over the outermost pieces, careful to avoid stepping on anything, particularly the fragile drawings, and stood in the center of the array Emmi had provided.

There, she spun slowly, slowly around, gazing at each picture before moving on. All traces of grief had fallen from her face, replaced by a profound expression of awed wonder.

I had to smile.

"I don't think she's going to want to give them back," I told Sileon.

"Don't be an ass, Deck," Jill said, proof that her trance was not as deep as I'd suspected. "These paintings don't belong to me. I wish I could return them to the museum they were stolen from, but that disappeared when Earth's inhabitants decided they no longer wanted to live a physical life. But even so, I can't keep these. They were meant to be shared with the people. And I'll find a way to do that."

"The Earthling is going to want her piece of the profit," Emmi pointed out.

"And I'll find a way to appease her. Maybe we can list her among the donors who recovered the pieces or something."

Emmi snorted. "You've got to be kidding."

"I don't know," Jill said. "I'll think of something. But this is going back. Every last piece of it."

"It's your funeral," Emmi replied.

"If necessary," Jill said. "I wouldn't be heartbroken if it comes to that. What do I have left to live for? My entire life was a lie, and everyone I knew a month ago is dead."

Then, she turned back and stared at a drawing. Not the Rembrandt drawing, so it had to be one of the ones by Degas.

Emmi walked over and squeezed my shoulder. "Welcome to my world," she said.

"What?"

"Brand new body. In no one's records. Technically, you've never had an alcoholic drink."

"Or any kind of drink," I said.

"And, just like me, you've never had sex," she said with a wink.

Sileon grinned. "Don't worry about that. I'll make sure it doesn't last."

And, just like that, I was the one who was blushing.

"I don't feel any different than I did before."

But even as I said it, I knew it wasn't quite true. I felt like I had more energy. The slight pain in my knee that I'd learned to live with after wrenching it a couple of years ago had disappeared, and I felt its absence with every step. Emmi smiled as if she knew what I was thinking.

"So now what?" I asked.

"Depends entirely on you," Sileon said.

"What?"

"There's only one thing we really need to do in Cassius Station, and that is to deliver Jill and her package. We'll be back in two days."

"We're not docked?" I asked, peering past the empty bay where the shuttle had been.

"No. We went on a loop. Things got… interesting in Cassius Station after you got captured. Some of the cyborgs are still alive. Hell, we think there's still a Hyde out there, not just one of the gang, but an actual Hyde family member. He's trying to bring everyone back together, but one of the other cyborgs also wants to lead. But The Earthling has been pulling back her territory, and there's news of dead cyborgs popping up all over the place. Security denies it, but there's a war on in Cassius Station, and all three sides have one thing in common. They don't like us right now."

"Jill, you want to walk into that?" I said.

"You're not going to talk me out of it," Jill replied. "I already told you. And besides, didn't you hear the lady? There's a Hyde still alive. I'm going to bust his ass. Hell, maybe I'll volunteer for the Cassius Station Security."

I took a look at her face again. Ten minutes earlier she'd been a wreck, trying to get over the death of her oldest friend—and a man I suspected felt more for her than either of them let on—then five minutes later, she'd been lost in artistic bliss. Now she looked determined as hell.

I shuddered. If she went through with her threat, I suspected that Cassius Station Security was going to find itself becoming a much more serious threat to the relaxed and enjoyable life one could currently live on the edges of Station society. That might mean the end of an era.

"So are you heading back?" I asked.

Jill looked around the room, her eyes lingering on each of the pictures. "Can I have a few days? Just to get my head right?"

The I exchanged a glance with Sileon. "Take as long as you like," I replied. "We can extend this loop a little."

"And us?" Sileon said.

"Sounds like we can't go back there for now," I said. "Unless we want to spend the rest of our lives looking over our shoulders. So… Copernicus?" I asked.

Sileon laughed. "Do you really want to go there? We've got an interstellar ship that can take us literally anywhere in human space. Are you seriously suggesting we go to the most boring of the known planets?"

"I haven't heard that the Wolf or Gliese colonies are any better."

"They aren't," Sileon replied.

"That kind of limits our options."

"Not really. Have you ever heard of the Bacchanalia?"

"What in the world is that?"

"It's like an empire," she said. "With noble houses and everything, like in the Tri-D dramas. Except this one is spread out over six star systems in a cluster about fifty light-years from here."

"Impossible."

"It's perfectly real," Sileon replied. "Except they haven't had contact with the official colonies in centuries."

"Sounds like a plan," I said.

"Can I come with you?" Emmi asked.

Sileon smiled. "I assumed you'd be with us. After all, we can't have the Earthling recycling you."

"Thank you," she said.

I looked into Sileon's eyes. "Are you sure you want me with you? You don't owe me anything. Hell, it's me who owes you. You saved my life."

Her face clouded over. "About that… I only copied you."

"Yep, and here I am."

"You don't get it. A copy means there's another copy. Still in the system. There's a version of you who will have to live out the sentence that judge imposed."

"You left me in there?" I asked. "What does that even mean?"

"To this version of you?" she said. "Nothing. To him? It means he's not going to be with me, and he's going to have some interesting times ahead. To me?" She held my gaze. "It means I couldn't bring myself to erase any version of you. Not even one that will never know I had the opportunity or remember anything about the time it was locked in storage. So never ask me if I'm sure I want you around. You're free to leave if you want. But if you decide to come with me, never ask me that again."

"I won't," I promised.

THE END

About the Author

Gustavo Bondoni is a Jim Baen Memorial Short Story Award-Winning novelist and short story writer with over five hundred stories published in fifteen countries, in seven languages. He has published several science fiction novels including two trilogies, six monster books, a dark military fantasy and a thriller. His short fiction is collected in Thin Air (2023), Pale Reflection (2020), Off the Beaten Path (2019), Tenth Orbit and Other Faraway Places (2010) and Virtuoso and Other Stories (2011).

In 2025, Gustavo won the Jim Baen Memorial Contest (to go with second and third places he'd garnered previously) and in 2018 he received a Judges Commendation (and second place) in The James White Award. He was also a 2019 finalist in the Writers of the Future Contest.

His website is at www.gustavobondoni.com

More intriguing Science Fiction from Guardbridge Books.

OUTSIDE
by Gustavo Bondoni

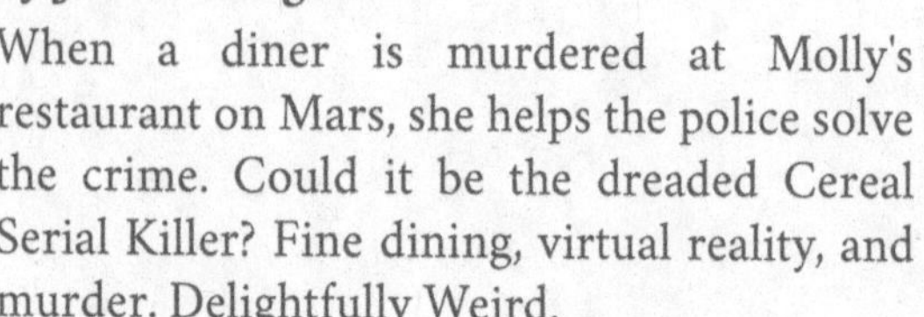

Earth is empty of humans. This surprising observation stymies Rome and his shipmates, crew of the starship come to re-establish contact from the colonies. Where have they all gone? Journey through real and virtual worlds, discover buried secrets and suppressed histories, and question what it means to be truly human.

Book 1 of the *Emily Plair Saga*, which sweeps across distant planets, space stations, and virtual worlds; disrupting societies, threatening humanity, and discovering what it is to really be alive.

Soul Searching
by Stephen Embleton

South African police use a device that can track souls in a harrowing search for a serial killer. But when one's soul can incriminate them before birth, can there be justice? NOMMO Awards Best Novel 2020 Finalist.

Sherlock Mars
by Jackie Kingon

When a diner is murdered at Molly's restaurant on Mars, she helps the police solve the crime. Could it be the dreaded Cereal Serial Killer? Fine dining, virtual reality, and murder. Delightfully Weird.

Now with a sequel, **P Is For Pluto**. Molly is opening a new branch on Pluto — send in the clones!